PRAISE FOR

The Last Policeman
Winner of the Edgar Award

"[The] plotting is sure-footed and surprising. . . . Ben H. Winters reveals himself as a novelist with an eye for the well-drawn detail."

—*Slate*

"Ben H. Winters makes noir mystery even darker: *The Last Policeman* sets a despondent detective on a suspicious suicide case—while an asteroid hurtles toward earth."

—*Wired*

"I love this book. I stayed up until seven in the morning reading because I could not stop. Full of compelling twists, likable characters, and a sad beauty, *The Last Policeman* is a gem. It's the first in a trilogy, and I am already excited for book two."

—Audrey Curtis, *San Francisco Book Review*

"I'm eager to read the other books, and expect that they'll keep me as enthralled as the first one did."

—Mark Frauenfelder, *Boing Boing*

"I haven't had to defend my love for science fiction in quite a while, but when I do, I point to books like *The Last Policeman*. [It] explores human emotions and relationships through situations that would be impossible (or worse yet, metaphorical) in literary fiction. This is a book that asks big questions about civilization, community, desperation and hope. But it doesn't provide big, pat answers."

—Michael Ann Dobbs, *io9*

"I've rarely been more surprised by a mystery novel than I was by this one—it's an unlikely cross-genre mashup that coheres for two reasons: the glum, relentless, and implausibly charming detective Hank Palace; and, most importantly, Ben H. Winters's clean, clever, thoughtful, and gently comic prose."

—J. Robert Lennon

"A solidly plotted whodunit with strong characters and excellent dialogue . . . the impending apocalypse isn't merely window dressing, either: it's a key piece of the puzzle Hank is trying to solve."

—*Booklist*

"This thought-provoking mystery should appeal to crime fiction aficionados who like an unusual setting and readers looking for a fresh take on apocalypse stories."

—*Library Journal*

"A promising kickoff to a planned trilogy. For Winters, the beauty is in the details rather than the plot's grim main thrust."

—*Kirkus Reviews* (starred review)

"Ben H. Winters spins a wonderful tale while creating unique characters that fit in perfectly with the ever-changing societal pressures. . . . [This] well-written mystery will have readers eagerly awaiting the second installment."

—*The New York Journal of Books*

"Extraordinary—as well as brilliant, surprising, and, considering the circumstances, oddly uplifting."

—*Mystery Scene Magazine*

"Exhilarating. . . . Do not wait for the movie!"

—*E! Online*

PRAISE FOR

Countdown City: The Last Policeman Book II

Winner of the Philip K. Dick Award

"Winters is a deft storyteller who moves his novel effortlessly from its intriguing setup to a thrilling, shattering conclusion."

—*Los Angeles Review of Books*

"As with the first Hank Palace novel (this is volume 2 of a trilogy), the mystery element is strong, and the strange, pre-apocalyptic world is highly imaginative and also very plausible—it's easy to think that the impending end of the world might feel very much like this. Genre mash-up master Winters is at it again."

—*Booklist*

"I always appreciate novels that have new and interesting approaches to traditional genres, and Ben H. Winters' two novels featuring Hank Palace fill the bill."

—Nancy Pearl, "NPR's Guide to 2013's Best Reads"

"Through it all Palace remains a likeable hero for end times, and . . . readers are left to wonder how he'll survive to tell his final tale."

—*Publishers Weekly*

WORLD OF TROUBLE

The Last Policeman Book III

by Ben H. Winters

Library of Congress Cataloging in Publication Number: 2014903377

ISBN: 978-1-59474-685-7

Printed in Canada

Typeset in Bembo and OCRA

Designed by Gregg Kulick based on a design by Doogie Horner
Cover photographs: (man) © Ibai Acevedo/Moment Select/Getty Images;
(meteor) © Ian McKinnell/Photographer's Choice/Getty Images; (building) ©
Hillary Fox/E+/Getty Images; (dog) © ideeone/E+/Getty Images
Production management by John J. McGurk

Quirk Books
215 Church Street
Philadelphia, PA 19106
quirkbooks.com

10 9 8 7 6 5 4 3 2 1

For Diana

". . . I'm gonna love you

till the wheels come off

oh, oh yeah . . ."

"And I won't let go and I can't let go
I won't let go and I can't let go
I won't let go and I can't let go no more"
—Bob Dylan, "Solid Rock"

Wednesday, August 22

Right ascension 18 26 55.9
Declination -70 52 35
Elongation 112.7
Delta 0.618 AU

"Are you here about the dust? Please tell me you're here to do something about the dust."

I don't answer. I don't know what to say.

The girl's voice is throaty and ill, her eyes looking out over a nose-and-mouth mask, staring hopeful and crazed at me as I stand baffled on her doorstep. Beautiful blonde, hair swept back out of her face, dirty and exhausted like everybody, panicked like everybody. But there's something else going on here, something not healthy. Something biochemical in her eyes.

"Well, come in," she says through her allergy mask. "Come on, come in, close the door, the door."

I step inside and she kicks the door shut and whirls around to face me. Yellow sundress, faded and tattered at the hem. Starved-looking, sallow, pale. Wearing not just the allergy mask but thick yellow latex gloves. And she's armed to the teeth is the other thing, she's holding two semiautomatics and has a smaller gun tucked in her boot, plus some kind of heavy-duty hunting knife in a calf sheath at the hem of the sundress. And I can't tell if it's live or not, but there is unquestionably a grenade dangling from a braided belt at her waist.

"Do you see the *dust*?" she says, gesturing with the guns, pointing into the corners. "You see how we've got a serious problem with the dust?"

It's true that there are motes hovering in the sunbeams, along with the garbage scattered on the floor, heaps of dirty clothing and open trunks spilling over with all manner of useless things, magazines and electrical cords and wadded-up dollar bills. But she's seeing more than what's here, I can tell, she's in the outer reaches, she's blinking furiously, coughing behind her mask.

I wish I could recall this girl's name. That would help a lot, if I could just remember her name.

"What do we do about this?" she says, rattling out words. "Do you just vacuum it, or—? Is that it—do you just suck it up and take it out of here? Does that work with cosmic dust?"

"Cosmic dust," I say. "Huh. Well, you know, I'm not sure."

This is my first trip to Concord, New Hampshire, since I fled a month ago, since my house burned down, along with much of the rest of the city. The chaos of those final frantic hours has died down to a grim and mournful silence. We're a few blocks from downtown, in the abandoned husk of a store on Wilson Street, but there are no jostling anxious crowds outside, no frightened people rushing and pushing past each other in the streets. No klaxon howl of car alarms, no distant gunfire. The people are hidden now, those that remain, hidden under blankets or in basements, encased in their dread.

And the girl, disintegrating, raving about imaginary dust from outer space. We've met once before, right here at this same small shop, which was once a used-clothing store called Next Time Around. She wasn't like this then, hadn't fallen prey to it. Other people are sick in the same way, of course, to varying degrees, different kinds of symptomatology; if the *DSM-IV* were still being updated and applied, this new illness would be added in red. A debilitating obsession with the gigantic asteroid on a collision course with our fragile planet. *Astromania*, perhaps. *Delusional interstellar psychosis*.

I feel like if I could only call her by her name, remind her that we have a relationship, that we're both human beings, it would ease her unsettled mind and make me less of a threat. Then we could talk calmly.

"It's toxic, you know," she's saying. "Really, really bad. The cosmic dust is real, real bad on your lungs. The photons burn your lungs."

"Listen," I say, and she makes a panicked gasp and rushes toward me, her assorted armaments jangling.

"Keep your *tongue* in your *mouth*," she hisses. "Don't *taste* it."

"Okay. I'll try. I won't."

I keep my hands at my sides, where she can see them, keep my expression neutral, soft as cake. "I'm actually here for some information."

"Information?" Her brows knit with confusion. She peers at me through clouds of invisible dust.

It's not her I'm here to talk to, anyway; it's her friend I need.

Boyfriend, maybe. Whatever he is. That's the guy who knows where I need to go next. I hope he does, anyway. I'm counting on it.

"I need to speak to Jordan. Is Jordan here?"

Suddenly the girl finds focus, snaps to attention, and the pistols come up. "Did he—did he send you?"

"No." I raise my hands. "No."

"Oh my God, he sent you. Are you with him? Is he in space?" She's shouting, advancing across the room, the barrels of the semiautomatics aimed at my face like twin black holes. "Is he doing this?"

I turn my head to the wall, scared to die, even now, even today.

"Is he doing this to me?"

And then—somehow—miraculously—the name.

"Abigail."

Her eyes soften, widen slightly.

"Abigail," I say. "Can I help you? Can we help each other?"

She gapes at me. Heavy silence. Moments flying past, time burning away.

"Abigail, *please*."

PART ONE

American Spirit

Thursday, September 27

Right ascension 16 57 00.6
Declination -74 34 33
Elongation 83.7
Delta 0.384 AU

1.

I'm worried about my dog.

He's limping now, on top of everything else, on top of the dry cough that rattles his small frame as he breathes, on top of the nasty burrs that have tangled themselves irretrievably in his matted fur. I don't know where or how he picked it up, this deep limp in his right forepaw, but here he comes now, moving slow out of the evidence room behind me, slipping through my legs and slouching with a pronounced foot-drag down the hallway. He shuffles away, poor little guy, nosing along the baseboard, his coat smudged but still white.

I watch him with deep unease. It wasn't fair of me to take Houdini along. A mistake I made without even thinking about it, inflicting upon my dog the rigors of a long and uncertain journey, the unhygienic drinking water and sparse food, the hikes along deserted highway shoulders and through fallow fields, the fights with other animals. I should have left him with McConnell and the others, back at the safe house in Massachusetts, left him with McConnell's kids, all the other kids, the other dogs, a safe and comfortable environment. But I took him. I never asked him if he wanted to come, not that a dog in any case could fairly weigh the risks and rewards.

I took him, and we crossed eight hundred fifty complicated miles in five long weeks, and the wear is showing on the dog, no doubt about it.

"I'm really sorry, pal," I whisper, and the dog coughs. I pause in the hallway, breathing in the darkness, staring up at the ceiling.

It was the same in the evidence room as in the rest of the place: thick coatings of dust on the shelves, filing cabinets turned over and emptied out. Odors of must and mildew. In Dispatch, on someone's desk between the blank laptops and the old foot-switch RadioCOMMAND console, there was an ancient sandwich, half eaten and crawling with ants. Nothing good, nothing helpful or hopeful.

We arrived very late last night and began our search immediately, and now it's three hours later and the sun is beginning to rise—dull pale beams filtering in through the glass-paned front door, down at the east end of the hall—and we've worked through most of the building and nothing. Nothing. A small police station, like the one in Concord, New Hampshire, where I used to work. Even smaller. All night I've gone through on my hands and knees with my magnifying glass and fat Eveready flashlight, taking the place room by room: Reception, Dispatch. Administration, Holding

Cell, Evidence.

Cold certainty slowly filling me, like dirty water rising in a well: there's nothing.

Officer McConnell knew it. She told me this was a fool's errand. "So you have, what, the name of a town?" is what she said.

"A building," I said. "The police station. In a town. In Ohio."

"Ohio?" Skeptical. Arms crossed. Scowling. "Well, you won't find her. Also, if you do? So what?"

I remember what it felt like, her being angry, justified in her anger. I just nodded. I kept packing.

Now, in the flat dawn light of the empty hallway of the empty police station, I make a fist with my right hand and raise it to a forty-five-degree angle and bring it down like the hammer of a gun, slam it backward into the wall I'm leaning against. Houdini turns around and stares at me, bright black animal eyes glinting like marbles in the dark.

"All right," I tell him. He makes a wet noise in the back of his throat. "Okay. Let's just keep looking."

* * *

A few feet down the hall is a plaque honoring the service of Daniel Arnold Carver, on the occasion of his retirement from the Rotary, Ohio, Police Department at the rank of lieutenant, in the Year of Our Lord 1998. Next to that commemoration is an upside-down horseshoe of construction-paper cards from local children: stick-figure cops waving gaily in bold Crayola colors, with

"Thanks for the tour!" written below in the neat handwriting of an elementary school teacher. The cards are dangling from fading twists of Scotch tape; the plaque is slightly misaligned and covered in a half inch of dust.

The next room is on the left, a few feet past the plaque and the kids' drawings. It's marked DETECTIVES, although the first thing I notice on entering is that there was only one detective. One desk, one swivel chair. One landline phone, with the cord cut, the receiver sitting unattached in the cradle like stage furniture. A long-dead flowering plant hangs from the ceiling: wilted stalks and clumps of brown leaves. A plastic water bottle on its side, half crushed.

I can picture the detective who once sat in this room, tilted back in the chair, finalizing the small details of a coming meth-lab bust, say, or cursing with crusty good humor at some ham-fisted directive from the know-nothings over in Admin. I sniff the air and imagine I detect the ancient stale odor of his cigars.

Her cigars, actually. Hers. There's a thick leather log book on the desk with a name neatly stenciled across the top right corner: Detective Irma Russel. "My apologies, Detective Russel," I tell her, wherever she may be, and toss a salute off into the air. "I should know better."

I think of Officer McConnell again. She kissed me at last, up on her tiptoes, at the door. Then she pushed me, a good two-handed shove, to send me off on my adventure. "Go," she said. Fondly, sadly. "Jerk."

The watery daylight is not fully penetrating the one dust-coated window in the detectives room, so I switch back on the beam of the Eveready and hover it over Detective Russel's log book and flip my way through. The first entry is from just seven months ago. February 14. On Valentine's Day, Detective Russel reported in neat cursive handwriting that rolling blackouts had been ordered for all municipal buildings countywide, and henceforth all record keeping would be done with pen and paper.

The entries that follow are a record of decline. On March 10 there was a small riot at a food pantry in neighboring Brown County, which spread quickly, resulting in "general civil unrest of unanticipated levels." It is noted on March 30 that the department's force-readiness levels are significantly depleted, at thirty-five percent of previous year's staffing. ("Jason *quit*!!!" Detective Russel notes parenthetically, the exclamation points bristling with surprise and disappointment.) On April 12, a "Bucket List rapist" was apprehended and turned out to be "Charlie, from Blake's Feed Supply!!!"

I smile. I like this Detective Russel. I'm not wild about all the exclamation points, but I like her.

I follow the neat handwriting down the run of months. The last entry, dated June 9—sixteen weeks ago—just says "Creekbed," and then "Heavenly Father keep a good eye on us, would ya?"

I linger for a moment, hunched over the notebook. Houdini pads into the room, and I feel his tail brush against my pant leg.

I take out my thin blue notebook from my inside pocket and write down *June 9* and *Creekbed* and *Heavenly Father keep a good eye on us, would ya?*, trying to write small, keep the words clustered together. It's the last one of these notebooks I've got. My father was a college professor, and when he died he left behind boxes and boxes of these exam-taker's notebooks, but I have used up many since entering law enforcement, and many more were lost in the fire that consumed my house. Every time I write something down I have this small rustle of anxiety, like what will I do when I run out of pages?

I close Detective Russel's desk drawers and return the log book to where it was, flipped open to the same page where I found it.

* * *

Also in my pocket, tucked in a red plastic Concord Public Library card sleeve, is a wallet-size copy of my sister's sophomore-year yearbook picture. Nico as a defiant and hip high-school student, in a ratty black T-shirt and cheap eyeglass frames, far too cool to have combed her hair. Her lower lip is jutted out, her mouth twisted: *I'll smile when I want to, not when some mope tells me to say cheese.* I wish I was carrying a more recent picture, but I lost them in the fire; the truth is, she's only eight years out of high school, and the photograph remains current, with regard to Nico Palace's appearance and affect. My body is itching to perform the familiar rituals, to flip the picture open to strangers—"Have you see this girl?"—to improvise a set of discerning follow-ups and follow-ups to the follow-ups.

Along with the photograph and the notebook, inside my

well-worn tan sport jacket are a few other basic investigative tools: a handheld magnifying glass; a Swiss army knife; a nine-foot retracting tape measure; a second flashlight, smaller and slimmer than the Eveready; a box of .40-caliber rounds. The gun itself, the department-issue SIG Sauer P229 I've been carrying for three years now, is in a holster on my hip.

The door of the evidence room clicks open and closed again, and I raise the flashlight at Cortez.

"Spray paint," he says, holding up an aerosol canister and giving it an enthusiastic shake-shake-shake. "Half full."

"Okay," I say. "Great."

"Oh, but it *is* great, Policeman," Cortez says, looking with childlike delight at this find, turning it over in his rough hands. "Useful for marking a trail, and easily weaponized. A candle, a paper clip, a match. Voilà: flamethrower. I've seen it done." He winks. "I've done it."

"Okay," I say again.

This is how he talks, Cortez the thief, my unlikely partner: like the world will go on forever, like he with his hobbies and habits will go on forever. He sighs and shakes his head sadly at my indifference, and slides past in the darkness like a phantom, away down the hallway in search of more loot. *She's not here*, whispers Officer McConnell in my ear. Not judging, not angry. Just noting the obvious. *You came all this way for nothing, Detective Palace. She's not here.*

The day is advancing. Dull gold sunlight inching closer to me down here at the far end of the dark hall. The dog, somewhere

I can't see him, but close enough that I hear him coughing. The planet wobbling beneath my feet.

2.

Next to the detectives room is a door marked MUSTER, and this room too is full of familiar objects, coat hooks hung with windbreakers, a well-broken-in blue ball cap, a pair of sturdy Carhartt boots with stiffened laces. Policeman street clothes. In one corner there's an American flag on a cheap plastic eagle-head stand. An OSHA workplace-safety information sheet is tacked to the lower corner of a billboard, the same sheet we had in Concord that Detective McGully liked to read aloud, dripping with disdain: "Oh, good, some tips on posture. We get frikkin' *shot* at for a living!"

Along the back wall is a dry-erase board on wobbly wheels with an undated exhortation, all-caps and triple-underlined: "STAY SAFE, ASSHOLES." I smile, half smile, imagining the weary young sergeant writing the message, hiding his own fear behind salty tough-cop cleverness. *STAY SAFE, ASSHOLES. Keep a good eye on us, would ya?* It hasn't been an easy time for law enforcement, this last set of months, it really hasn't.

I push through a door at the back of the muster room into an even smaller space, a kitchenette slash break room: sink, fridge, microwave, round table and black plastic chairs. I open the fridge and push it closed immediately against a wave of warmth and foul odor: soured food, spoiled food, rot.

I stand in front of the empty vending machine and peer for a moment at my funhouse reflection in the Plexiglass. There are no snacks in there, just the bare coils like empty winter branches. But the glass is not smashed, like all the world's glass seems to be these days. No one assaulted this machine with a bat or a Carhartt boot to rob it of its treasures.

Presumably this machine was emptied out ages ago, maybe by Detective Russel or by her disappointing friend Jason on his way out—except, when I crouch down, take a knee and look closely, I find a plastic fork holding open the black horizontal door at the bottom where the food comes out. I shine my light on it, the fork dramatically bowed, the tensile strength of its hard plastic holding up precariously against the weight of the snack trap.

Holy moly, is what I'm thinking, because this could be exactly what I'm looking for, unless it isn't.

Because theoretically, of course, a plastic fork could remain in that bowed position for a long time, for months even, but on the other hand, one of the many suspensions my sister earned during her rocky career at Concord High School was for performing the same trick: rigging open the vending machine in the teachers' lounge and looting all the candy bars and potato chips, leaving behind just the low-fat yogurt bars and a note: *You're welcome, fatties!*

When I catch my breath I gingerly remove the fork. I have a dozen sandwich bags in my pocket, and I slip the fork into one of the bags and the bag into my sport-coat pocket and move on.

The kitchenette's two slim cupboards have been rummaged. Plates broken and disarrayed; bowls tossed onto the floor. Only two coffee mugs are still intact, one reading PROPERTY OF ROTARY POLICE DEPARTMENT, the other I'M THROUGH WITH LOVE; FORTUNATELY THERE'S STILL SEX. I smile and rub my bleary eyes. I miss cops, I really do.

Was she here? Did Nico take the candy?

The gooseneck spout of the sink is in the on position, angled up sharply to the left, as if someone came in for a glass of water, forgetting that the municipal supplies have stopped. Or perhaps the water went out right in the middle of someone using the sink. Some cop in the break room after a long and treacherous shift, filling up his cup or washing his face, her face, and suddenly, whoops, no more water for you.

The sink is full of blood. It's a deep-walled sink with a basin made of stainless steel like the handle, and when I look down into it the sides and the bottom are covered with a rust-red explosion of blood. The drain is clotted and thick with it. I look again at the gooseneck spout, closer now, shining the light, and find the faint smudged patches: red, bloody palms clutching and jerking the handle.

STAY SAFE, ASSHOLES.

Above and behind the sink, bolted to the wall, is a horizontal rack hung with three knives. All of them are stained with blood, up and down, freckled from hilt and blade. A clot of dread and excitement forms in the base of my gut and floats like a bubble up into my throat. I swing around, moving quickly now, heartbeat thrumming, back through the muster room and out into the hallway, and now the sun is all the way up outside, casting a muted ochre glow through the glass door and I can see the floor clearly, see where the trail of blood runs down the hallway. Discrete spots, leading plain as bread crumbs from the kitchenette sink through the muster room, pass the dry-erase board and the flagpole, all the way down the hall to the front door of the station.

My mentor Detective Culverson, my mentor and my friend, he called it *walking the blood*. Walking the blood means walking with the escaping suspect or the fleeing victim, it means "you find the trail and see what songs it wants to sing you." I shake my head, remembering him saying that, most of the way joking, purposefully hokey, but Detective Culverson could turn a phrase, he really could.

I walk the blood. I follow the steady line of drops, which appear on the tile at six- to eight-inch intervals all the way down the hallway and out the glass door, where the trail disappears in the thick mud just outside the building. I stand up in the gloomy daylight. It's raining, a sputtering indecisive drizzle. It's been raining for days. When Cortez and I got here late last night it was squalling hard enough that we were biking with our jackets tugged up over our necks and the backs of our heads, like snails, a blue tarp tied tautly over all our stuff in the Red Ryder wagon trailing behind. Wherever the bleeding person went from here, there is no trail left to sing about it.

Back at the bloody sink in the break room, I open my small blue notebook to one of its last fresh pages and draw a rough annotated illustration of the knives behind the sink. Butcher's knife, twelve inches; cleaver, six inches with a tapered spine; paring knife, three and a half inches, with the brand initials W.G. inlaid on the handle, between the rivets. I sketch the blood pattern on the knives and in the basin of the sink. I get down on all fours and walk the blood again, and this time I note that each of these drops is oblong, less a perfect circle and more an oval with a pointy end. I go again, third time, nice and slow, running my big Sherlock Holmes magnifying glass along the trail and now I'm seeing that they *alternate*: an oblong droplet pointing this way, and then one pointing that way, one eastward droplet, one westward, all the way down the hall.

I was a detective for only three months, promoted out of nowhere and dismissed just as abruptly when the CPD was absorbed by the Department of Justice, and so I never received the higher-level training I would have in the normal run of a career. I am not as versed as I might wish in the finer points of crime-scene forensics, I cannot be as sure as I would like. Still, though. Nevertheless. What I've got here is actually not one trail but two; what the alternating droplets record are two separate instances that someone passed along this corridor either bleeding or carrying a blood-stained object. Two journeys in opposite directions.

I go back to the kitchenette and stare once more into the red mess in the sink. There is a fresh jitteriness in my gut, a new chaos in my veins. Too much coffee. Not enough sleep. New information. I don't know if Nico's here, if she was ever here. But *something* happened. Something.

* * *

It was not the impending end of the world that drove a wedge between my sister and me, it was our diverging responses to the end of the world, a bedrock disagreement regarding the basic reality of what is happening—i.e., whether it is happening or isn't.

It *is* happening. I'm right and Nico is wrong. No set of facts has ever been as rigorously vetted, no set of data points so carefully analyzed and double-checked, by as many thousands of professors and scientists and government officials. All desperate for it to be wrong, all finding it nevertheless to be right. There are some uncertainties on the fine points, of course, for example regarding the composition and structure of the asteroid, whether it is made up primarily of metals or primarily of rocks, whether it is one monolithic piece or a pile of agglomerated rubble. There are, too, varying predictions as to what exactly happens, postimpact: how much volcanic activity and where; how fast the seas will rise and how high; how long it will take for the sun to be dimmed by ash and for how long it will remain shrouded. But on the core fact there is consensus: the asteroid $2011GV_1$, known as Maia, measuring six and a half kilometers in diameter and traveling at a speed of between thirty-five thousand and forty thousand miles per hour, will make landfall in Indonesia, at an angle from horizontal of nineteen degrees. This will happen on October 3. A week from Wednesday, around lunchtime.

There was this computer animation that got a lot of traction early on, a lot of "likes" and reposts—this was over a year ago, midsummer of last year, when the odds were high but not yet definite; when people were still at work, still using computers. This was the last wild flowering of social networking, people looking up old friends, trading conspiracy theories, posting and approving of one another's Bucket Lists. This cartoon, this animation, it depicted the world as a piñata, with God wielding the stick—God in his Old Testament iteration, with the big white beard, Michelangelo's God—whacking away at the fragile globe until it burst. This was one of a million versions of the coming event that ascribed it, however cutely, to God's will, God's vengeance, the interstellar object as Flood 2.0.

I didn't find the cartoon all that clever; for one thing, the piñata image is way off. The world isn't actually going to explode, fly off into pieces like shattered pottery. It will shiver from the impact, to be sure, but then continue in its orbit. The oceans boil, the forests burn, the mountains rumble and spew lava, everybody dies. The world keeps turning.

The crux of our falling out is that Nico imagines that she is going to prevent Maia from impacting. She and some friends. The last time we spoke at length was in Durham, New Hampshire, and she filled me in on all the details about her secret underground group and their secret underground plans. She was leaning forward, talking fast and passionate, smoking her cigarettes, impatient as always with her narrow-minded older brother, stolid and disbelieving. She told me how the path of the asteroid can be diverted by a pinpoint nuclear explosion, detonated at a distance of one object-radius from the asteroid, releasing sufficient high-energy X-rays to vaporize some portion of its surface, creating "a miniature rocket effect" and changing the trajectory. This operation is called a "standoff burst." I didn't understand the science. Nico, it seemed clear, didn't understand it either. But, she insisted, the maneuver has been gamed out in classified exercises by the United States Department of Defense and has a theoretical success rate of more than eighty-five percent.

She went on and on, me trying to listen with a straight face, trying not to laugh or throw my hands up or shake her by the shoulders. Of course the information about the standoff burst is being suppressed by the evil government, for purposes unknown—and of course there is this one rogue scientist who knows how it's done, and of course he's being held by the government in a military prison somewhere. And—of course, of course, of course—Nico and her pal Jordan and the rest of the cabal have a plan to set him free and save the world.

I told her this was delusional. I told her this was Santa Claus and the Tooth Fairy and she was being a fool, and then she disappeared and I let her go.

This was an error, and I see that now.

I'm still right and she's still wrong, but I cannot just let her be gone. Whatever she thinks, whatever she's doing, she is still my baby sister and I am the only person left with a stake in her welfare.

And I can't abide the idea of our final bitter exchange remaining the last conversation to take place between her and me, the last two members of my family who ever will exist. What I need now is to find her, see her before the end, before the earthquakes and the high water and whatever else is coming.

I need to see her so badly that it is like a low rolling heat in my stomach, like the fire in the belly of a furnace, and if I don't find her—if I don't manage to see her, hug her, apologize for letting her go—then it will leap up and consume me.

3.

"Knives? Really?" Cortez looks up. His eyes gleam. "Are they big and sharp?"

"Two of them are big. The third is a paring knife. I don't know about sharp."

"Paring knives can be surprisingly effective. You can do some serious damage with a paring knife."

"You've seen it," I say. "You've done it."

He laughs, winks. I rub my eyes and look around. I've caught up with Cortez in the three-car garage, the last unexplored area of the station. No cars left in here, just stuff—engine parts, broken pieces of tools, other miscellaneous junk that's been forgotten or left behind. It's big and echoey, smelling of old spilled gasoline. The sun comes in refracted through two grungy glass-block windows along the north-facing wall.

"Knives are always useful," says Cortez cheerfully. "Sharp, dull.

Take the knives."

He gives me a congratulatory salute and goes back to what he's doing, which is rifling his way along the wire shelving units in the back of the room, across from the big garage doors, looking for useful objects. Cortez's features are strangely large: large forehead, large chin, big glowing eyes. He has the jollity and the fierceness of a pirate king. The first time we met he shot me in the head with an electric staple gun, but our relationship has evolved in the subsequent months. On this long and complicated journey he has proved himself to be endlessly valuable, skilled at picking locks, siphoning fuel and reviving dead vehicles, discovering stores of resources in a resource-depleted landscape. He is not the sort of sidekick I ever would have predicted for myself, but the world has been reordered. I never used to think I'd have a dog.

"The knives are covered in blood," I explain to Cortez. "I'm leaving them where I found them, for now."

He glances at me over his shoulder. "Cow's blood?"

"Maybe."

"Pig?"

"Could be."

He waggles his eyebrows insinuatingly. We've eaten what we brought, what we stumbled upon or bargained for along the way: snack-type food, jerky strips, a big thing of honey-roasted peanuts in tiny foil bags. We caught fish in the Finger Lakes in improvised nets, salted them, and ate those for five days. All we've been drinking is coffee, working our way through one massive sack of arabica beans. Cortez rigged up a manual pencil sharpener into a grinder; we measure out cups from the barrels of spring water we took with us from Massachusetts; we boil up the coffee in an old carafe over a camp stove, strain it through a mesh spatula into a hot/cold thermos. It takes forever. It tastes terrible.

"Can you make coffee?" I ask Cortez.

"Oh, yeah," he says. "Great idea."

Cortez stands, stretches, takes the necessary items from his golf bag and gets set up, while I think about blood. Two trails, one running out of the kitchenette and one running back.

Coffee on the boil, Cortez goes back to rummaging for treasure, working his way down the shelving system, lifting each object to the light, quickly assessing, evaluating, moving on.

"Training manual," he says. "Porno mag. Empty shoebox. Sunglasses. Broken." He tosses the mirrored state-trooper-style shades over his shoulder, shattering them further on the patterned-concrete floor of the garage. "Holsters. Could use these, maybe. Oh, goodness. Goodness gracious, Policeman. Binoculars."

He holds them up, bulky and black, points them at me like a birdwatcher.

"Bad news," he says. "You look like shit."

He takes the binoculars. He takes a bag full of cell phone batteries. I've stopped asking Cortez what good it all is, all of the collecting and acquiring and sorting. It's a game to him, a challenge: keep gathering up useful objects until the world caves in and no one has any use for anything.

I am aware of the possibility, of course, that it is Nico's blood on the knife, in the sink, on the ground. It is too early to think about that, too early to reach that sort of conclusion.

The most likely scenario, after all, is that this blood is the blood of a stranger, and these knives are totally unrelated to my current investigation. It's just some terrible act of violence among uncounted terrible acts of violence occurring at an accelerating rate. We saw a lot of this on our journey, met people who confessed, whether in tearful remorse or in fierce defiance, to some unconscionable deed. The old lady standing guard over her grandson in an abandoned grocery store, who whispered how she had shot a stranger for six pounds of frozen hamburger meat. The couple at the truck stop that caught someone trying to steal the Dodge pickup they'd been living in, and in the ensuing confrontation ran him over.

We called them red towns, the worst of the places, the communities that had fractured into chaos and lawlessness. We had different names for the different kinds of worlds that the world has become. Red towns: violence and grief. Green towns: pleasant, playing at make-believe. Blue towns: uneasy calm, people hiding. Maybe National Guard or regular army troops on scattered patrol. Purple towns, black towns, gray . . .

I cough into my fist; the claustrophobic garage smell is getting to me, the reek of ancient cigarettes and exhaust. A grimy concrete floor in a black-and-white checkerboard pattern. A thought is twitching to life. Dim and uncertain. I sniff again, drop down onto all fours, digging my knees and palms into the hard concrete floor.

"Policeman?"

I don't answer. I take a crawling step forward, toward the middle of the room, head angled down, staring at the floor.

"Have you gone mad?" says Cortez, clutching a battered steel money box under his arm like a football. "If you've gone mad you're useless, and I'll have to eat you."

"Can you help me?"

"Help you what?"

"Butts," I say, peeling off my sport coat. "Please help me find cigarette butts."

I crawl across the floor, from the back of the room out toward the garage doors, my shirt sleeves pushed up, my palms getting filthy. I use my magnifying glass, following the checkerboard pattern across the concrete: light squares, dark squares. After a moment Cortez shrugs, sets down the steel box, and we settle in, side by side like grazing cows, moving in slow patterns, staring at the floor.

There are plenty of butts, of course: the floor of the parking garage, like all such places, is littered with the stubs of dead cigarettes. We hunt through the dust and grime of the floor and gather up all we can find and then I come up to a squat and sort them into two piles, checking each one carefully, holding it up and squinting at it in the light before consigning it to its place. *Possibles* and *not possibles*. Cortez whistles while he works, occasionally murmuring "madness, madness." Most of the cigarettes are either generic, having no marking on the filter, or home-rolled, just twists of thin white paper with crusts of tobacco leaf spilling out the side.

And then, after ten minutes—fifteen—

"There it is."

There. I reach down and pluck up the grimy little twist of paper, the one I was looking for. I hold it up to the flat gray light.

There.

"Ah," says Cortez. "A cigarette butt. I knew we could do it."

I don't answer. I found it, as I knew in my secret policeman's heart that I would. A single cigarette butt, snarled and torn, smashed to a ragged brown by the grind of a heel, shredded-leaf guts spilling out around the dirty wrinkle of the wrapper. I hold the stubbed-out butt carefully between two fingers like the broken body of an insect.

"She's here." I stand up. I look around the room. "She was here."

Now it's Cortez's turn not to answer. He's still staring at the floor—something else has caught his attention. My heart is heaving in my chest, swelling and receding like a tide.

The cigarette market, like all markets for addictive goods, was violently disrupted by the impending end of civilization: skyrocketing demand and vanishing supply. Most smokers, old and new, have made do with foul-tasting generics, or scrounged enough loose tobacco to roll their own. But my sister, my sister Nico, has managed somehow always to be in possession of her favorite brand.

I hold the butt up high. I sniff it. This object must be considered in combination with the plastic fork suspended in its struggle to hold open the door of the vending machine, and the conclusion to be heard from these two objects, these two small objects singing together, is that this is real. Poor addled Abigail didn't pick the police station in Rotary, Ohio, at random from all the buildings in all the world. Nico really came here, she and her merry band of conspiracists and would-be heroes. I would almost say that she left the butt on purpose, maybe even kept smoking all these years on purpose, in defiance of my nagging, just so that she could leave this clue behind. Except I know that she kept smoking all these years because she was addicted to nicotine, and also because she enjoyed pissing me off.

"She was here," I say again to Cortez, who is muttering to himself, feeling along the floor with a forefinger extended. I slide the butt into a baggie and carefully place it in my coat pocket. "She *is* here."

"I'll go you one better," he says, looking up from the square of concrete he's squatting on. "This is a trap door."

* * *

I've been playing hide-and-seek with Nico for our entire lives.

The weekend after the funeral—the second funeral, our father's, early in June of the year I turned twelve—the movers were roaming around the house, boxing up my little life, carrying out my stash of comic books and my baseball glove and my twin bed, all my worldly store lifted out to the truck in one trip. I realized with a start that I hadn't seen my baby sister for hours. I flipped out, charged through the house in a panic, ducking past the movers, throwing open the doors of the dusty empty closets, charging down to the basement.

Out on the streets of Concord I clomped through patches of mud from the midsummer rain, up and down side streets, calling her name. I found Nico at last in White Park, giggling, hiding under the slide, getting sunburnt in a light summer dress, scratching her name in the dirt with a stick. I glowered and crossed my skinny arms. I was infuriated, already a roil of emotions from the move, the grief. Nico, age six, reached up and patted my cheek. "You thought I was gone, too, didn't you, Hen?" Hopping up, taking my big hand between her two little ones. "You did, huh?"

And now here I am in Rotary, Ohio, less than a week to go, bent forward at the waist with my fingers twitching, pacing like a lunatic in a circle around Cortez the thief, staring at his broad back where he's hunched over a trap door trying to figure how to lift it.

The secret door in the floor of the garage is a surprise, except it's not a surprise. This is one of the things people are doing, people all over the world, digging holes or finding holes and climbing down inside them. The United States Army, according to rumor, has created vast networks of lead-lined bunkers for the evacuation of top brass and key executive branch officials, a reinforced underground universe extending from beneath the Pentagon all the way across Arlington. The city of West Marlborough, Texas, embarked on a three-month "all-city dig" to create a massive safe space for all city residents beneath a local high-school ball field.

The relevant experts, in general, have been politely skeptical of such enterprises—of all the governments, the neighborhoods, the millions of private citizens digging into their Cold War–style redoubts. As if one could ever dig deep enough to withstand the blast. As if you could take enough groceries down there with you to survive when the sun disappears and the animals all die.

"Son of a bitch," mutters Cortez. He's using my magnifying glass, peering, tapping the smooth stone floor with his big knuckles.

"What?" I say, and then erupt in a coughing fit, overcome by excitement, anxiety, exhaustion, dust. I don't know what. My throat burns. I'm standing right behind him, peering over his shoulder, shifting on my feet. Time is passing while we stand here, minutes are rushing past like stars flying by at light speed in a science-fiction serial. I check the time on my Casio. It's 9:45 already. Can that be right?

"Cortez," I say. "Can you open the door or not?"

"It's not a door," he says, sweating, pushing his thick black hair out of his eyes. "That's the problem."

"What do you mean, it's not a door?" I'm speaking too rapidly, too loudly. My words jangle back at me. I feel like I'm going crazy, just a little bit. "You said it was a door."

"Mea culpa. A door has a handle." He jabs his finger at the floor. "This is a lid. A cover. There is an opening in the ground here, probably for a staircase, and somebody covered it over."

Cortez points to four places on the floor where he claims to see the ghostly remnants of post holes, the foundations of a stair rail. But even more telling, he says, are the four panels of the concrete itself: two dark and two light, laid more recently than all the others.

"That's the lid," he says. "Those four pieces are one piece. They had a hand mixer, they poured a slab, they stamped and stained it to match the pattern of the floor and cut the edges to fit, and then they lowered it in." He hands me back my magnifying glass. "You see where it's cut?"

I can't, though. I can't see any of this. I just see a floor. Cortez stands and cracks his back, turning all the way this way, then all the way the other. "The pattern was hand-corrected along the edges. The rest is machine-sawed. This here is done by hand. See?"

I squint at the floor; I open my eyes as wide as they can go. I'm so tired. Cortez sighs with weary amusement and then hustles over to the big garage door.

"Here," he says, and pops the lock and flies it open. "You see *that*?"

And the room is suddenly alive with tiny particles, all around, millions of tiny pieces dancing in the empty air.

"Dust."

"Yes indeedy. Concrete is just tiny stones packed very tight. Someone uses a chop saw or a walk-behind to correct the edges of a lid, for example, and it makes a lot of dust. Like this."

"When?" I say. "When did they do it?"

"You're going to hyperventilate, Policeman. Your head is going to fall off."

"When was it?"

"Might have been yesterday. Might have been a week ago. Like I said—concrete makes a *lot* of dust."

I squat down. I get up. I reach into my pocket, feel the photo of Nico, the fork, the cigarette butt now encased in a sandwich baggie. I squat again. My body refuses to be still. I feel coffee sluicing through me, bubbling black and nervous along my veins. The dust is stinging my eyes. I think I can see it now, the hairline fracture between the door and the floor. Nico is down there. Nico and the rest of them. She and her cadre arrived here and have built themselves some sort of ersatz headquarters, under a layer of smoothed rock in an old garage. Waiting down there for the next stage of the scheme to unfold—or have they given up, are they waiting now like ostriches, heads in the dirt below the station?

"Let's put a handle on it," I say to Cortez. "Lift it up."

"We can't."

"Why not?"

"Because it would require strength, which we do not have."

I look down at my body. I have always been a thin man, and now I am a thin man after a month of granola bars and coffee. Cortez's weight loss has resolved his fighter's frame to a coil of sinew, but he's hardly Mr. Universe—stronger than me, in other words, but not strong.

"A handle doesn't help," he says. He is slowly rolling a cigarette of his own, layering in tobacco from a pouch he keeps in the golf bag.

"So what do we do?" I say, and he laughs, watching me pace.

"I'm thinking, man. I'm pondering. You keep walking in circles. Eventually you will fall over, and that will be amusing."

I do it. He is joking, teasing me, but I do, I keep walking, I can't stop, I circle the lid in the floor like an orbiting star. My thoughts run back to my sister's close compatriot, the one I tried to track down in Concord: Jordan, last name unknown. Jordan was introduced to me by Nico at the University of New Hampshire, when she went there with me to help on a case; he held, she suggested, some vague but critical position in the hierarchy of her conspiracy. What struck me about Jordan was the ironic overlay in everything he said. While Nico's relationship with their secret revolution was always so earnest—they really *were* going to save the world—with this kid

Jordan I always got a sense that he was playacting, posing, having a grand old time. Nico didn't see, or didn't want to see, this attitude in him, and their relationship therefore was just one more thing to make me uneasy. The last time I saw Jordan, Nico was already gone, a helicopter had borne her away, and he gleefully hinted to me about more secrets, deeper levels, aspects of their intrigues to which Nico was not privy.

And then when I went back to find him, to demand of him where the hell she had gone, I found Abigail instead, baffled and abandoned Abigail, and from her I got here—to Ohio, to Rotary, to a door in the floor.

"We have to get down there."

"Well, I'll tell you," says Cortez. "It might be impossible."

"We *have* to."

Cortez blows his smoke rings and the both of us stare at the floor. Jordan is down there, I know that he is, and Nico is down there too, separated from me only by this layer of cold rock, and all we have to do is peel it up and out of the way. I breathe—I sing a line of something—I am trying to get my feverish and overextended mind to slow, stop galloping long enough to make a plan, develop a strategy, when my dog races into the room, skidding on his small heels, claws scrabbling on the concrete. There's something wrong. He's barking like mad, barking to wake the dead.

4.

"It's probably a possum," says Cortez, breathing hard as we charge like maniacs through the woods. "Stupid dog probably wants to show you a squirrel."

It's not a possum. It's not a squirrel. That much I can tell from the way that Houdini is hurtling forward, all sparked up, racing and bounding despite that limp, a distinct stutter step as he careens through the undergrowth. We run after him, Cortez and I, through the dense woods that back up against the police station, crashing through the brush like the world is on fire. It's not a possum or a squirrel.

We tumble down a westward slope, along the muddy bank of a small creek, deeper into the woods, and then at last we come out in a small clearing, a leafy mud-specked oval maybe twenty-five feet around. Cortez and I step over a line of high bushes to get in there while Houdini noses under, tearing new cuts in his hide, not caring. Cortez has a hatchet clutched tightly in one fist, and there is, I know, a sawed-off shotgun in the deep inside pocket of his long black coat. I draw my own weapon, the SIG Sauer, and hold it out ahead of me two-handed. The three of us form a semicircle at the edge of the clearing: man, dog, man, all panting, all staring at the body. It's a girl, facedown in the dirt.

"Christ," says Cortez. "Christ almighty."

I don't answer. I can't breathe. I take a step into the clearing, steady myself. The image disappearing, reappearing, my vision clouding and unclouding. The girl is fully clothed: Denim skirt. Pale blue top. Tan sandals. Arms thrown out in front of her as if she had died swimming, or reaching for something.

"That her?" Cortez says quietly. In three strides I'm across the clearing to the body, and by the time I get there I know that it's not—the hair is wrong, the height. My sister has never worn a jean skirt. I manage the word: "No."

My body floods with relief—and then, immediately, guilt, crashing in like a second wave while the first is still ebbing. This girl is not my sister but she is somebody's sister, or daughter, or friend. She is somebody's something. She was. Facedown in the dirt in the woods, arms extended. Caught after a chase. Six days to the end.

Cortez steps up next to me, the hatchet clenched like a caveman's club. We're a quarter mile into the stillness of the forest and you can no longer see the one-story police station behind us, or the small town of Rotary that is down the hill on the other side of the woods. We might as well be miles deep into timberland, lost in a green-brown fairy world, surrounded by wildflowers and mud and the curled yellow leaves that have drifted down to coat the forest floor.

I kneel beside the body of the girl and roll her over, gingerly brush the dirt and wood chips off her cheeks and out of her eyes. She's Asian. Pretty. Fragile features. Black hair, pale cheeks. Thin pink lips. Small gold stud earrings, one in each ear. She's been in a fight; her face shows multiple lacerations and bruises, including a black eye, the right eye, swollen almost shut. And the girl's throat is cut from end to end, one side to the other, a terrible slash beginning at a point just beneath her right ear and traveling in a curved line to a point just below her left. The sight is flatly horrific, the red vision of her throat's insides, wet and raw, gashed out of the pale white flesh. Blood is dried in clustered drips along the length of the wound.

Cortez takes one knee in the mud beside me and murmurs: "Our Father, who art in heaven." I glance at him questioningly and he looks up, smiling but uneasy.

"I know," says Cortez. "I'm full of surprises."

I'm looking at the corpse, at her neck, thinking about the rack over the kitchen sink, butcher's knife, paring knife, cleaver, everything splattered and stained with blood, and then I am about to stand up and she breathes—a tiny but distinct movement of her chest, and then another. Rise and fall.

"Whoa—" I say, "Hey—" and Cortez says "What?" while I scramble to find her pulse point, inches below her Adam's apple, under the horrible wound. There it is, the faint cry of a pulse, a thready gallop under my fingertips.

She has no business being alive, this kid, throat slit and lying in the woods, but there you go, here she is. I bend my head down close and listen to the shallow breaths. She's desperately dehydrated, tongue thick and dry and lips cracked.

Very carefully, very gently, I lift the girl and arrange her weight in my arms, supporting her head in the crook of my arm like a newborn baby's.

"It's my fault," I whisper, and Cortez says, "What?"

"It's all my fault."

We're too late. That's the feverish understanding that's burning its way up my neck and my face, standing here cradling this victim: whatever happened out here has already happened and we missed it and it's my fault. We took too long to get here from Concord, made too many stops, always my decision, always my fault. A girl, ten miles outside of Seneca Falls, she came screaming out of the woods beside the roadway: she and her brother had been trying to free the animals from the local zoo, the poor beasts were trapped and starving, and now a tiger had cornered the brother and run him up a tree. All of this one long terrified rush of words, and Cortez said it was a trap and to keep driving the cart—we were in a golf cart, we found it at a country club in Syracuse—but I said I couldn't do that, I said we have to help her and he asked why and I said "she reminds me of my sister." Cortez laughed, opened his door with the sawed-off trained on the girl. "Everything reminds you of your sister."

The episode with the tiger cost us half a day, and there were more, too many more, red towns and gray towns. In Dunkirk we pulled a family from a burning apartment building in the fiery wreck of downtown but then we had nowhere to take them, no way to offer them assistance of any kind. We just left them on the firehouse steps.

It's spitting rain, ugly and cold. Late morning. The dog is moving in anxious circles among the trees, the dirt, the clumps of yellow leaves. I hold the sleeping girl close in my arms like a honeymooner, start the walk back to the police station. Cortez goes ahead of us, swinging the hatchet, clearing brush and branches from the path. Houdini limping along behind.

5.

We called it Police House because that was the name the kids picked for it, a big isolated country house in western Massachusetts, near a dot on the map called Furman. A bunch of cops and retired cops and their kids and friends have banded together there to live out the last run of days in relative security, in the company of like-minded individuals. That's where I was living, along with Trish McConnell and her kids, along with a handful of other old friends and new acquaintances, before I left to find my sister.

Among those in residence at Police House, on the top floor, is a tough old bird with close-cropped gray hair named Elda Burdell, known as the Night Bird, or just the Bird. Officer Burdell retired at the rank of detective sergeant two years before I joined the force; at Police House she has eased into the roles of unofficial dean and resident sage. Not the leader, but the person who sits in the attic in her armchair drinking Pabst Blue Ribbon from a stack of cases she showed up with, dispensing advice and wise counsel about everything. The kids ask her which berries are safe to eat. Officer Capshaw and Officer Katz had the Bird settle a bet about what the best lures are for catching trout out of the fast-moving stream a quarter mile from the house.

Late on August 23, the day after my trip to Concord to visit Abigail, I took the long walk up the stairs to the attic to discuss a couple of matters related to my planned departure.

The Night Bird offers me a Pabst, which I decline, and we speak quickly about the necessary arrangements, and then she gazes at me with a half smile while I linger at the doorway, one foot in, one foot out.

"Something else on your mind, son?"

"Well—" I hesitate, rubbing my mustache, feeling ridiculous. "I just wanted your take on something."

"Fire away." She leans forward with her hands draped between her legs, and I launch in, I give it to her as briefly as I can: the rogue scientist formerly attached to Space Command, the supposed nuclear stockpile waiting somewhere in the United Kingdom, the standoff burst.

The Night Bird holds up two fingers, takes a short sip from her beer can, and says, "I'll stop you there. You're going to ask if a standoff burst is plausible."

"You've heard of it?"

"Oh boy, oh boy, Officer. I've heard of *all* of them." The Night Bird sets down the Pabst and reaches out a thick palm. "Hand me that, will ya? The red binder there."

As it turns out, Officer Burdell's made a study of all the various scenarios; she's been collecting all the sober theories and glittery-eyed Hail Mary pitches and gauzy counterfactuals, all the off-the-wall ideas presented as possible world savers.

"The standoff burst, kid, you're talking about a top ten fantasy. Top five, maybe. I mean, you got, what, you got your push/pull fantasies, your gravity tractor fantasies, your Enhanced Yarkovsky Effect fantasies." She flaps open the binder to a particular page, gazes with amusement at the long columns of figures. "People do get a hard-on for that Enhanced Yarkovsky Effect. Probably the funny name. But it won't work. They never got the numbers right on all that magnetic field shit."

I nod, okay. All the science is boring me, I want yes or no. I want answers. "So, but the—the standoff burst?"

The Night Bird clears her throat, cocks her head at me sour for a second, not liking to be rushed.

"Yes," she says. "Same story. It would take calibration and it would take hardware. The calibration, maybe, maybe this Space Command guy has some good numbers, maybe he's figured out the target velocity and that, but no one's got the hardware. Gotta have a highly specialized delivery system, built specific to this thing. To the material strength, the porosity, the velocity. Maybe there's a chance someone builds the right launcher, does the math, if the sumbitch was a couple years out. If it was ten years out, you could nudge it enough that by the time it gets close it sails by, it's a miss." She angles forward in the armchair. "But you're telling me someone thinks they're gonna do it with a standoff burst *now*?" She looks at her watch, shakes her head. "What are we—a month? Month and a half?"

"Forty-two days," I say. "So you're saying there is no chance?"

"No. Listen. Officer. I am saying there is less than that. There is less than no chance."

I thanked her politely for everything and went downstairs and finished packing.

* * *

"You know, I hate to say it," says Cortez, carefully constructing a hand-rolled cigarette. "But this is a very attractive girl."

I look at him sharply. There is nothing in either his tone of voice or his salacious expression to indicate that he does, in fact, hate to say it. He's needling me is what he is doing, saying exactly the thing I will find most unsettling. Other people have enjoyed teasing me in the same way: my old friends, Detectives McGully and Culverson. Nico, of course. I get it. I know what I'm like.

"I'm just saying." Cortez lights a smoke and enjoys a long, satisfied inhale, contemplating the girl's slim body with open appreciation. I don't say anything, not wanting to give Cortez the satisfaction of even a joking rejoinder, no mild "ha-ha" or straight-man rolling of my eyes. I scowl, waving cigarette smoke away from the unconscious young woman, and he stubs the thing out on the floor.

"Oh, dear Palace," he says, and he yawns and stands up. "I'm going to miss you when I'm in heaven and you're not."

I'm sitting on the toilet, beside the girl, whom we've laid out on the thin bare mattress, her hands tucked at her sides. The bed is just inside the bars, inside the actual cell part of the holding cell, along with the toilet and the sink and mirror. Cortez is on the other side of the room, the good-guy side, in the thin space between the bars and the door leading out to the hallway. That's the only place I could find a ceiling hook for the saline bag, so that's where it's hung: on the good-guy side of the room, the sterile fluid dripping out of the bag, looping down through its tubing, through the bars and into the girl's arm. When we left Police House, the Night Bird assembled a first-aid kit for me: reams of gauze and boxes of aspirin and bottles of hydrogen peroxide, plus two liters of saline in two one-liter bags and an IV start kit. When I told her I had no idea how to administer it, she scoffed and said just follow the instructions on the kit. She said it practically administers itself.

Cortez follows my gaze up to the bag of fluid. "Doesn't look like it's coming out, does it?"

"Well, it's dripping at the top, see?"

"Did you do it right?"

"I don't know. But it's dripping."

"What happens if you did it wrong?"

I don't respond, but the answer is that she won't get fluid and she'll die. I check the Casio and it's 4:45 in the afternoon. The watch was given to me, along with a rushed hug, by Trish McConnell's daughter Kelli. "Mom is mad at you," she said, and I said, "I know," and she said, "I am, too," but nevertheless she snuck the watch into my pocket, and I've been wearing it. When you press the side button it glows a pleasant blue-green. I love the watch.

This girl does not appear to have been sexually assaulted. I checked—swiftly and gingerly and with the minimum possible physical contact, murmuring apologies, but I checked. Neither does she have abrasions at the wrists or elbows that would be consistent with having been bound. Just the throat, plus the contusions and lacerations to the face, along with other signs of violent struggle: bruises on her knuckles and shins, two torn fingernails. I collected tissue samples from under her nails with a tweezer and placed them carefully in one of the sandwich bags. Detective Palace's Miniature Roving Evidence Locker. I cleaned and dressed the wound to her throat, applying Neosporin in a thin glaze along the wide obscene mouth of the cut. I ended up using too much gauze, extending the bandaging on either side well beyond thc edges of the wound, reaching around to the back of her neck. It looks like her head has been cut off and reattached. The girl's hair is perfectly black, falling away in two matted curtains from her face.

I stand up from the toilet, turn away for a minute, waver on my feet. I'm starving. Exhausted. In my hand is the sleeping girl's bracelet. It was in her shirt-front pocket, not on her wrist. Delicate fake gold, the sort of cheap token you get at a mall chain store, the kind of thing boys buy for girls in high school. There are charms dangling from it: a music note, a pair of ballet slippers. A tiny silver cluster of flowers, delicate and lovely.

"Irises?" I murmur to myself.

"Lilies," says Cortez.

"You think?" I feel the small weight of the chain in my palm.

"Maybe they're roses."

"Lilies," he says again and yawns.

I study the girl's blank face and decide that her name is Lily. That's why she has the bracelet. I need for her to have a name, for right now.

"My name is Henry Palace," I whisper to Lily, who can't hear. Cortez gazes at me with amusement. I ignore him. "I need to ask you a few questions."

She doesn't answer. She's unconscious. I'm not sure what else to do. I have a weird sudden need to lie down on that mattress myself; a weird wish that it was me instead of her. I watch her breathing: shallow breath in, shallow breath out. I hold the bracelet in my palm, dull in the dirty gold light of the small gray cell.

Cortez pushes off from the wall and leans against the bars and starts talking, absently, casually.

"My mother was in a coma once. State hospital. Just two days. They brought her lunch and dinner, even though she was eating through a tube. Oversight, I guess. Or some dumb rule. Me and my brother ate it. It was good, too, compared to the food she usually provided for us."

He laughs. I give him a half smile. I am never quite sure, when Cortez rolls out one of his long, involved stories, how true it is, how embellished, how much fabricated from whole cloth. The first time I met Cortez he was holed up in an ersatz warehouse on Garvins Falls Road, sitting on a pile of loot, which was subsequently taken from him by his erstwhile romantic and business partner, Ellen. He has told me three versions of that story, all with substantively different details: she caught him unawares and chased him out with a hatchet; she tricked him in a bargain; she had another lover, who showed up with some friends and cleaned the place out.

He's wandered back into the cell now and he stands beside the small toilet, examining his wide, uneven face in the mirror. I ask him how his mother ended up in the coma.

"Oh." He cracks his knuckles. "You know. I cut school one afternoon to go home and smoke some weed, and I found her and her boyfriend, and the boyfriend was choking her. His name was Kevin. He had been a marine. He was choking her with two hands, like this." Cortez turns from the mirror and mimes the gesture, knuckles knitted together around an imaginary neck, eyes bulging.

"That's awful."

"He was a bad man, Kevin."

"So she was choked, and lost consciousness?"

He makes a vague gesture. "She was on crack also. They both were."

"Oh." My eyes flicker back to the sleeping girl. "What about her? I'm presuming an OD."

"Bite your tongue." Cortez presses his hand to his chest, mock horrified. "She's not that kind of girl. Someone slashed her. She bled out. She—I don't know. Her organs shut down."

"No." I've been turning this over, trying to remember the medicine of it. Not my specialty. "If a person bleeds enough to lose consciousness then they keep bleeding until they die, unless someone is present to staunch the wound."

Cortez frowns. "You sure?"

"Yes. No." I am trying to remember. "I don't know."

I shake my head in self-disgust. Why don't I know? In five years, I might get to be good at this, at being a policeman. Ten years, maybe.

Cortez turns back to the mirror. I squeeze my knuckles into my eyes, trying to resurrect lessons from basic first-responder trainings. Academy courses, professional readiness seminars. The throat is a narrow place clustered with vital structures—meaning that, whatever else has befallen this girl, she is in one respect extremely lucky: whoever sawed into her throat stopped shy of transecting the carotid artery, stopped shy of the jugular vein, the delicate piping of the trachea. A simple blood test could reveal whether some illicit substance is additionally involved here, but at this point a simple blood test is a concept from an alien universe, it's science fiction. Mass spectrometry and immunoassays and gas-liquid chromatography, all of it belongs now to a bygone world.

And the fact is that what Cortez said actually has the ring of truth. *Not that kind of girl.* But neither was Peter Zell that kind of guy. Nobody is the kind of person they used to be.

I study Lily's calm face, and then look up again at the saline bag. I think some is gone now. I think she's beginning to rehydrate. I hope so.

"Don't worry, Sherlock," says Cortez. "We'll just wait for her to wake up and we'll ask her what happened. Oh, unless it takes more than a week. If it takes more than a week, we're fucked."

He laughs again and this time I give it to him, I laugh too, I roll my eyes and shake my head. Next week, we'll all be dead. This station will be a pile of ash, and all of us inside it. Ha-ha-ha. I get it.

* * *

I leave Lily sleeping and Cortez smoking and tromp back through the woods to the crime scene.

If Detective Culverson were here, he would do a quiet, focused reenactment—walk it through, play all the parts. The girl was splayed out, facedown, pointing westward. Which means she was running from this direction, tripped here perhaps—fell forward this way. I pantomime her last desperate running steps, throw my hands forward like Superman. Imagine falling and landing, do it again, falling and landing, sensing behind me the shadowy form of my pursuer, knife in hand, bearing down.

There are plenty of distinct footprints in the thick mud of the clearing, but they're from two hours ago, from us: the squared-off heel of my traveling Doc Martens, the wedge of Cortez's cowboy boots. I can even see the circuitous routes of Houdini's paw prints, dancing circles around the scene. But the ground around the girl is an indistinct mush of scuff marks, ambiguous indentations, ground-down leaves and clots of mud. Black traces in the surrounding brown. All signs of the assailant buried or washed away from the crime scene by the wet weather of the past two days.

I trudge back through the woods to the station, emerge onto the gravelly driveway that horseshoes through what was once a neat municipal lawn and is now an ugly field. Uneven beds of zinnias surrounded by overgrown grass like an advancing army. In the center of the lawn are two flagpoles, two flags rustling listlessly in the light rain: the United States of America, the state of Ohio. I search as carefully as I can through the lawn, dividing it into a grid in my mind and moving through sector by sector. I find things that might be clues and might not be: a mound of peanut shells, a tangled half-foot length of twine. In a sector just north of the Ohio state flag I find three evenly spaced divots in the mud that look to have been left by tent poles.

When I've completed the grid I stand for a long time under the flags with my hands on my hips, rain in my eyes like tears, rain dribbling down my nose and chin. There is a level of tiredness where your body feels tender, like a bruise. Your throat hurts; your eyes sting. The hunger intensifies it—you feel shriveled, sort of, bent, burnt, hardened. Like the crust of something, the rind.

Budgeted for today I've got three little bags of the honey-roasted peanuts, plus a green apple from a basket we took from a Residence Inn in Penfield. I eat one of the apples rapidly, like a horse. I almost eat one of the bags of peanuts and then I decide to save it for later.

Two overlapping trails of blood; two passages down the corridor; one going out and one coming back.

Lily is attacked inside the kitchenette. She runs, blood singing out of her neck, perpetrator chasing after, and manages to lose him in the woods. Collapses in the clearing where we found her. Assailant goes back inside, blood still dripping off his three knives. Hangs them up and disappears.

Disappears, though, what does that mean? It means he goes

underground. Through the hole in the floor of the garage.

Right? Detective Palace, isn't that right?

Right, except how does the determined and murderous perpetrator fail to track down a defenseless, hundred-pound girl, stumbling through the woods and bleeding from the neck?

Right—except why, and how, is he juggling three knives?

I stare up at the sky and clench my teeth and fight back a fresh wave of panic and guilt and desperation because I will probably never know. This mystery, along with my sister's, will remain unsolved forever. It *is* the right place, the police station in Rotary, Ohio, it's the right place but now it's the wrong *time*, we're too late, we didn't get here in time to stop this girl from being attacked and we didn't get here in time to stop my sister from slipping down through the earth and away. My fault. All my fault.

I rub my forehead with the heel of my hand, staring at the edge of the station lawn where it becomes the woods, seeing her, our nameless sleeping girl, racing through the darkness, hand clutched at her throat, trying to scream, unable, blood exploding from her wound.

* * *

It was not a trap after all. There really was a small-town zoo and these two well-meaning foolish teenagers really had freed the animals and the girl's brother really was now trapped by a tiger. This was in early September, about two weeks ago, sixteen days maybe, halfway through our tortuous journey. Seneca Falls was a gray town, uneasy calm, people out in the streets, some armed, some not armed, some in groups and some alone, everybody grave and on edge. Ten miles out of town is where we spotted the girl waving her arms, and we put her in the golf cart and drove at top speed, shivering and jolting over back roads to this tiny zoo and there he was, tank top, jean shorts, barely sixteen and scared out of his head, quavering out on a top branch, his fidgeting weight bending the branch low to where the animal was snarling up at him. Mangy coat stretched thin over the rickety ribs.

"What are we going to do?" said the girl, and I said, "Well—" and Cortez brought down the animal with one shotgun blast in the center of the nearer flank. The boy yelped and dropped out of the tree into the dirt, beside the dead animal. Gore and steam rising out of its exploded orange side. Cortez jammed his gun away and looked at me and said, "Can we go now?"

"Wait, wait," the sister said, rushing after us as we clambered into the golf cart. "What are we supposed to do now?"

"If I were you," said Cortez, "I would eat that tiger."

* * *

"*DO NOT DRINK THE WATER IN THE MUSKINGUM RIVER WATERSHED . . . DO NOT DRINK THE WATER IN THE MUSKINGUM RIVER WATERSHED.*"

Cortez is in the dispatch room, standing mesmerized in front of the old foot-switch RadioCOMMAND, a solid black piece of dispatch-specific communications equipment, relaying the same emergency-band warning message over and over. It's a calm voice, the kind of dull affectless tone you used to hear waiting for tech support: press one if you're calling for help setting up your device . . .

"Check this baby out," says Cortez. "Still kicking."

"Oh, sure," I say, feeling a rich wash of nostalgia. "These machines are indestructible. And it would have been installed with multiple battery backups." I'm remembering the same console at Concord PD. It was rendered obsolete by the digital laptop systems that were installed a couple years before I took the oath, but somehow no one ever wheeled it out of Dispatch, and it sat there in the corner, black and shiny and immovable, a monument to traditional police work.

The message coming out of the Rotary RadioCOMMAND shifts: "*FIRST-AID CENTERS HAVE BEEN ESTABLISHED IN THE FOLLOWING COMMUNITIES . . . FIRST-AID CENTERS HAVE BEEN ESTABLISHED IN THE FOLLOWING COMMUNITIES* . . ." and then the lady starts to list them, good old-fashioned Norman Rockwell town names: "*CONESVILLE . . . ZANESVILLE . . . DEVOLA . . .*"

I run my finger along the dusty top of the machine. It's a beautiful piece of police equipment, the RadioCOMMAND console, it really is.

"*FIRST-AID CENTERS HAVE BEEN ESTABLISHED IN THE FOLLOWING COMMUNITIES . . .*"

We stand there side by side, Cortez and I, listening to the charmless recital of town names. It is creating this low wistful feeling in my heart, the woman's voice, the drone of the machine, and I think it may simply be that I miss information. For most of my life the world was awash with news, with reports of things happening; and then in the last year they blipped off the radar, one by one, the *Concord Monitor* and the *New York Times* and then television, the whole concept of television, and the Internet with its ceaseless froth and churn, all of it just gone. For a while back in Concord, before my house burned down and I left, I had a ham radio tuned to someone named Dan Dan the Radio Man, and I listened to him all through the Mayfair Commission hearings. Dan Dan reported out the last round of IPSS legislation, hurriedly passed by the rump Congress, nationalizing grain silos and redesignating all national parks as camps for the internally displaced.

On the road you could get only the swirl of gossip and unconfirmed reports, the nervous trading of rumors, speculation, and fantasy. Someone says that the Hoover Dam has been dynamited by downstream Nevadans desperate for fresh water. Someone waves a paper, supposedly a copy of one signed by the president, declaring the United States to be "a sovereign and enduring nation, retaining in perpetuity its privileges over all territory currently encompassed." Someone says that the city of Savannah has been "taken" by catastrophe immigrants from Laos, who have turned the town into a fortress and are shooting white people on sight; someone else says no way, it's Roanoke where that happened, it's totally Roanoke, and the CIs are from Ethiopia.

And now here we are, this is what's left of the outside world:

packaged sandwiches and Band-Aids are being handed out under a tent somewhere in Apple Grove, Ohio.

"*THE 'BUCKEYES HELPING BUCKEYES' PROGRAM WILL CONTINUE THROUGH IMPACT AND BEYOND,*" says the RadioCOMMAND. "*THE 'BUCKEYES HELPING BUCKEYES' PROGRAM WILL CONTINUE THROUGH IMPACT AND BEYOND.*"

I turn to head back outside, and a great rush of sparkles and stars paint the inside of my eyelids, and I stumble and catch the doorjamb and hold myself steady.

"You okay?" say Cortez, and I wave over my shoulder, *I'm fine*, here I go. But when I let go of the doorjamb and try to walk again I get another fireworks head rush, and this time I'm seeing bloody splatter patterns burned across my retinas. A girl facedown in a field. A door in the floor. A rack of red knives behind a red sink. A candy machine emptied of its candy like a gutted animal.

"Palace?"

I take a step—I'm very tired. I fall down.

6.

"Henry. Hey. Get up."

That voice. I wake up and that's it—mystery solved. Nico is simply present, her eyes flashing in the darkness like a cat's. She is kneeling at my side where I'm lying on the ground, waking me up like she used to wake me up to make her breakfast, poking at my chest with two fingers, sticking her face right up close into my face. "Henry. Henry. Hen. Hen. Henry. Hey. Hen."

She jabs a thumb over her shoulder, at Lily, the unconscious girl next to me on the thin jail-cell mattress. Cortez must have hauled me from the dispatch room and laid me down beside her in the bed.

"Who's your friend?" says Nico.

I start to talk, to say *oh, Nico, I thought you were dead* but she puts one finger over her lips to hush me, and I obey, I hush, I stare at her in silence. The smell of Cortez's cigarette lingers in the room.

"So, listen," says Nico, and just the sound of her voice is forming the heat of tears in my eyes. "It's happening. It's a go." She looks exactly as she did the day of the yearbook photo, the picture in my jacket pocket: she's grown her hair back out and she's wearing her glasses again, her old ones, from when she was in high school. I can't believe she even still has them. I want to leap up and hug her. I'll put her on the handlebars of the bike, I'll put Houdini in the wagon to ride behind us. I'll take her back home.

"Everything went exactly as planned," she's saying. "They brought him down here. That scientist, the one I told you about? We've got him. We're going to England in the morning, and he and the team he knows there will initiate the standoff burst. Show that asteroid who's boss." I mouth the words back to her, astonished: "Show that asteroid who's boss." She smiles. Her teeth glow white. "It's all going to be *fine*," she says.

I have objections, I have a lot of questions, but Nico presses one flat hand over my mouth, shaking her head, flashing impatience.

"I'm telling you, Hen. I'm telling you. It's all wrapped up like a beef burrito." One of the dopey expressions our father used to use, one his favorites. "It's all squared away. Nothing to worry about."

This is incredible. Incredible! They did it. Nico did it. She saved the world.

"Listen, though. In the meantime, keep an eye on your goon. I don't trust him."

My goon. Cortez.

They never had the pleasure of meeting, those two. They

would have liked each other. But Nico never met him. Never heard of him. A pool of melancholy blooms in my chest and rushes out into my body like deep-blue blood. It's not real. I'm dreaming, and as soon as I know that I am dreaming, Nico fades like a Dickens ghost and is replaced by my grandfather, sallow and sunken, hollowed-out cheeks and staring eyes, sitting in his ancient leather armchair sucking on an American Spirit, muttering to himself.

"Dig a hole," he says. "Dig a hole."

* * *

The smoke is real. Fresh cigarette smoke, rolling down the real police station hallway through the thin cell bars and into my dream. My grandfather really did smoke American Spirits, the same as Nico. Or, rather, Nico smokes them, the same as him. He would curse after each one, say "stupid goddamn things" even as he drew the next one from the pack, fidgeting it with irritation between two old fingers. A man who did not like to enjoy things.

It's not him smoking now; he's been dead some years. It's Cortez, somewhere in the building, working on another butt.

Neither was I really on the thin mattress, tucked in snugly beside our sleeping assault victim; I'm right where I fell down, on the floor in Dispatch, in the shadow of the RadioCOMMAND. I can feel it, still, the warm dream feeling of her hand pressed flat over my mouth, Nico's hand.

I stand quickly, then buckle from the pins and needles in my legs, reach out and steady myself on the wall with a flat hand. It's

5:21. It's morning. How long did I sleep? I follow the curling stink of the smoke and find Cortez back in the cop-car garage, squatting in the center and examining the ground. Our portable coffee rig is erected on one of the shelves, stray grounds clinging in clusters around the mouth of the urn. There's a thermos at Cortez's side with steam rising around its edges, mingling with the cigarette smoke.

"Oh, good morning," he says, without looking up.

"We have to get down there."

"No kidding." He grunts, slides down onto his stomach. "I'm working on it."

"Can we get down there?"

"I'm working on it," he says again. "Have some coffee."

I find my steel thermos on the shelf behind me, the one with my name Sharpied on the side, and I pour myself a cup. My dream was obvious wish fulfillment, a classic: Nico's alive, the threat of the asteroid is ended, Earth survives, I survive. But what about my grandfather, muttering from his deathbed, "Dig a hole"? His actual last words. He said that. Cortez has his face against the floor, one eye opened, one eye closed, cigarette dangling from the corner of his mouth while he slowly runs the claw of his hammer along the concrete, squinting at the invisible fracture between the lid and the surrounding floor.

I sip my coffee; it's hot and bitter and black. I wait ten seconds. "So what do you think? Can we get down there?"

"You're a very focused individual."

"I know. So what do you think?"

He just laughs, and I stop, I wait, I demand patience of myself. Cortez wants the same thing I do, as badly as I do. I want to get into the hole because that's where my sister is, my sister or individuals possessing information as to her whereabouts; Cortez wants to get into the hole because it is there. He wants in because he is locked out. His hair is a mess, out of its ponytail, rolling in tangled clumps down his back. I've never asked him, in so many words, why he came along on this fool's journey in search of my errant sister, but I think this is the answer: to do things like this, to do what he loves with what time is left. I am a question mark pointed at a secret, Cortez is a tool aimed at the stubborn places of the world.

"So?" I say. "Can you—"

"Yes." He heaves himself to standing and flicks his cigarette away, adding one more butt to our gathered piles.

"Yes? How? How?"

"Wait and I'll tell you." He smiles and then digs out tobacco for a fresh smoke, pats his pants for papers, rolls the thing slowly, torturing me. And then, at last: "It's a wedge, not a flat lid, is my guess, which means we couldn't lift it up even if we weren't a couple of skeletons."

"So?"

"So we crack it instead. First choice is a gas-powered jackhammer, which we don't have and won't get."

I'm nodding, nodding like crazy, and my mind is running and gunning, ready to roll. This is what I want. Specifics. Answers. An agenda. I've set down my coffee, I'm ready to run out of here and go get what we need.

"Second choice?" I say.

"Second choice is a sledgehammer." He takes a long drag on the cigarette, grins languorously while I wait in desperation. "And I know where to get one."

"Where?"

"Why, at the store, of course."

At last—at last—he explains. He clocked the hammer when we rummaged through a SuperTarget two days ago, the last stop we made, three highway exits before Rotary. The SuperTarget was among five other stores, massive and fortresslike, spread out across a vast parking lot: a Hobby Lobby, a Home Depot, a Kroger grocery, a Cheesecake Factory.

"It was a Wilton," Cortez says. "Big twelve-pounder. Good grip on it." He's leaning against the wall, shaking his head. "And I left it behind. I remember, because I picked it up and I almost took it but then I didn't. I thought, we won't use it. It'll weigh down the wagon and we just don't need it." He sighs and exhales wistfully, like a man dreaming of a lost lover. "But I remember it. A big lovely Wilton with a fiberglass handle. Do you remember it?"

"I—sure." I'm not sure. I remember the SuperTarget pretty well, rows and rows of empty shelves, scented candles and bath towels scattering the smudged tile floors, plumbing fixtures smashed on the ground like broken toys. The grocery aisle ravaged as if by packs of beasts. A big sign, must have been months old, that said NO MORE AMMUNITION THANK YOU SO MUCH.

"But what if it's gone?" I say. "What if someone else has taken it?"

"Well, then we won't have it," Cortez says. "Just like now."

I chew on the end of my mustache. The point of the sarcasm is that if we go in search of the sledgehammer and don't find it, we will have lost nothing, but in fact he is wrong, because we will have lost time. Time is what we will have lost. How long to get down there on the bike, how many hours to find the hammer, to secure it to the wagon, to bike it back?

Cortez knows exactly where it is. He remembers the aisle and the shelf: aisle 9, shelf 14. That's how his mind operates. It's in the rear of the store, past the gardening supplies and the plumbing section. I hear it again in his voice as he describes the route, that deep vein of regret, for having left the hammer behind, for having been caught for once in his life without the necessary tool for the job.

"You stay here," I tell him. "You watch the hole."

"Okay," he says, saluting me, settling cross-legged in the center of the garage. "I'll watch the hole."

* * *

On my way out I stop in the holding room, gratified to see that the 1.5-liter bag of saline solution is empty, sagging and curling at the top like a flattened balloon. The area around the needlestick in Lily's extended right arm seems just fine also, no purple radius of traumatized tissue around the entry point. Lily, or whatever her name is. Poor girl. Somebody's something. I step into the cell with her and run my finger gently along the length of her lips; they're dry still but not nearly so dry, not deathly dry. She's taking fluid.

"Good job, kid," I say to her. "Good for you."

Except for the not inconsiderable problem that if Lily is taking fluid she should be passing it, and she is not. There's no urine, which is warning me of something but what exactly I don't know, because my medical training is limited and specific, first responder material, crime scene material: administering rescue breaths and patching wounds and minimizing blood loss. Piecing together bedside medical clues is uncharted territory. It's a crossword puzzle in a language I don't know.

I stand up on a chair and I carefully unhook the bag and switch it out, and that's all she wrote for my saline-solution supply. Whatever else is going on with this girl, I have reached the limits of my ability to affect medical intervention. At this point her condition has become binary; she will either die or not.

"You're going to be okay," I tell her. "You're going to be fine."

And that's it, I'm ready to go, except for a sharp jag of memory, a flash from last night's dream: Nico, scowling and untrusting, whispering urgently, *keep an eye on your goon.*

Disturbed, uneasy, I look back down the hallway at the garage, where he is sitting, smoking, waiting. It's not fair; it was a dream; Nico doesn't even know the man. But then neither do I, exactly. He is good company, and I have taken advantage of his various competencies, but I suddenly feel how far I am from really knowing him—certainly from knowing him enough to trust him.

And meanwhile, the girl: asleep, vulnerable, alone. I picture Cortez's crooked smile, his eyes dancing along Lily's recumbent figure, admiring her like a bowl of fruit.

It's an old-fashioned jailer's key they've got here, hanging on an old-fashioned hook. I push closed the door of the cell area, give it a good shake to make sure it's closed and locked. Then I take the key off the hook and toss it through the bars, where it lands and skitters to the back wall of the cell.

Wednesday, August 22

Right ascension 18 26 55.9
Declination -70 52 35
Elongation 112.7
Delta 0.618 AU

I've got Abigail calmed down now, I've got a conversation going, I've got lucidity flickering in and out of her eyes.

I showed her my badge and my gun, explained that I am a retired Concord police officer working on a case, not an alien trailing a veil of cosmic dust, not someone from NASA here to inject her with antimatter. We're at a small, rickety table in the back of the store, in the same back room where I once sat behind Jordan and watched him access the Internet, access the NCIC database, subjected myself to his taunting contempt to gain his help on my case.

We're sitting at the table and Abigail is telling me haltingly, tiredly, that Jordan is not here and she does not know where he is.

"He is supposed to be here. We were supposed to be here together. Those were our instructions."

"Instructions from who?"

She shrugs. Her body movements are jerky, pained. "Jordan talked to them."

"To who?"

She shrugs again. She is staring at the table, pushing a torn corner of a piece of paper around with her finger, first this way and then another, like she is moving it on an invisible game board.

"What were the instructions?"

"Stay—stay here."

"In Concord?"

"Yeah. Here. Resolution had been found. At a base. Gary, Indiana."

"Resolution. That's the scientist? Hans-Michael Parry."

"Yeah. And the others were going to find him, go to the last phase, but we were to stay." She looks up, sticks out her bottom lip. "Me and him. But then Jordan went away. Gone, gone. I was alone. And then the dust started to float in." She stammers. "It—it—it just floated in."

It's like she reminds herself of it, of her invisible torment—she starts looking this way and then that, scowling into the corners of the room, rubbing at her skin where it's coated with the cosmic dust.

"And when was this? Abigail? When did he leave?"

"Not that long. A week ago? Two weeks? It's hard because then the dust started coming. Coming on in."

"I know it's hard," I say, and I'm thinking, stay with me, sister, just a bit further. We're almost there. "So the group, when they left, they were traveling to Gary, Indiana?"

She scowls, bites at her lower lip. "No, no. That's where they found Resolution. But the recon spot was in Ohio. A police station in Ohio."

Ohio. *Ohio.* As soon as she says it I know that's where I'm going, as soon as she says the word—that is the target. The last known location of the missing individual. Nico is in Ohio.

I move forward in my seat, nearly toppling the table with my eagerness.

"Where in Ohio? What town?"

I wait for her to answer, holding my breath, teetering on the edge of discovery, like a drop of water on the side of a glass.

"Abigail?"

"I can feel the planet spinning. That's also happening. It makes me dizzy and nauseous. But I can't stop *feeling* it. Can you—do you understand that?"

"Abigail, what is the name of the town in Ohio?"

"First you have to help me," she says, and reaches out her hands in their latex gloves and covers my hands. "I can't do it. I'm too scared to do it."

"Do what?" I say, but I already know, I can feel it pouring out of her eyes. She pushes one of her semiautomatics across the table to me.

"I know the name of the town. I have a map. But then you do it and do it fast."

PART TWO

Blue Town Man

Friday, September 28

Right ascension 16 55 19.6
Declination -74 42 34
Elongation 83.1
Delta 0.376 AU

1.

Here is how I know that she's not dead: because she's never dead. Like that time I found her in White Park, tucked fairylike in the shade beneath the slide, after Dad's funeral. *You thought I was gone, too, didn't you, Hen?* And she was right, I had thought so, and she's given me periodic occasion to think so ever since. Since the year that our parents died I have carried this foretaste of her doom like a sourness in my stomach, this cold certainty that one day she too would slip away: one of her dimwitted underachieving boyfriends would involve her in a drug deal gone wrong, or the junk-shop motorcycle she drove around her sophomore year would catch a patch of ice and flip, or she would simply be the kid who drinks too much at the party and is carried off in a stretcher while the others stand like cows, staring and swaying in the red flash of the emergency lights.

And yet again and again she has managed to swim successfully through the tides of her life, a fish flashing through the dark foam, even in these last terrible months. It was not her, but her deadbeat husband, Derek, who disappeared, sacrificed to the murky goals of her crackpot organization. And it was not her but me who nearly died in a fort in southeastern Maine, shot in the arm on the hunt for a missing man. It was Nico, that time, who rescued *me*, coming up over the horizon in that shocking, impossible helicopter.

Still, though. Nevertheless. Now she's gone again, and the fear grows in my gut like illness, the knowledge that she is dead somewhere or dying, and I have to remind myself that always, always she has been okay. Not a scratch on her. She's somewhere. She's fine.

* * *

Only one road leads from the police station down into the town proper, and, this being the heart of the American Midwest, that road is called Police Station Road: a pastoral quarter mile of gentle downhill pavement, snaking past horse fencing and a country-red barn. A windmill is off to the right, back from the road a ways, listing rightward as if someone tried to push it over and then got bored. Houdini lies coughing in the basket on the handlebars. The empty wagon rattles along behind us, waiting for its load.

It's sunrise, drizzling still, and with the muted rain-wet golds and scarlets of the trees, with the crickets calling to one another, the crows doing their plaintive cawing, I find myself imagining for a minute what a peaceful world this'll be when the people are gone, when the paved expanses are reclaimed by wildflowers and the birds have the full use of the sky.

I know, of course, that this is just another dream, another piece of widely held wishful thinking: the virginal and pastoral postapocalyptic world, wiped free of mankind's dirty cities and loud machines. Because these auburn Midwestern trees are going to burst into flames in the first burning moments. Trees around the world will go up like dry tinder. In a short time the clouds of ash will block the sun, put a hard stop to photosynthesis, snuff out all lushness. The squirrels will burn up, the butterflies and the flowers, the ladybugs crawling in the tall grass. Possums will drown in their holes. What is about to happen is not the reclaiming of Earth by a triumphant Mother Nature, a karmic repudiation of humanity's arrogant ill stewardship.

Nothing we ever did mattered one way or another. This event has always been in the cards for man's planet, for the whole scope of our history, coming regardless of what we did or didn't do.

* * *

"Rats," I say, spiraling down the exit ramp, as the massive parking lot comes into view below me. "Rats, rats, rats."

The SuperTarget has been taken. I see people with machine guns wandering around on the roof of the store and I instinctively start counting them—one, two, three, four, . . .—although even one person with a machine gun on the roof of a big-box store is plenty. Five metal staircases, those wheeled stair sets that move up and down the aisles to help customers access high shelves, have been rolled out of the store and pushed to the parking lot entrances, stationed like guard towers. There's someone at the top of each staircase. Closest to me is a trim middle-aged woman in a red softball jersey, a red bandana holding back a tumble of black hair, a machine gun of her own.

I get off the bike and raise my hand to the lady with the gun and she raises a hand back and then she shouts, "hey-*yuh*," and from the far side of the parking lot someone on one of the other moving staircases—also in a red jersey, though I can't tell from here if it's a man or a woman, young or old—calls back in kind, "hey-*yuh*," and then there's another call and then another, the syllables carried around in a ring, and at last a white Dodge pickup roars around from the back of the store, belching vegetable-oil exhaust and kicking up gravel off the pavement. The truck screeches to a halt a few feet from me, and I step backward and raise both hands.

"Good morning," I call out.

There is a squeal of feedback from a bullhorn mounted on the roof above the driver's seat. I wince. The woman in the guard tower winces. Then someone starts talking through the bullhorn from inside the truck.

"Is this your—" The voice is swallowed in a new burst of feedback, and then there's a muttered "oh, hell" and an adjustment of the volume. "Is this your place?"

"No." I shake my head. He means the parking lot—the store—did I, or did I and some band of compatriots, maybe all dressed in sensible blue pants and tan blazers to keep track of each other, like these guys are all in softball jerseys, did we already call shotgun on this SuperTarget? Did we declare it to be our base, our temporary encampment, or were we intending to pick the bones of the shelves for food or entertainment for the last week before impact?

"No," I say again. "I'm passing through." The woman on the moving staircase is watching with mild interest. I'm keeping my hands in the air, just in case.

"Oh, okay," says the voice through the bullhorn. "Yeah, us too."

The people on the roof of the building have clustered at the edge, watching me. Machine guns, red jerseys. From the corner of my eye I can see around the corner to the backside of the SuperTarget, where there's a blur of figures busy at the loading dock. They're cleaning it out. Box loads, full pallets wrapped in clear plastic sheeting. There wasn't much left in the store when we were there, but what there was is coming out. I feel a flash of desperation. All I need is that sledgehammer.

"There's an item in there," I say. "Something I really need."

"Well—" Another squealing tide of feedback. "Oh, for heaven's sake," the man says, and the sound stops abruptly as he shuts off the bullhorn and opens the driver's side door and leans out. Glasses, mild expression. Red jersey also, with the name ETHAN stitched above the breast pocket. A soft paunch on an athletic build. He looks like somebody's middle-school basketball coach.

"Sorry. Stupid thing. What is it that you need?"

"A sledgehammer. There's one in there. A Wilton with a fiberglass handle." I step forward to him, make eye contact, smile and raise a hand, like we're meeting at a barbecue. "I really need it bad."

"Well, huh. Okay, hold on." He scratches his cheek, uncertain, raises one finger, and leans back into the truck. I hear him talking on a CB or a walkie-talkie. Then he leans back out and peers at me smiling while he waits for an answer from whoever decides. He'd say yes, I can see it. Were it up to just Ethan I'd be good to go. It's still raining; endless steady mild rain. I run my hands over Houdini's fur. I take a look at the woman on the moving staircase, and she's looking off into space, bored, letting her mind wander. A year and a half ago she would have been checking e-mail on her phone.

The walkie-talkie blares from within the truck, and Ethan leans back in and listens for a moment, nodding. I watch his face through the windshield until he pokes his head back out.

"Listen, bud. You got anything to trade?"

I make a rapid internal inventory of my possessions: Jacket and pants, shoes and shirt. Notebook and pen. A loaded SIG Sauer P229 and a box of .40-caliber shells. A tattered high-school yearbook photo of a missing girl.

"Not really," I say. "Unfortunately. But that sledgehammer. The truth is, it's mine."

"What do you mean, it's yours?"

I don't know what to say. I saw it first? I need it real bad?

"One thing," I say, hearing my voice travel into a pleading, desperate upper register. "It's just the one thing."

Ethan rubs his chin. He feels bad. Everybody feels bad. "What about the wagon?" He looks up at our friend in the guard tower, who looks skeptical. "Maybe you could trade us that wagon."

I look down at the battered Red Ryder. We brought it from Concord. The wheels are bent.

"The thing is, if I give you the wagon, I can't get the hammer back to where I need it."

"Well, heck, then." The man sighs. "You got a, uh—what do you call those again?"

"Catch-22?" says the woman on the staircase.

Before I can say something else, someone shouts "hey-*yuh*" from the loading dock, and then someone else yells it from the roof, and then the man at the next staircase over yells it, too, and Ethan's gotta run: he pops back into the truck and pulls the door closed and does a rapid three-point turn in the parking lot and heads back the way he came. The woman with the bandana looks at me, tight-lipped, and shrugs, *what can ya do?*

"Shit," I say softly.

Houdini barks his rattling phlegmy bark, and I bend to scratch his ears.

* * *

I don't know what happens if I go back without the sledgehammer.

Cortez will have more tricks up his sleeve, or else he won't, and if he doesn't we sit on our hands drinking weird bad coffee and making disjointed conversation until Wednesday around lunchtime, when the conversation stops and everything stops.

The town of Rotary is small, but it's bigger than Pike, where the SuperTarget was. It's bigger than anything else around. There's got to be a hardware store.

There's a church spire and another one, there's the fat onion bulb of a water tower with the word ROTARY painted in mile-high letters in the classical small-town style. Autumn dogwoods along the sidewalk, leaves orange and red, branches drooping with rain. No people, no sign of people.

It's got to be here: towns like this one still have hardware stores, or they did until last year, the mom-and-pop operations, beloved by the locals, losing money every year. There will be a sledgehammer at the hardware store, a row of them, a display, and I will take one and strap it in the wagon and mule it back up Police Station Road.

We go from door to door up Main Street: ice cream store, pizza parlor, pharmacy. A bar with an old-timey saloon theme called the Come On Inn. No one anywhere, no signs of life. "Blue town," I say to Houdini as we're poking around an abandoned ice cream shop. He's nosing into an empty box of sugar cones, trying to get his teeth into something that's food. There is a utility closet in the basement of the one-story redbrick municipal building, with an acrid reek of ammonia and mop water, a stack of bright orange safety cones, countdown hatch marks scratched in the wall by some bored custodian. No sledgehammer. No tools of any kind.

* * *

We called the towns with color names because of the package of multicolored Post-it Notes that Cortez had; he had them left over from his Office Depot warehouse. When we left a town behind us we would assign it a color, just keeping track, just to keep ourselves amused. All the degrees of dissolution, the differing extents to which each town or city had collapsed under the weight of all this unbearable imminence. Red towns were those seething with active violence: towns on fire, towns beset by marauding bands, daylight shootings, food foragers and food defenders, homes under siege. Only occasionally did we encounter active organized law enforcement: you'd see National Guardsmen patrolling red towns in small clusters, whether officially or unofficially it was hard to say—brave young kids, hollering for order, firing their guns into the air.

Becket, in the Berkshires, was a red town: ten teenagers tailed us on puttering mopeds, chanting for blood like savages. Stottville, New York, was red. De Lancy, Oneonta. Dunkirk, the town where we saved the small family from the fire but left them defenseless on the firehouse steps—bright red.

Green towns were just the opposite, communities where it seemed like some sort of agreement had been made, spoken or implied, to plug along. Folks raking leaves, pushing strollers, waving good morning. Dogs on leashes or bounding after Frisbees. In Media, Ohio, we were astonished to hear the SpongeBob SquarePants theme song being sung lustily by three hundred or more people in a public park at dusk. After the sing-along everyone hung around on the village green: there was a knitting circle, a book club, a demonstration on making candles and another on making bullets. A local sport-shooters association had organized a hunt-and-gather system, traversing the local woods and farmland to bring back venison and beef and distribute it by priority: women and children, the old and the infirm.

A sure sign of a green town was some sort of a garbage system. A trash pyre burning outside the city limits, or even just a dump still in use, people hauling their bags of refuse down there, going out of their way for the mutual benefit. If we didn't see garbage heaped on curbs, Cortez and I, when we rolled into a certain spot, we knew that town was okay for a night of rest.

Black towns are empty. Blue towns feel empty, but they're not, they're just so quiet they might as well be. They're empty except for occasional scurrying, nervous souls darting from one place to another, some feeling safer in the day, some at night. Peeking out of windows, clutching guns, measuring out what they've got left.

By noon we have worked our way through downtown, and Houdini and I reluctantly turn our search to private homes. I set the protocol as knock, wait, knock again, wait again, push in. I find houses cluttered with small personal items: unseasonal clothing, waffle irons, trophies, the sorts of things people leave behind when they leave in an emergency. But tool sheds are empty, like the fridges, like the pantries and the gas cans. At one tidy little aluminum-sided one-story I knock, wait, knock again, wait again, push in, and find a tiny, very old man asleep on an armchair, with a faded *Time* magazine spread out on his chest, like he fell asleep a couple years ago and is about to wake up to a terrible surprise. I tiptoe backward out of there and creep the door shut.

Blue town. Classic blue town.

* * *

It's two o'clock now on the Casio. At some point the sun has burned the clouds away. Time passing and passing.

The thought comes from nowhere, unbidden, big as a hovering spaceship, filling the sky: *She's dead, back there. Back there in the woods. Somewhere I didn't see her.*

Or else she's down in that hole and she's not coming out because she doesn't want to, and what I'm doing here is I'm wasting time until the end.

Keep walking, Hen. Keep searching. Do your job. She's fine.

On Brookside Drive, six short blocks from the American Legion hall, is a small brick ranch house, partially surrounded by some kind of blast wall, a ten-foot-high barrier of concrete. Serious business, like this modest one-story home is an American embassy in Baghdad or Beirut. Thick concrete, smooth face, with slits in the surface, as if for arrows. This fortification was built to withstand not the end, but the events leading up to the end. Thieves. Bandits on the road.

"Hello?" I call up toward the slits. "Hello?"

The sky erupts with the deafening clatter of machine-gun fire. I drop down to my knees. Houdini goes bonkers, chasing himself in a wild circle. Another rip of live fire.

"Okay," I say, yelling into the muddy lawn, where I threw myself down. "Okay."

"I still have the right to defend my home," says a voice, thick and hoarse and slightly manic, from somewhere beyond the wall. "I still have the right to my home."

"Yes, sir," I say again. "Yes, sir, I know."

This is a blue-town man. I can't see his face, but I can feel his fear, his anger. I look up slowly, very slowly, and get a good look at the gun muzzle, long and stiff like the nose of an anteater, poking through one of the slits.

"I'm going," I say, "I'm sorry to bother you," and I go, I crawl away, nice and slow, butt up in the air and hands down.

Worming my way out of there takes me right past the base of the wall, and I see where the man who built it—whoever built it—put a tradesman's stamp in the stone. It's a single word, colored in a deep somber red: JOY.

2.

The only suicide victims I find in Rotary are in a screened-in sunporch on Downing Drive: gunshots, husband and wife, a pitcher of lemonade on the glass-topped front-porch table between them, sugar crystals clinging to the sides, lemon wedges rotting at the bottom. The husband still holds the rifle, clutched between his hands, sunk into his lap. I get a quick read on the scene, instinctively, without even wanting to. He was the shooter, he killed her first, cleanly, and then himself; he took one high on the cheek—a first try, a miss—and then a second shot, under the chin and correctly angled.

I feel a quick swell of good feeling toward the dead man, the bottom of his face a red hole, for having honored their bargain. First his wife and then himself and he followed through, as promised. The lemonade pitcher buzzes with bees, attracted to the fading sweetness.

They don't have a sledgehammer. I check their garage, and then even inside, in the closets. It's just not a common household item.

Houdini and I step down off the porch on Downing Drive into a warm wafting smell, buoying up off the road and surrounding us, and I swear we look at each other, the dog and I, and obviously he can't talk but we do, we say it to each other: "Is that fried chicken?"

Saliva fills my mouth, and Houdini begins whipping his little head this way and that. His eyes are shiny with excitement, like glossy marbles.

"Go," I say, and Houdini bolts for the source of the smell and I bolt after him. We're sprinting along a side street I had not yet explored, a long narrow one-laner dwindling westward off of Elm Street. More shuttered small houses, a filling station with the pumps torn from the ground. As I run after the dog my stomach starts to growl and I laugh a little, a little jagged riff of madman laughter, contemplating the possibility that this is some sort of desert-island mirage: the madman running for the hazy sight of water, the tall hungry policeman hurtling after an illusory bucket of chicken.

The road slopes upward a little, passes through a couple of stoplight intersections, and then to the right is a parking lot—at the center of which, disconcertingly, is the instantly recognizable form of a Taco Bell. The garish exterior in purple and gold, the cheap stucco walls, one of a million such small purpose-built structures that bloomed in the outskirts of small towns in the last half century of American civilization. But there is no question of it being cut-rate Mexican, the smell now billowing thickly around Houdini and me. It's fried chicken, rich and smoky and unmistakable. I wipe my chin. I'm drooling like a cartoon character.

There's music playing, too, that's the other odd thing. We are crossing the Taco Bell parking lot, slowly, me first with gun drawn, Houdini behind me at my pace, inching forward at my feet, and we hear big beat-driven music blaring from the restaurant—from behind the restaurant, it sounds like—raucous music, fuzzy guitars, sing-shout vocals.

I stop moving and whistle sharply at the dog, and he grudgingly heels beside me. I take a good look at the building, smashed windows showing plastic booths inside, linoleum tables, napkin dispensers. The front doors are propped open by a telephone book.

It's the Beastie Boys. The music, blaring from the other side of the parking lot. It's "Paul Revere," from that really big Beastie Boys record. The chicken smell wafts toward us on the breeze, along with the music.

"Sit." I point at the dog. "Stay."

He obeys, more or less, making small fidgety motions while I edge along one side of the tacky little building. "Hello?" I say, back to the wall, gun up, tiptoeing my way around. "Who's there?"

Nobody answers, but I can't be sure I've made myself heard above the music. I was never a huge Beastie Boys fan. I had a friend, Stan Reingold, who was into hip-hop for about a week in junior high school. A bunch of years ago I heard that he had enlisted and ended up in Iraq with the 101st Airborne. He could be anywhere now, of course. I raise the SIG Sauer to chest level, take a big step over the hedges and into the drive-through lane.

I no longer seriously suspect that this is a mirage. The smell of the cooking chicken is too strong, mingling with the gritty tar odor of the asphalt, damp from the rain. Maybe it's some sort of a trap, someone luring unsuspecting passersby with party music and delicious smells and then—who knows?

My view of whatever is going on back here is blocked by a gigantic RV, twenty-five feet long, backed up to the rear of the restaurant and extending perpendicularly out into the parking lot. The massive boxy vehicle is up on blocks, doors all wide open, windows down. Articles of clothing are draped over the windshield and across the popped front hood. There are red stripes along the long tan sides, and the legend HIGHWAY PIRATE is airbrushed in fanciful calligraphy along the flank. The music is coming from inside the RV, it seems like. Houdini gives a small yelp at my feet—he gave up on waiting. I bend down and pat him on the neck and hope he stays quiet. He's not really a very well-trained dog.

The music stops, there is a breath of silence, and then it starts again, Bon Jovi now, "Livin' on a Prayer." We keep moving, Houdini and I, we creep along the side of the RV, and when I come around the back of it I can see the parking lot, and there is a man there with a shotgun pointed at my head.

"Stop in your tracks, brother," he says. "Quit movin' and tell the dog to quit."

I quit moving and thankfully Houdini does, too. There are two of them, a man and a woman, both half naked. He's shirtless in boxer shorts and flip-flops, dirty brown hair in an overgrown mullet. She's in a long, loose flowery skirt, red hair, black bra. Each of them has a beer in one hand and a shotgun in the other.

"All right, brother, all right," says the man, squinting at me. Big sweaty biceps, ruddy forehead. "Please don't make me blow your head off, all right?"

"I won't."

"He won't," says the woman, and she takes a pull off her beer. "I can tell. He's a good boy, right? You're a good boy."

I nod. "I'm a good boy."

"Yes. He's gonna be real good." She winks at me. I stare at her. It's Alison Koechner. The first girl I ever loved. The lean white body, wild curls of orange hair like ribbons on a gift.

"I'm Billy," says the man. "This one's Sandy."

"Sandy," I say, and blink. "Oh."

Sandy grins. That's not Alison. She looks nothing like her. Not really. What is wrong with me? I clear my throat.

"I'm sorry to stumble in on you like this," I say. "I mean no harm."

"Shit, man, neither do we," says Billy. His voice is warm and boozy, soaked in laughter and sunshine.

"No harm in the world," says Sandy.

They clink their bottles together, both still smiling, both still holding their shotguns, raised and pointed. I smile back uneasily, and then there's a long moment, everybody assured of everybody else's good intentions, everybody nevertheless frozen with guns drawn. The way of the world. Behind Billy and Sandy, between their RV and the back of the Taco Bell, is the little private universe they've created. A big old charcoal grill, heavy and black and belching smoke like a steam engine. A rickety beer-making apparatus, a tangle of plastic hoses winding around cylinders and barrels. And there, behind a low wire fence, running around on a ragged layer of straw is a bustling tribe of chickens—rushing past and around each other on their weird alien feet, cackling like merrymakers on a parade ground, waiting for a concert or an execution.

Billy breaks our tableau, stepping forward one step, and I retreat one step, aim the SIG at his face. He squints and pulls his head away, mild annoyance, like a lion ducking back from a mosquito.

"Here's the story, brother man," he says. "I got the beer and I got the gun, you can see that, right? You can take the beer and hang out for a bit, we'll even feed you somethin' before you shove off. We got a chicken on the cooker right now, since it's coming up on suppertime. It's a big one, right, baby?"

"Right," she says. "Claudius." She grins. For a confusing half second I think she's calling me Claudius and then I realize that's the chicken. "Three birds a day," she says. "It's how we keep track of the countdown."

Billy nods, "That's right." Then he sniffs, tosses his hard-rock hair. "Or, option B, you do anything hilarious, you try and fox one of our chickens, and Sandy'll shoot you dead."

"Me?" she says, laughing with astonishment.

"Yeah, you." Billy smiles at me, like we're in on this together. "Sandy's a better shot'n me, especially when it gets later and I got a buzz on."

"Shit, Billy," she says. "You always got a buzz on."

"Like you don't."

This woman looks nothing at all like Alison Koechner, it is clear to me now. The resemblance has receded like a tide.

"Well, brother?" says Billy. "A beer or a bullet?"

I lower my gun. Sandy lowers her gun, and then at last Billy lowers his and hands me the beer, which is warm and bitter and delicious. "Thank you," I say, as the two of them step back and gesture me into the courtyard. "My name is Henry Palace." The dog shuffles in behind me, staring warily at the fat feathery strangeness of the chickens.

A new tune is blaring from the speakers, something heavy metal, something I don't recognize. There are two hammocks suspended on ropes between the restaurant and the RV, swaying above paper plates littered with old chicken bones. Chinese lanterns are hung from the trees around the edges. The speakers are mounted on the outside of the vehicle; the engine is on and idling, powering the tunes, the lights, the world.

I wonder in passing how Trish McConnell is doing, back at Police House. Dr. Fenton, at Concord Hospital. Detective Culverson; Detective McGully, wherever he ended up. Ruth-Ann, my favorite waitress at my favorite restaurant. Everyone back somewhere in time, doing something else.

"Serious, though, man," says Sandy, laying a hand on the small of my back. "You fuck with our chickens, and we blow your mopey face off."

* * *

The chicken is delicious. I eat a polite portion, but Billy and Sandy tell me to take more so I take more and feed a bunch to Houdini, who eats with vigor, which is nice to see. I offer up three bags of honey-roasted peanuts as a side dish, which my hosts accept with delight, raising a series of enthusiastic toasts to my generosity.

They've been living here, "at this particular location," for about a month, maybe six weeks, they don't know for sure. It's their third site, though. "Third," says Billy, "and you gotta figure last, right?" The chickens they rustled up from their second site, a farmhouse between here and Hamlin, the next town down the highway coming up from the south. They're snug on the hammock and I'm on the ground beneath them, sitting with my back against the vehicle while we enjoy the last of the peanuts. The chickens, Sandy says with a happy shake of her hair, were "a goddamn gift from the gods, man."

"We got sixteen of the little emperors left, at this point," she says. "Three chickens a day times five days equals fifteen."

"Plus a bonus chicken," puts in Billy.

"Oh, yeah, right, bonus chicken." Sandy squeezes his arm.

They're nice to listen to, these two; they're like a little show, a mild comedy. Their pleasure in each other combines with the twilight and the misting rain to create a kind of anesthetizing fog, and I lean my head back and exhale, just listening to them talk, finishing each other's sentences and laughing like kids. They hang out all day, they tell me, smoke cigarettes, fool around, drink beer, eat chicken. They both grew up here, as it happens, right here in Rotary, Ohio, went to prom together at Cross-County High School, but they hadn't resided here as adults. Billy had lived "just about everywhere," he'd done a little time, was out on parole—"still on it, officially," he says, and snorts. Sandy for her part had gone to a two-year college in Cincinnati, married a "world-class dingleberry," got divorced, ended up waitressing at some diner outside Lexington.

They got back in touch in the early days of the threat, back in late spring or early summer of last year, when the odds of impact were low but rising fast; low but high enough to start looking up lost loves and missed opportunities. "We found each other," says Billy. "Facebook and that shit." Summer burned away into fall, the odds inching up and up and up. The world started to slip and tremble, Billy and Sandy wrote each other funny e-mails about hooking up again, seeing the world out together.

"But by the time the damn thing got to be a hundred percent, the stupid Internet was gone." Billy tosses his hair. "And I had never gotten her damn phone number—what a bonehead, right?"

"Yep," says Sandy. "Course, I never got his, either."

He grins at her, and she grins back, tilts her head, drinks her beer. He's telling the story and she's popping in now and then, adding detail, gently correcting, stroking his sweaty biceps. I am aware of an insistent internal voice telling me to keep moving on, stay on target, find a sledgehammer and get back to that garage—but I find I'm rooted in place, my back planted against the RV, my knees drawn up, slow-drinking that same first beer, watching the sunset color the tops of the trees. Houdini's head a furry white teddy bear in my lap.

"So basically I said, screw it," Billy says. "I fired up the Pirate and drove down to find her. And can I tell you something—sorry, man, what . . ."

"Henry," I say. "Or—Hank."

"Hank," says Sandy, as if she was the one who asked. "I like that. Crazy part is, I was all packed. I was waiting for him."

"You fucking believe it? She was waiting for me. Says she knew I'd be coming to find her."

"I did," she says, nods firmly, a mild drunk smile in her eyes. "I just knew."

They shake their heads at their mutual good fortune, clink the long glass necks of their beers. I watch their small movements, Billy making a little ashtray out of tinfoil and tapping his cigarette into it, Sandy doing a modified, seated version of the Robot to some old-school beatbox hip-hop number coming from the speakers on the RV.

I close my eyes for a minute and drift in and out of a doze. On some level, of course, I am aware that my illogical insistence on certain ideas regarding my sister—in particular my dogged belief not only that she is alive, but that I will find her and bring her home to a city that doesn't even exist anymore—that all of this magical thinking has extended itself, grown outward like the halo of light around a candle. If Nico has managed to stay alive by clinging to her crazy idea that the asteroid crisis is avertable, that the threat can be eliminated, then maybe she's right. Maybe the whole thing isn't going to happen.

Nico's fine. Everything is going to be fine.

I blink awake after a minute or two, shake a crick out of my neck, and get out my notebook and get to work.

No, Billy and Sandy have no sledgehammer. No gas-powered jackhammer or drill. What they've got is fuel, enough to keep the RV running another couple days, just for the tunes; they've got beer and they've got chicken and that's about it.

Then I figure, what the heck, and I reach into my pocket and take out the yearbook picture from the plastic Concord Public Library sleeve and unfold it carefully, because it is beginning to crumble around the edges.

No, they haven't seen her. They haven't seen many people at all, and definitely no adult version of this high-school girl with the glasses and black T-shirt and the wry expression. No one like that around here at all.

3.

Billy and Sandy's little campground takes on a shabby glamour at night; they spare enough power to light the lanterns and do some close dancing under the yellow globes, weaving in and out of the cooker's fragrant plumes. Sandy bobs her head lightly to the booming rock and roll, her long tangled red curls moving up and down, Billy's hands wrapped around her waist like a life jacket.

I stand up and brush the dust off my pants and watch them in the starlight glimmer and think about my dead parents. Maybe it's missing Nico, looking for Nico, maybe it's just the intensity of these days, wondering on some level what they would have made of it all.

Every gorgeous New Hampshire September, when the leaves were in the first flush of turning and the sky woke up perfect blue, day after day, my father would say something like: "September is the queen of months. Not just here—everywhere. Everywhere in the world. September is perfect." He's standing out front with his glasses pushed up on his forehead, leaning forward with his palms flattened on the wood rail of the porch, breathing in the crisp smell of someone burning leaves a couple doors down. And then my mother, shaking her head, giving him that gentle *tsk-tsk*ing smile. "You've never been anywhere else. You've lived in New England your entire life."

"Oh, sure," he says. "But I'm right." Kisses her. Kisses me. "I'm right." Kisses little Nico.

The next chicken is named Augustus and he will be served at midnight, but I've got to get going. I've got work to do. I look past the RV, out at the street, and the street looks so black.

Billy wanders back over to their ramshackle Rube Goldberg brewery to fill up his bottle, leaves Sandy swaying on the dance floor, and I find I have one more line of questioning to pursue.

"What do you know about the police?" I ask him.

"Say again, Hank?"

He gazes at me while beer foams out of the dirty tap into his bottle.

"Local law enforcement. In Rotary, I mean. Do you know anything about the police around here?"

"Oh, they're total assholes. Like all cops."

He clocks my expression and snorts, spraying liquid out of his nose. "Oh, no!" He laughs, swipes beer off his chin with the back of his hand. "I had a weird feeling about you, I totally—" He cuts himself off, hollers to Sandy, who is swaying, eyes closed, mumbling along with Metallica's "Enter Sandman." "Sandy, he's a cop!"

She keeps her eyes closed, raises one hand in an absent thumbs-up, keeps on swaying.

"Listen, man, don't bust me on the open container, all right?" He's laughing, he can't believe it. "It won't happen again."

"I'm not a cop anymore," I say. "My position was eliminated."

Billy pulls another big swig. "Shit, you know what? That's what everyone should say. Whole planet, man." He snorts. "Our position has been eliminated."

"So," I say. "The local cops."

He shakes his head. "Yeah, like I said, no offense, man, but the cops around here were just your classic bully cops. They were when I was growing up, anyway, and it only gets worse, you know?"

"How long did they keep working?"

"With the big news, you mean?" Billy considers this, runs a beer-wet hand through his hair. "About two fucking seconds, most of 'em. Even the chief, Mackenzie, first-class pig that guy was." He turns again. "Hey, Sandy, remember Dick Mackenzie?" Another eyes-closed thumbs-up from Sandy. "Pig, right?" Her thumb raises higher.

"Shit, man," Billy says, turning back to me. "As soon as this got to be a serious thing, it was fuck it like a bucket for most of those guys."

That's the same story I got from Detective Irma Russel's big leather log book—I can see it clearly, the notebook page where she wrote *Jason quit*, triple exclamation points. That's how I ended up with my own brief employment as a detective in the Concord Police Department, Adult Crimes Unit. People quit, people died. A slot opened up unexpectedly. Silver lining.

"Guess some of 'em kept at it a while, though," says Billy. "The good ones. Till the riot."

"The riot?" I'm interested now. I squint to focus, shaking my head, shaking off the mild effects of my one beer. "What riot?"

"Prison riot. State pen."

I blink. "Creekbed."

"Right, that's right. This was—man—Sandy, do you remember, when was Creekbed?"

"May," she calls.

"Nah." Billy scrunches his face. "June, I think."

"June 9," I tell him.

"If you say so."

I nod. I do say so. Irma Russel's last entry, June 9, neat handwriting, *Heavenly Father keep a good eye on us, would ya?*

"This is from a buddy of mine who heard about it from a guy he knows, a meth head that was in there, who bragged about it apparently, sick fuck. Way the meth head says, everyone still walking around with a badge got sent down there to Creekbed State Penitentiary. I guess the guards had took off, left the bars locked, you know, and the inmates were getting cuckoo for Cocoa Puffs down there. Started basically thinking everyone'd forgotten about 'em, and they were gonna die in there."

Right. Which they would have—like caged rats—like Cortez's mom's boyfriend Kevin, the ex-marine. All the people who'll be caught somewhere when Wednesday comes: all the prisoners, all the elderly or incapacitated on life support, those morbidly obese people who can't leave the house without a piano mover. Everybody, really, all of us, trapped in place, like the damsel in distress in the old movie, tied to the tracks with the train barreling down.

"So they set the damn place on fire," says Billy.

"The cops?"

"No, man, the bad guys. My buddy's buddy and his pals. There were like a couple hundred or more in there." Billy's beer is empty again; he presses the spigot to refill it. "They set their own joint on fire, just to call some attention, and whatever cops was left around here, the cops and the fire folks, the what do you call 'em—ambulance guys. All went down there. And then I guess things—uh, things got real nasty." He looks over his shoulder at Sandy, and then leans in to continue the conversation sotto voce, as if to protect her from such conversations, from wasting a moment's thought on this stuff. "Real nasty. As soon as a couple of 'em were rescued they were taking guns off the cops, shooting at the cops, the firemen and all. Locking folks in the fire, you know, just for . . ." He shrugs. "Just 'cuz."

He looks down into his bottle. "I mean, I don't like cops"—he laughs a little—"no offense, like I said. But this . . ."

He trails off, clears his throat, tries to pull the glimmer back into his smile.

"Anyway, so that was about it around here, as far as police. Since then it's every man for himself, you know?"

"Yeah," I say. "Sure. I know."

"That about the story where you came from?"

"Yeah," I say, and I can see it, Concord on fire, the statehouse dome gleaming red with flame. "Just about."

Red towns, blue towns, black. It's almost over. It's almost here.

I record the conversation about Creekbed in my little blue

notebook: the date, the sequence of events. I am considering as I write whether there might be some crossover here, some connection to Nico and Jordan's group and their presence in Rotary, Ohio. What I know is that Nico was summoned out here as of mid-July, after this scientist with the clandestine plan was located in Gary, Indiana. Even if that much of it is true, which it probably is not, it is hard to imagine Jordan and his allies mustering the resources and strategic thinking to arrange a prison riot, a terrible fire, just to clear the few cops remaining from the Rotary, Ohio, police station.

Still, though, I write it down. The thin pages of my notebook are smudged with new question marks.

My grieving for Detective Irma Russel I condense into five seconds. Ten seconds. Not my story. Not my case. Still, though, you can picture it, the fiery prison, rescuers rushing in, gunshots, flames, people pounding on cell walls, screaming and burning behind thick glass doors.

"Oh, and Billy, what I wanted to ask: Do you know anything about the station itself?"

"Nah."

"When it was built? Whether there's a basement?"

"Man, I just said I don't know anything about it." Billy's big tailgate-party smile wavers. Sandy wanders over to the home-brew setup, smiling vacantly. Billy is asking himself, how long am I supposed to give this guy? How many minutes out of however many minutes remain for the stranger with the notebook and the questions, who can offer nothing in return?

"Thank you, Billy," I say, and close my notebook. "You've been very helpful."

"No sweat, brother," he says, walking away. "I gotta go and kill Augustus."

* * *

Now it's time to leave, it really is. The moon is up.

But I stand inside the RV with Sandy, watching Billy select and slaughter the final chicken of this twenty-four-hour period. Houdini remains outside, at the edge of the coop, his chin lowered in his paws, staring warily at Billy as he stalks among the waddling birds. Now there's nothing left. Billy has got long yellow gloves on, pulled up almost to his elbows, and a heavy butcher's apron over his bare upper body, tufts of black chest hair sprouting up over the top of the apron. The coop looks new; the crossbeams, connecting from post to post to post and strung with chicken wire, are of pine wood, smooth and regular two-by-fours, newly cut and precisely measured. The posts themselves are concrete. At the base of one of the posts of the coop is stamped a small three-letter logo, the single word JOY in all caps.

"Hey. Hey," I say suddenly. "Hey, Sandy. That chicken coop."

"Nice, huh?" She's transfixed, watching Billy in his yellow gloves lift doomed Augustus out of the crowd.

"Sandy, who built that coop for you all?"

"The chicken coop?"

"Yes, right. Who built it?"

"This guy," she says through a yawn. "This Amish guy."

"Amish guy?"

Billy and the chicken a blur at the periphery of my vision. My mind rushing and racing. Billy lifts the bird by the neck, lifts it high as if considering the weight. Houdini's eyes follow the squawking, flapping victim.

This Amish guy, Sandy says, Billy encountered down in Rotary proper. "He was in town, putting up signs, basically. Odd jobs, concrete work. Will work for food, you know." She looks at me, sees my intent expression—concrete work, I'm thinking, just two little words, concrete work—she keeps talking. "It was funny, actually, I was just telling Billy we had to make ourselves a coop for these damn things, and he says he's got no idea how to do that. Half hour later, we run into these guys."

"These guys? There were more than one of the Amish guys?"

"No. One Amish guy. A big guy, older guy, big thick beard, black with gray in it. Must have come from down county, that's where they live out here. But he had a couple of foreigners with him, you know?"

"Foreigners, as in CIs."

"Yeah. Exactly. CIs. Confused-looking sons of bitches. Chinese maybe? I don't know. But they didn't say a word, they just worked. Worked hard, by the way. The Amish guy, though, he was calling the shots."

"Did you get his name?"

"You know what? I did not. I know Billy didn't. I think we just called him Amish Guy for the four hours he was here. He didn't laugh, but he answered to it."

Billy presses the chicken's small pinched face down on the top of an upside-down wooden crate to hold it still. The chicken angles his head upward by instinct so it seems to be staring straight ahead, while Billy's big hand steadies the wriggling round body. He brings the axe down in one long sweeping arc, slams the blade through the chicken's tiny neck, and blood shoots out in all directions. Billy turns his head away, just for a second, an expression of pure horror and disgust. The chicken's body jumps and he holds it steady with his hands. Houdini comes to life, barking like mad, watching the twitching corpse of the chicken, the blood spouting from the open neck.

I pick up the pencil again and I get back into it with Sandy, taking everything down, writing quickly, all the new information, progressing rapidly toward the end of the notebook. Amish guy, up from down county—how far away is down county?—down county is forty miles. Two catastrophe immigrants on the crew with him—Asian men, anyway—but you're sure he was the boss—he was the boss. Concrete work—you asked him to do the coop in concrete—no, he suggested it, he knows concrete, the hell do we know . . .

My fingers gripping the pencil in the old familiar way, my heart doing the thing it does when I'm working, soaking up facts like a sponge, really gunning and going. Sandy's eyes are wide and amused as I nod and nod and echo her words, circle back to get things right, breathing fast, experiencing a welcome burst of self-confidence, a belief in myself as possessing the instincts and the intelligence to do this work properly. Five years? Ten?

I realize that my eyes are closed, I'm thinking hard, and then I open them and find that Sandy is staring at me—no, not staring, gazing, looking me over with a kind of abstract interest, and for a brief strange second it's like she can see into my skull, watch the thoughts in there rotating and spiraling and orbiting each other in patterns.

I clear my throat, cough slightly. There is a trickle of sweat running down her chest, disappearing into the space between her breasts.

"What was her name?" she says.

"Who?"

"The woman. Any woman. One of the women."

I blush. I look at the floor, then back up at her. She had reminded me of Alison Koechner, but it's Naomi that I say. I whisper the name—"Naomi."

Sandy leans forward and kisses me, and I kiss her back, pressing myself against her, my excitement about the investigation rolling over, accelerating, transforming into that other big feeling, that exhilarating and terrifying feeling—not love, but the thing that feels like love—bodies rising to each other, nerve endings opening up and seeking each other—a feeling I know, even as it floods into my veins and my joints, that I will probably never feel again. Last time, for this. Sandy smells like cigarettes and beer. I kiss her hard for a long time and then we pull apart. The moon is up and full and bright, coming through the kitchen windows of the RV.

Billy is there. He's watching in silence, holding the chicken by the stump of its neck, the plump body rotating in his fist, steam rising from the hot dead animal. Billy's taken off his apron and there is a slick of sweat on his neck and shoulder muscles, blood flecked on his bare chest, blood splattered along the hem of his underpants. He smells like charcoal and dirt.

"Billy," I begin, and Sandy shivers slightly beside me, drunk or fearful, I don't know. How absurd it'll be if I just die here, right now, the end of the line, how ridiculous to die on day T-minus five from a shotgun blast in a lover's triangle.

"Hang out another half an hour," he says. "Eat more chicken."

"No, thanks."

"You sure?" he says. Sandy crosses the small space of the RV kitchen, hugs him around the waist, and he squeezes her back while he holds the chicken aloft. "I just gotta pluck him."

I could stay, I really could. I think that they would have me. I could stake out a space in the dirt by the Highway Pirate, slump down low in it, and wait things out.

But no, that's not—that's not going to happen.

"Thank you. Really," I say. New facts. New possibilities. "Thanks a lot."

PART THREE

JOY

Saturday, September 29

Right ascension 16 53 34.9
Declination -74 50 57
Elongation 82.4
Delta 0.368 AU

1.

The way I figure it, if Cortez's take on the spatial mechanics of the police station garage is correct, and that's a thick wedge of concrete wiggled into that floor like a cork in a bottle, then they can't have done it themselves. Someone was there after Nico and her gang went down, and presuming that everyone in the group descended together, then it was someone else—someone who was hired and paid for the gig, contracted to roll the seal across the tomb.

Thus I am aware of a concrete job that was recently performed in this area, and I am aware of a group of men who were out offering themselves for odd jobs generally, but specializing in concrete.

That's enough. Away I go, rolling south on State Road 4 in the middle of the night.

"Twenty or thirty miles," says Billy, "that's where the Amish farms start to crop up, the fruit stands and that. You can't miss it." Houdini's in the wagon and my fat Eveready is duct-taped between the handlebars, sending a joggling uneven light down the highway ahead of us.

As I pedal I can picture Detective Culverson chuckling at me and my rookie logic. I can see him, across our booth at the Somerset Diner, looking at me with quiet amusement, rolling his cigar from one side of his mouth to the other. I can hear him poking at the holes in my theory like a loose tooth.

He asks his pointed questions in his mild voice, rolls his eyes at Ruth-Ann, the waitress, who joins him in teasing good old Hank Palace before bustling off for more coffee.

But the Somerset Diner finally closed, and Culverson and Ruth-Ann are back in Concord, and I have no other direction to point myself but forward, so here I go, State Road 4 due south toward "down county." I let myself sleep in an empty rest stop, sleeping bag rolled out under a YOU ARE HERE map of the state of Ohio, alarm on the Casio set for five hours.

When Sandy asked for a name I said "Naomi" without thinking—even though Alison Koechner is the girl I loved the longest and Trish McConnell is the one I left behind, I said "Naomi" right away.

I think about her in the quiet moments, the moments created by the absence of television and radio and the bustle of normal human company, the moments not filled by investigatory reasoning or by the low churn of fear.

I met Naomi Eddes on a case and tried to protect her and couldn't. One night together was what we got, that's pretty much what it was: dinner at Mr. Chow's, jasmine tea and lo mein noodles, and then my house, and then that was it.

Sometimes, when I can't help it, I imagine how things might otherwise have ended up for us. Possible futures surface like fish from deep water; like memories of things that never got to happen. We might one day have been one of those happy sitcom households, cheerfully chaotic, with the colorful alphabet magnets making bright nonsense words on the refrigerator, with the chores and yard work, getting the kids out the door in the morning. Murmuring conversations late at night, just the two of us left awake.

Not worth dwelling on.

It's not just a person's present that dies when they die, when they are murdered or drowned or a giant rock falls on their head. It's the past, too, all the memories that belonged only to them, the things they thought and never said. And all those possible futures, all the ways that life might have turned out. Past and future and present all burn up together like a bundle of sticks.

Most likely scenario, though, all things being equal, had Maia never darkened the sky: I would have just ended up alone. Like Dectective Russel, clean desk, no pictures, notebook bent open, putting in the hours. Dutiful detective at forty, wise old department hand at sixty, docile old codger at eighty-five, still turning over cases that he worked years ago.

* * *

All the Amish roadside groceries look the same: creaking wooden bins, empty baskets. All of the fruits and vegetables, of course, are long gone; ditto all the cakes and pies; all the Amish honey and Amish cheese and Amish pretzels.

For ten miles or so there are what feel like dozens of these places, and at each I get off the bike and check carefully for concrete work. In one place, slim round posts holding up the wood roof; in another place a set of handsome rounded steps leading from the racks outside to the little store. Over and over again I slide my aching body off the bike and kickstand it and get down on all fours to scour an abandoned farm stand, looking for a red stamp that bears the single word JOY. Over and over Houdini heaves himself out of the wagon and roots around next to me as if he knows what we're looking for—the two of us together pushing past empty wicker shopping baskets and wads of thin discarded receipt paper.

A day of this. Almost a whole day of nothing, finding nothing, and then it's late afternoon, and each time I get back on the bike I think maybe that's it, maybe I can't go any farther, but I can't go back, what if I go back with nothing? My body is aching, and I'm starving, the chicken meals are a distant memory, and all the faded signs for pie and pretzels are not helping in the least.

"Okay," I say to Houdini, at the sixth or eighth or hundredth of these little abandoned useless roadside stands. "Okay, now what?" There's Cortez, back in Rotary, waiting impatiently, sitting cross-legged atop the secret door: *Well?* There's Detective Culverson, at the Somerset of blessed memory, puffing wryly on his cigar. *I don't want to say I told you so, Stretch.*

Except then there it is—a quarter mile farther down State Road 4, with just enough daylight left to see it—there it is. Not stamped on a post in the dirt after all, or at the base of a step, but above my head, written on a billboard, right up there in red letters literally ten feet tall. JOY FARMS.

And then, below it, in slightly smaller letters: CLOSED AND DESERTED. And below that: JESUS = SALVATION.

There's another of the farm stands just beneath the sign, and a few minutes of investigation reveals a narrow byroad leading perpendicularly off into the cornfields behind it. I pause, looking back and forth between the sign and the road, and then I just grin, grin until my cheeks tighten, just to feel what it feels like, just for a second. And then I aim the bike down the byroad.

After a quarter mile winding through rows of corn the byroad narrows into a path, and when it narrows more it becomes impassable for the wagon, so I dig out the Swiss Army knife and use the Allen wrench to uncouple it, and then I leave the wagon behind and keep riding, deeper into the fields. After ten or fifteen minutes the clouds open and begin to spill rain across my forehead. The bike wheels get slick and wobbly on the wet path. I squint and wipe my eyes, wipe them again, pedal more carefully, slow down. The narrow path winds through the corn until I am confronted by a crossroads, and then another. Arbitrarily I choose my route, feeling after more time has passed that I am lost in a tangle of dirt passages, the rain now pouring steadily, confusing my way. I stand up on the pedals and angle forward a little bit, trying to cover Houdini with my body—Houdini who has somehow managed to fall asleep. Deeper I go, down this gravelly one-lane path, and it's harder going, the rain really coming down now, pouring down through my eyebrows and soaking my cheeks, and I look away for a minute at the sodden patches of corn, and when I turn my eyes back to the path there is a tall wide man in a black hat, seated on a horse, right in the center of the path just a few feet away, sheets of rain parting across his face, a hunting rifle raised and aimed.

"Hey," I start, and he fires the rifle in the air.

My face jerks back from the noise and I pull the handlebars hard to the right, wheeling and angling the bike sharply and careening off the road and smashing into the bent cornstalks. I tumble off the bike, watch Houdini bounce out of the basket. I scrabble for cover with my hands over my head. Two more shots. Each of them a loud, distinct *kaboom*, like he's shooting at me with a cannon.

"Hold on now," I call out from the ground, clutching the sides of my head, shouting. "Please." Crawling among the stalks and the sheets of rain. Heart pounding. The dog raises himself unsteadily, soaked by rain, looks around and barks.

The shooting has stopped. I'm on the ground. I'm unhit, unharmed, getting rained on, half hidden among the rows. I can see the horse hooves clopping toward me, splashing into puddles.

"Go," calls the stranger.

"Wait," I say.

"Go now." I grab the white T-shirt the dog had been sitting on, pull it from the basket and wave it, signaling surrender, peace, hang on a damn second. The hooves are still coming toward me, faster, cutting through the rows—Houdini barks at the wondrous size of the horse.

"Wait—" I say again, and throw my hands up before my face

as I realize what's happening, but it's too late—horse and rider are directly above me, and the huge front hoof arcs across the sky and slams into the side of my chest like an iron. For a second or two I feel nothing, and then suddenly everything, my whole body detonates with furious sparking pain, and I am in motion, flipping over like a pancake, rolling over fast, front to back.

My forehead lands in the dirt, facedown, like the girl in the clearing, that dead girl we found who turned out not to be dead.

What was her name? Lily. Her name was Lily. No—it—wait—what was it—it's dark out here. I taste dirt in my mouth. I'm losing consciousness. I can feel it. I grit my teeth and push back against darkness. I hear the dog barking, shouting, the rain splashing in sheets all around us.

The pain seizes me again and I scream, but the man on the horse can't hear me—he's way up there, Zeus in the saddle, and me all the way down here, my head all gummed up, one thick pulse of pain. I flip myself over, blink up at the dark storm-filled sky. The man with the black hat, he's got the rifle in one hand, the horse's reins in the other hand, he's like a painting from a battle scene, cavalry charge, avenging horsemen. "My name is Palace," I try to say, just moving my mouth, my tongue lolling free, and rain falls into my mouth and I think about those turkeys you hear of that die from drowning, staring idiotically, open-mouthed, up into the rain. The horse shuffles agitatedly to and fro, the man steadies him with the reins. My dog is dodging confusedly around the feet of the larger animal. Wild pinpricks of light are exploding across the black horizon of my vision, and my mouth gapes open, rain pouring in.

I fumble again for words and fail, can't speak.

My assailant, the Amish man in the black hat, is saying "easy, girl, easy" to his horse, and then he slides down off the saddle and his boots land in front of my eyes in the dirt. I am staring at his boots. Feeling new tenderness in my side. A broken rib. Maybe a number of them.

"You must leave," says the man, crouching down, his face filling my vision. Big eyes, thick black chinstrap beard streaked with gray.

"I just need to ask you a couple of questions," I say—try to say—I don't know if I say it or not. I gurgle.

The man pulls back, stands up straight. Along with the gun he carries a pitchfork on a strap across his back. A long wooden handle with three pointed tines, a simple, brutal implement. He towers over me Satanlike: the beard, the pitchfork, the glare. I just need to ask him a couple of questions. I open my mouth and my mouth fills with blood. Blood is washing down my face; my forehead must have split on a stone on the path. This is bad. This is a problem. Blood on my face from a cut in my head, blood choking up to drown me from my insides. Blood on the knives and in the sink.

The man takes the pitchfork down off his back, jabs me in the chest with one curving prong, like a cop rousting a drunk. It's definitely more than one rib. I can feel them, clawing my insides like spiny fingers.

"You must leave," he says again.

"Wait, though," I manage, heaving breath, peering up at him. "Wait. I need to ask you a couple of questions."

"No." His brows darken. Rain drips down around the brim of

his hat. "No."

"I'm looking for a man or men who—"

"No. Stop." He pushes at me again with the pitchfork, right in the chest, and the pain dances up my rib cage, into my brain, like a fork of lightning. I picture myself pinned to the road, wriggling, stuck into the ground like an insect. Still, I talk, I keep talking, I don't know why.

"I'm looking for someone who did some concrete work."

"You must leave."

The man starts muttering to himself in a foreign language. Swedish? No. I try to remember what I know about Amish people. German? The man bows his head, clasps his hands together and keeps talking in the low, guttural stream of speech, and while he is doing that I struggle to my feet, get dizzy, fall down.

Blood covers my eyes now, and I wipe it away with my knuckles. I lean forward and heave awful breaths, my throat as dry as insulation, my stomach clenching and unclenching. I'm wondering where the Asian guys are, his employees or friends. I shake my head to try and clear it, and I am rewarded with a new pulse of pain and disorientation. "I'm looking for some men who did concrete work at a police station, up in Rotary." I talk slowly, word by word, while blood dribbles out of the sides of my mouth, like I'm a monster who just ate something.

The Amish guy doesn't answer, he keeps talking to his joined hands. He's praying, or maybe he's crazy, maybe he's just talking to himself, channeling voices. He appears to be a man teetering on the edge of something. He's tall and sturdily constructed, with a wide chest that looks as if built with broad wood beams. Thick beard, thick gray hair beneath the hat. Wide, strong neck. A face stern and lined, the face of the underground king in a scary tale for children.

The rain comes down in billowing curtains, blowing hard across his face. The pitchfork trembles in his clenched fist.

"Please," I say, but then the man lowers the pitchfork and raises the rifle instead.

"Forgive me," he says. "Jesus Christ, forgive me."

I bury my chin in my chest, wriggle my head away from the nose of gun. Still—still I am afraid to die. Even now. I smell it, the rank smell of my own terror, billowing up around me like a fog.

"Jesus Christ, forgive me," he says again, and I'm pretty sure he isn't asking me to forgive him, he's not saying "Jesus Christ" for emphasis. He's asking Jesus Christ to forgive him, for whatever he's done, for what he's about to do.

"Sir," I say, as quickly and clearly as I can manage. "My sister is missing. I have to find her. That's all. I have to find her before the end of the world."

The old eyes widen, and he crouches and puts his face right down next to mine. Lays down the rifle and gingerly wipes blood from around my eyes with his fingertips. "You mustn't say those words."

I'm confused. I cough blood. I look around for Houdini, and my eyes find him a little space away in the corn, stumbling and rising, stumbling and rising, shaking raindrops from his dirty coat.

The big man walks to the saddlebag, unbuttons it and takes out a small sack. He dumps out the contents, charcoal briquettes, and they fall with a series of horse-manure thuds onto the gravel path.

"Sir?"

He lifts the bag above me, and I flinch. It's such an archaic word, *saddlebag.* When did I even learn that word? The world has become so strange.

"You mustn't, mustn't say those words," he says, and then he pulls the bag down over my head and cinches it tight.

* * *

The big, thick-necked Amish man doesn't kill me. I suffer a long terrible moment lying on the ground, my head encased in darkness inside the bag, waiting for him to kill me. Over the rush of the rain I hear him moving around, back and forth to his horse, boots on the road, muted clanks—he's putting down his gun and pitchfork, he's gathering things from the bags.

My arms are bound loosely behind me, wrist to wrist. His hands shove in under my armpits and lift me like a broken doll and set me on my feet. He pushes me in a direction, and we begin to walk. Through the rows, crunching over small slippery mounds of rotting husks, the brush of dead stalks against my legs and hands.

"Please," says my captor, each time I slip or stumble, his strong hands shoving urgently at my back. "You will continue."

I am trapped inside the thick stale odor of the briquettes, the canvas of the bag scratching at my face and scalp. The woven fabric is not enough to blind me completely. I get fleeting glimpses of the cornfield, flickers of moonlight peeking in through the material.

It might be the same man, the man that Sandy described, or it might not be. How many burly sixtysomething Amish men must there be, black beards flecked with gray, out here "down county," guarding their farmsteads from strangers on the road? What are the odds that this is the right place—the right man—that he can answer my questions? What are the odds that he is about to shoot me and leave my body in an unsown field?

"Sir?" I begin, turning my head slightly, still walking. How even to ask? Where to begin?

But he makes a harsh Germanic shushing noise, like *ech*, repeats what he said before: "You will continue."

I continue, I stumble forward through the cold rain in my mask of darkness.

I hear a sharp nervous yelp, just behind me at waist level. I hadn't realized he was carrying the dog. I twist in my restraints, try to separate my wrists from each other inside the tight encircling rope.

"If—" I say, and my captor says, "Quiet."

"If you shoot me," I say, "then please—" I can't say it. "Please take care of my dog. The dog is ill."

He's not listening. "Quiet," he says. "You must be quiet."

We walk for close to half an hour. I lose track of it. I am lost in the pain of my broken ribs, the pain of my cut forehead, lost in worry and darkness and confusion, tromping at gunpoint through the fields. I keep waiting for the Amish guy to stop walking and order me to kneel. I think of Nico, of Sandy and Billy, and then of McConnell and her kids back at Police House, working jigsaw puzzles, catching fish for dinner. I should have stayed with those guys. Should have stayed with Cortez at the police station; stayed with Naomi Eddes at Mr. Chow's, flirting over greasy lo mein. A million places I should have stayed.

* * *

"Sir?" At last we stop walking and I try again: "Sir?"

The man doesn't answer. From where he's now standing, a few yards away, a new noise, a rattling chain. I squint, make out dim shapes through the sack.

He's taken us to a building—a house? I stand in the rain, shivering, waiting. Then the distinct creak of a rusted door being pulled open. A massive door. Not a house. A barn.

He grabs me again beneath my armpits, firm but not rough, and lifts my body and thrusts me forward through the doorway. The smell of it is immediate and unmistakable: horse manure and warm stale hay. He lays my wounded, exhausted body on the ground and binds my legs as he has my wrists.

"Sir?" I say, jerking my head around, looking for his face through the burlap. He's moving again. Back to the door. "I don't want to take your farm, I don't want food. Do you hear me? I'm not that kind of person. Sir?"

"Forgive me," he says, quietly, almost whispering, and it's the same as before: he's not talking to me. It's not my forgiveness that interests him. I stumble around in a circle, a frightened animal, blind and bound. I start to cough, and I taste my own spittle and the heat of the inside of the bag.

"Don't leave me here," I say. "Please don't do that."

"I will bring you food," says the man. "If I can. I may not be able to."

Hot panic now, panic and fear and confusion: I feel like a man trapped in a cave, in the rubble of a building collapse. If the old man leaves me here, then that's it, my investigation ends right now and never will I know what happened to my sister. The asteroid will careen into the earth and catch me wasting away, hooded and hungry in a dilapidated barn.

The man comes over and kneels beside me, and I flinch as I feel something press against my head. It's a knife blade—he's cutting the sack away from my scalp, peeling it off like a caul. The world is revealed, only marginally more visible than when I was hooded. A moonlit barn, dark and cobwebbed and warm. The smell of horses and horse shit. I take three long gasping breaths and find the man's face and stare him in the eye.

"You can't leave me here."

"It is four days only," he says, pointing at the sky. "Only four days."

He places the dog gently at my side. Houdini immediately begins to lap the dirty water of a puddle.

"Have mercy," I say to the man. He draws his hand down along his face, surveys me lying in the dirt.

"This is mercy," he says, and then he goes. The rattle of a chain, tying the barn door closed. The loud crunch of the Amish guy's boots through the cornfields, quieter and quieter as he walks away.

2.

Country silence. Country darkness.

Don't fall asleep, Henry. Don't go to sleep.

That's the first thing. The first thing is simply to stay awake. The second thing is to keep things in perspective. Surviving challenging circumstances, I have found, is very often a matter of keeping things in perspective. The last time I found myself in a situation like this, left high and dry like this, I hadn't merely been kicked by a horse, I'd been shot. I'd taken a sniper's bullet high in my right arm, which ruptured the brachial artery, and that was bad, that was definitely real bad. I was bleeding out in a tower watching the day fade to night, until my sister came to rescue me on a helicopter, of all things, the blades swicking against the sunset, the big loud thing lowering to get me.

This time she won't come. Of course not—I'm supposed to be rescuing *her*.

The first step is easy. Now that I'm not being force-marched through a field in the rain, now that the mask has been pulled from my eyes and I can concentrate, it takes all of five minutes to pry my wrists far enough apart to access the knots with my long fingers and worry the knots open and free my hands. A couple of minutes more and my legs are free also, and I can get up and stagger about the barn.

Where'd they get it, I think suddenly. That helicopter. The troubling thought appears as it has on occasion before, floating to life unbidden like a laughing ghost . . . if they're such hapless dimwits, Nico's pals, if they're deluded losers chasing their illusory asteroid-foiling scenario like children playing dress-up—then where'd they get a *helicopter*? Where, indeed, did they get the Internet access that Jordan allowed me the use of, that last night in Concord; the same night he stood, smug and taunting, telling me there was more to it than I could possibly know. More than *Nico* could possibly know . . .

Leave it. Come on, Palace, leave it. Stay focused. It doesn't matter right now, obviously. Now I need to keep working. I need to get out of the barn.

I walk around, a couple of wobbly circuits, sniffing in the corners like an animal, getting a sense of the place. It's a barn, is all, a barn like all barns. A big abandoned drafty room, maybe thirty feet by sixty feet, split into three sections: feeding stations on either end, where the animals were slopped or given their oats, and then in the middle the smaller area for hay storage. Walls constructed of wooden planks, old but sturdy, securely joined. Peaked roof. Racks on the wall where once the tools were hung. A ladder to a loft, six flat wooden rungs leading up. I stop and breathe, holding one hand over my nose.

The fetid humidity of the place is like another person trapped in here with me, a dismal clinging presence tracking my steps.

Whatever animals once resided here, it can be presumed, have long ago been taken out for slaughter. Plenty of hay, though, piles of it, old and stale and cracking in bales and loose piles.

There is only one entrance, the big double barn door, which I know to be chained from the outside. And I can tell from here that the trio of tiny windows, letting in moonlight up on the loft level, are too small to accommodate a grown man—no matter how thin, no matter how desperate to squeeze through.

"What else, Detective?" My voice is tired, too, worn and gray. I clear my throat and try it again. "What else?"

There's nothing else. Houdini has given in to sleep and lies curled into himself beside his small puddle. I try the door, just to try. I grab the handle and shake it, hear the mocking jangle of the chains on the other side.

I step away from the door. Under the thick odor of the barn I smell myself; days of sweat, of fear, faint stale whiffs of burnt chicken and charcoal.

There was a barn on the edge of my grandfather's property when we were growing up, one of several outbuildings no longer in use. Some ancestral Palace, in the mists of New Hampshire history, had kept horses, but all that remained by the time my sister and I found the place—by the time it became one of her innumerable hideouts—all that was left was old hay, rusted instruments, the earthy odors of manure and sweating animals.

I found her out there once, drinking whiskey she had siphoned from Grandfather's stash, the day she was supposed to be taking the SAT.

I smile to myself now, in the darkness of the Amish barn. One thing about Nico, she never apologized. Never lied.

"Aren't you supposed to be taking the SAT?" I asked her.

"Yuppers."

"So what are you doing?"

"Drinking whiskey in the barn. You want some?"

I did not want some. I dragged her home. Reregistered her for the test, drove her myself.

Hide-and-seek, our whole lives.

Houdini is up, rustling around in the hay, chasing after a mouse, batting helplessly at the ground. I watch the little mammal escape the clutches of my addled dog, watch it slip through the tiny gap beneath the bottom edge of the slat. I get down on all fours beside the dog, sniff at the hole. A whisper of cool air from outside; the smell of the grass of the farm. But it's a mouse hole. A bare smudged circle in the ground.

I stare at the hole.

It would take a long time, but I could do it. Give me a month, maybe. Give me a year. Give me a year and give me a shovel and I could bust right on out of here, worm myself through and emerge gasping like a jailbreak prisoner on the other side. Just give me time.

I go back to the door and throw one shoulder against it and it does not give at all, just shudders and throws me backward and I land in the hay with my broken ribs screaming. I struggle up and try it again, and the pain is even worse—and again—and again. I imagine

Cortez back in Rotary, working on the sealed floor, while I work on this chained barn door, the two of us pushing and pushing, and wouldn't it be something if he was somehow on the opposite side of this door, and I'll smash through just as he smashes through and we'll tumble into each other like slapstick comedians.

I turn away from the door, hunched over and heaving breaths, my sweat dripping from my forehead into the dirt and the hay. Houdini meanwhile is utterly outclassed by the mouse. It runs right by his nose and he watches it, his wet eyes flickering as the thing scampers past.

* * *

I climb slowly, wincing with each step, my rib ends jabbing at tender spots in my lungs or intestines. Then I'm poking my head up over the lip of the loft and what's up here is a private universe, the second hidden paradise I've stumbled upon in two days. Four bales of hay arranged into a semicircle around a three-legged wooden stool. *Milking stool*, some old part of my memory announces. *That right there is a milking stool.* I manage to wrestle my ungainly battered body the rest of the way up, to examine the small transistor radio seated on the stool. A plastic metal rectangle with a circular mesh face over the speaker, antenna like a stiffened tail, jutting up at a sharp angle.

I lift the radio, feel the weight of batteries inside. Flick it on—nothing—it's a paperweight. I switch it off. I set it back down.

I can see a little better up here; I'm closer to the row of tiny roof windows, and the moon is getting higher and brighter. On the hay-strewn floor of the loft, nestled facedown beside one of the bales, is a small handheld mirror. I lift it and examine my face in the smudged and cloudy glass: a haggard and gaunt old man, eyes red-rimmed and sunken. My mustache is overgrown, the rest of my beard coming in uneven, like wild grass on a cliff. I look crazy, lycanthropic. I lower the looking glass.

There are cigarette butts in a little wooden cup. Like a dice cup, from a board game. I tip the butts out into my palm. Store bought, generic, hand-rolled. Months old. Dried out by summer heat. Stale and crumbling.

I take a look back down at the main floor. Houdini is asleep. No sign of the mouse. I'm the only one left awake, way up high; surveying my domain—the suffering king of the spooky old barn.

I settle down on one of the bales of hay, fight fiercely against a fresh urge of tiredness. A dead radio, a bunch of old smokes, a smudged mirror. This was someone's hideout, someone's private place, sometime not too long ago. A young Amish girl by herself in the darkness of the barn, smoking secret cigarettes and listening to forbidden music from somewhere far away.

I can't help it, I'm picturing this kid looking like Nico, like Nico as she was in high school, doing her own sneaking off, her own romantic dreaming, sipping Grandfather's eye-watering spirits out in the barn. It's like what Cortez said, about me, about the girl with the tiger problem, *everything reminds you of your sister.*

I have an idea, a terrible idea, but as soon as I think of it I know that it's what I'm going to do. The only thing I can do, really, the only option available.

There was a fire in the jail. Creekbed Penitentiary. The quick unbearable story that Billy told me. The prisoners were getting restless and desperate because the world had abandoned them, left them trapped, waiting forgotten until the end.

My terrible idea is radiant and bright.

I cannot stay in here for three days, growing hungry and going mad with waiting. I cannot suffer four nights and three days and then still die not knowing where she is or why.

I have to do this next thing, and whatever happens as a result is just what happens, and that's all there is to it.

"How did you light them, kiddo?" I ask the phantom of the girl in the hayloft. "How did you light your smokes?"

It doesn't take long to find them. Black twisted stumps of matches like tiny little burned-down trees, surrounding the dirt beneath the bale. The rest of the matches are close by, two half-used-up books tucked together beneath one of the legs of the stool. The matchbooks are as old as the cigarettes, the sticks crumbling and breaking. But I try one, and it lights right away.

I stare at the dancing match light until it burns my fingers and I blow it out. Maybe this is rash. Maybe it's all a hallucination, maybe I've dreamed up the whole thing: an issue in the prefrontal cortex, neurons firing wild. Nico is fine. I'm fine. I was given an early retirement from the Concord force, late last year, because I was succumbing to some genetic predisposition for mental illness, driving my department Impala up onto the sidewalk, screaming to strangers about an interstellar object the size of the one that killed the dinosaurs.

Not so, though. It isn't so.

It's out there. Closer, now. Closer than the sun; closer than Venus. Our nearest neighbor, the author of our destruction. Accelerating in accordance with Kepler's third law: the closer it gets, the faster it comes. A ball player hurtling for home, a horse breaking into a gallop when it smells the barn.

I've got to get out of here.

I climb down the ladder and scoop Houdini up under my arm, carry the poor sick dog uncomplaining, struggle him up to the loft and lay him down. I kick out one of the small windows easily, one fake karate-chop kick with the strong side of my body. Before I can think about it too much I toss the dog out the window, and he barks as he falls end over end, his body catching as I had planned it on the bank of shrubs below. He scrabbles on the uneven surface of the hedgerow, tumbles forward and lands with a *whomp* in a patch of mud. Looks up at me, confused.

I toss a salute down to the dog, light another match from the matchbook, and set the hay on fire.

* * *

It happens a lot faster than I thought it would, old dry hay and wooden timbers, much faster than I in my rashness and desperation had really contemplated. One small fire touching off new small fires in all directions, small fires growing together and becoming large, dancing up, reaching for the rafters. I retreat, stumble backward, miss the ladder and roll down from the loft onto the hard dirt floor, landing flat, flipping over and moving as fast as I can away from the growing fire up there, my black shoes pulling through the barn-floor mud.

Immediately I regret my plan. I crouch in a corner staring up in horror, watching the burning embers float over the edge of the loft, float and then rain. The fire is literally raining down, sending sparks and small twirling pieces of hay over the edges of the loft. The black and gray of the midnight barn has erupted in red, and after all this was a mistake—better to starve and die in the barn than burn. I race to the door and pound on it hard, the heavy wooden beams thudding against my fist, while the floor of the barn turns to fire all around me, new gouts of flame, now it's like hell's floor, patches of burning ground on all sides.

The heat is crowding in, splinters tumbling down from the roof, the roof beginning to crack above me. If it's going to work, if anyone is going to see it, they'll see it now—it will get no brighter, I don't see how. It's a furnace in here, I'm here in a furnace. In the last instant, I grab like a maniac at the handle of the barn door, pulling, knowing it's useless but pulling, and the pain on my hands is instant and intense and scalding, and I hear this weird distant screaming—a screech, a call, a cry. Is it me? Is that me screaming? I think that it is, I think I'm screaming.

3.

There is no strange swim back up from unconsciousness this time, no sneaky dreams of Nico. I'm just awake, looking from left to right in a small warm room. I'm on a bed. The room is beige, off-white. A wooden door. The bed has a quilt on it, lovely and plain.

The first thing I do is cough. Taste smoke and ash in my throat. I cough again, louder, violently, my body buckling upward, cough so hard and so loud that my stomach starts to ache. When I have recovered, managed to take three normal slow breaths, I realize that I am still dressed, T-shirt and shoes and long pants. Fully dressed under the covers like a little kid whose parents carried him, sleeping, in from the car.

I cough one more time, look around for a glass of water and find a pitcher and a cup. I pour myself a cup and drink it, then pour the rest and drink that, too. It's a bedroom. Wooden bed frame and wooden nightstand and four undecorated walls. Plain white muslin curtains, pulled back from the single plain window and tied with twine. I can taste smoke inside my lungs, I feel heavy with it, like there was a fire inside my mouth and esophagus that was doused with thick wet foam. There is also a new nasty pain on the palms of my hands—I look down and see that both hands are thickly bandaged, mummy hands. Beneath the bandages, they burn and sting. I groan, try to roll my body slightly, one way and then the other, shift out of the discomfort. It feels like I should probably be dead by now.

When my grandfather said "Dig a hole" he was in hospice, at the very, very end, the absolute last thing he said before he died, the last event of his life. I was sitting beside him waiting, as we had been waiting for months, more or less. Grandfather's breaths rolling in and out on rusty wheels, in and out, each one emerging with more difficulty than the last. His eyes staring straight up at the ceiling, his cheeks hollowed out, body twitching. Neither one of us were churchgoers, but I felt that as the responsible adult I needed to ask: did he want me to get someone? "Someone?" he said, even though he knew what I meant, but I pressed on, fulfilling my obligations, trying to get everything down according to procedure. "Someone," I said. "A priest. To do last rites." He laughed, with effort, a low, gasping chuckle. "Henry," he said. "Dig a hole."

I shift on the bed. It feels better now—marginally better. I can move.

There's my sport jacket. Folded nicely at the foot of the bed. I stand up, waver a little, unfold the coat and slip it on. My little treasure trove is still in the inside pocket: The picture of young Nico. The butt of the American Spirit. The plastic fork. My notebook, nearly full. Only thing missing is the SIG. Everything else still in its place.

I pick up the jug and tilt it back and swallow the last drops of the water.

There's no mirror in the room, no pictures, no paintings. The Casio says 5:45, but the information seems abstract; incomplete. Five forty-five when? How long have I been under? It's an uncomfortable relationship you develop with sleep, at a time like this, it feels like every time you close your eyes you could wake up on the last day of the world.

I get up and out of the bed, relieved to find that I can walk with only a little difficulty. I cough again on the way to the door, try the handle and find it locked from the other side, as I had a feeling it would be—but as soon as I rattle it, someone cries out on the other side.

"He's awake!" A woman's voice, relieved, joyous even. "Praise God! The boy is awake."

The boy. Is that me? A scrape of a chair, then another scrape. Two people out there, sitting in the hallway, waiting for me. A vigil. The second voice I recognize.

"Be still. Stay." Old man, thick neck, beard. The creak of his boots approaching the door. I hear the lock click open, and I step back, my heart tightening. I remember his hands at my back in the cornfield, shoving me forward. The door sneaks open, letting in a sliver of light from the hallway. He is there, my assailant from the roadway, black coat, large body, just outside the door.

It's the voice of the woman, though, that travels in. "Friend," she begins. "We must ask. Are you ill?"

"I—" I stand in the quiet room, confused. Am I ill? Obviously, I am not well. I have been burned. There is smoke in my lungs. I have been kicked by a horse, and my forehead is split. I am hungry, and exhausted, and worn. But am I ill?

"Friend?" she says again, the voice of a woman in her early old age, firm and maternal and insistent. "You must tell us. We will know."

I stare at my side of the door. "I'm sorry," I say. "I don't understand."

"She means to ask whether you suffer from the plague."

The old man's words are slow and purposeful. He wants to make sure I get his meaning. But I don't. I don't think I do.

"Excuse me," I say. "What?"

"Whether you are stricken like so many others."

Stricken. A word from another time. Saddlebag. Milking stool. Stricken. I feel my cheeks with my mummy hands, half expecting to find boils or welts, some new biblical form of suffering written on my face. But it's just my same face, thinned out by travel, mustache thick above my lip, wild stubble across my chin.

The man speaks again. "Here we keep ourselves isolated from the illness. We need to know whether you have been afflicted."

Slowly I bring my hand down from my face, while my mind races, trying to work this through. Stricken—afflicted. I begin to nod, I begin to think I've got a line on the situation here, and I'm already trying to figure out how to navigate my way through, how to get what I need and get out.

I clear my throat. "No," I say, and cough. "No, sir, no ma'am, I am not afflicted. Can I please come out of the room now?"

* * *

If there are any Amish people in the state of New Hampshire I've never come across one, and so my entire concept of Amishness is from culture, the cartoon version: black hats, black beards, horse-drawn buggies and candles and cows. Now she opens the door, an old woman in a faded purple dress and black bonnet, and beside her the old man, just as formidable a presence in daylight: tall and wide-bodied in a white shirt, black pants, and suspenders. Estimable chinstrap beard, black with streaks of gray. Broad forehead and large nose, eyes wary and staring above a carefully set mouth. The woman meanwhile has one hand clasped to her mouth in startled joy that I am alive, that I am well, like I am her own long-lost child.

"Come now," she says warmly, beckoning me forward, "come on. Come along to everyone."

I trail along behind her down a sunlit wood-floor hallway, and she is speaking quietly in English the whole way, thanking God and murmuring praise, but not the old man—he's just a pace behind me, and when I glance at him he just looks back at me wordlessly and grave, his silence an unspoken warning. Quiet, boy. Hold your peace. The house smells like cinnamon and bread, warm and welcoming and calm. We pass three doors, two of them open to neat bedrooms like the one I was in, one closed tightly shut with a light on underneath.

Our destination is a vast sunlit kitchen, crowded with smiling people in plain dress, and as soon as I enter with the older couple everybody gasps.

"He's okay!" shouts a little boy, no more than eight years old, and then the woman standing behind him bends and hugs him around the neck and says "Praise be to God," and then the packed room explodes in celebration, everybody hooting and clapping their hands. "He's alive!" they call, and clasp each other tightly. "Thank God!" Older men, younger men, girls and women, a legion of chattering children in long pants or long plain dresses, everyone embracing and gazing at me with excitement and frank fascination, their hands fluttering at their sides or raised high toward the rafters. Everybody singing out the happy news to each other, repeating the words "Alive!" and "Awake and well!" the news of my good health tossed joyfully about like rice at a wedding. The men seize my hand, one after another, young men and middle-aged men and one ancient doddering grandfather. The women don't approach, but smile warmly, ducking their heads in murmured prayer.

I stand, quiet and confused, like an idiot savant, mute among the ruckus, unsure what I'm supposed to do. After a minute or so I raise one wrapped hand slowly, palm out, give a sort of awkward wave, and then lower it again. It's strange, it's so strange, there is an undeniable *Twilight Zone* quality to the whole thing, like here I am, a visiting god set down in an alien land.

"Sit now," cries the old woman merrily, the one who first came to fetch me, raising her voice among the group, shooing the whole tribe into the adjacent dining room. "Let us eat."

I let myself be guided through the bustle to a seat; I am smiling at everyone, playing up my exhaustion and confusion but paying careful attention—watching the old man, watching him watch me, my mind churning and rolling and popping. I am wondering about the pair of Asian men, the quiet immigrant laborers that Sandy described. They're a secret is what I'm thinking, one of my new friend's secrets. Wherever they are, they're not invited to lunch.

Everyone arranges themselves around the circular tables in the long dining room adjacent to the kitchen. Napkins are spread on laps, and water is poured into cups from wooden pitchers. The women in their bonnets and shawls and ankle-length dresses, the men in plain white shirts without buttons, black shoes, beards. Everyone smiling at me, still, from all over the room, peering at me in my exhaustion and dishevelment.

Lunch is served: a sparse meal, loaves of bread and cooked vegetables and rabbit, but it's food. I try to tabulate the people, sort out the relationships: the old man, my captor; three men in their late forties or fifties, who would be his sons or sons-in-law, a generation younger, same beards and coats, same stern faces, not yet grayed and lined. And women of that middle-aged set, the wives and sisters—five of them? Eight? Daughters and daughters-in-law, slipping in and out of the kitchen, carrying out platters and plates, pouring water from wooden pitchers, whispering smilingly to each other, straightening the bonnets and collars of a seemingly infinite number of small children. One bright-eyed six- or seven-year-old with big funny ears is gaping at me, and I turn and waggle one thickly bandaged hand and say "Hiya." He smiles like crazy, turns away and rushes back over to his siblings and cousins.

Everyone at last is seated, and, suddenly, at no announcement or signal that is apparent to me, the room becomes silent and everyone closes their eyes and bows their heads.

We're praying; we're supposed to be praying. I keep my eyes open and look all around the room. I can see into the nearer corner of the kitchen, where there is a butter churn, wood-paneled and sturdy, the handle poking out of the basin, drops on the sides showing recent use. Eggs on the counter in a wooden bowl. It's as if I found an escape hatch after all—you just have to travel back in time to a colonial village, where the death of our species is still four hundred years into the future.

One of the girls, I discover, is doing the same thing as me: a young teenager with red cheeks and strawberry blonde hair in simple braids, peering around the table with one eye open while everyone else prays. She catches me catching her, blushes, and looks at her food. I smile, too. You never really think of Amish people as being people, they're this weird otherworldly category and you lump them all together in your mind, like penguins. And now here they are, these specific human people with their specific human faces.

The old man clears his throat, opens his eyes to say "Amen," and the room comes to life again. Happy small conversations, the muted clink of silverware, the rustle of napkins. Though my body hurts, though I struggle to swallow, every bite is delicious, warm and savory. And then at last the old man settles his silverware carefully beside his plate and looks at me with unnerving frankness. "We thank the good Lord God for you, friend. We are glad you are here and you are welcome." I mutter "Thank you," nodding carefully. He left me to starve. He deposited me hooded and fearful into the barn and tied me up to die.

He stares evenly back at me, challenging, calm—as if daring me to call him out: who would they believe?

"No one has used the south barn for many months, since the beginning of the trouble," says someone from the far end of the table, a matronly middle-aged woman with dark hair, one of the daughters or daughters-in-law. "And Father has kept it locked."

The black-bearded old man nods at the detail. The south barn, I'm thinking. The trouble, I'm thinking. They mean this illusory plague, they mean a different kind of trouble than everyone else. The title "Father," I'm gathering, is as much honorific as literal. The man who shot at me on the path is the respected patriarch, the elder sage of this family or gathering of families. The others bow their heads slightly when he speaks, not as if in worship but as a mark of deference.

"You, friend," he says now, turning to me, speaking slowly and evenly. "We wonder, did you climb up into the south barn through its window and light a match for a cigarette or for light and put the match down carelessly? Is that what happened?"

The same challenging expression, cold and clear.

I take a sip from my water glass, clear my throat. "Yes, sir," I say, giving it back to him, striking a truce. "That's what happened. I lit a match so I could see and put the match down carelessly."

Father nods. A murmur passes across the table, the men whispering to each other, nodding. The children at their separate tables have mostly lost interest, they're eating and chattering idly to one another. The only decoration in the room is a wall calendar, spread open to September, a line drawing of a mostly bare oak, the last leaves tumbling to Earth.

"And if we may ask, sir, you are fleeing from the pandemic?" This from one of the younger men, a sturdy character with a beard and face to match his father's.

I answer him tentatively. "That's right. Yes. I have traveled from my home to escape it."

"God's will," he murmurs, and the rest of them say it too, look down at their plates, "God's will."

Father stands now, draws up to full height, and places his hand on the shoulders of one of the children. "It is through God's grace that Ruth saw the fire from her bedroom window, way off in the distance, and awoke the house."

All eyes turn to the girl whom I saw cheating during the prayer. Her cheeks go from rosy red to bright pink. A couple of the smaller children giggle.

"Thank you, young lady," I tell her, and I mean it, but the girl doesn't respond, she keeps her eyes trained on her plate of stewed vegetables. "Answer our guest, Ruthie," says her grandmother gently, nodding to the girl. "Our guest said thank you."

"Thanks be to God," says Ruthie, and the others nod their approval, the men and the women and even the littlest kids, murmuring in uneven chorus, "Thanks be to God." I have nailed down the number of people in the room at thirty-five: six adult men and seven women, plus twenty-two children ranging from toddler to late adolescence. They don't know. I look at the old man, I look around the room at this silent happy family, and I know that they don't know. These people don't know about the asteroid at all.

You mustn't say those words, he told me. When I said that I had to save my sister before the end of the world, he said *you mustn't say those words*.

They don't know and you can see it on their peaceful Amish faces, that bloom of happiness you just don't see anymore. Because of course a pandemic would be an absolute calamity, some deadly virus stalking the land, and you would huddle up with your family and shut out the world until it ended, but then it would—it would have an ending. A pandemic runs its course and then the world recovers. These people in this room don't know that the world will not be recovering, and I can see it, as they finish their lunch and say more prayers and rise, laughing, to clear the plates. I can feel it, a feeling I never had occasion to notice until it disappeared, the odorless colorless presence of the future.

"I would speak with our guest alone," says the old man abruptly. "We will walk the property."

"Atlee," says his wife, the old woman. "He is tired. He is wounded. Let him eat and return to bed."

"Thank you, ma'am, but I'm feeling just fine."

That's not true; I feel like I've been hit by a garbage truck. My side hurts each time I swallow or take a full breath, and my hands, within the last ten or fifteen minutes, have begun to burn again beneath their bandages. But I want information, and speaking alone with this man Atlee is the only way to get it. "Thank you, though, for supper, and for everything, Mrs. Joy."

The old woman's eyes pop open with surprise, and a bright wave of laughter ripples through the room.

"No, young man," she says. "Our surname is Miller. Joy is—" She leans to the plain-faced daughter seated beside her, and they exchange whispers.

"Joy is an acronym," says the daughter. "A way of living. You are to set your mind first to Jesus, then Others, and lastly to Yourself."

"Ah," I say. "Oh."

Atlee takes me by the elbow. "Now," he says quietly. "We will walk the property."

4.

The butt of Atlee Miller's pitchfork thunks in the gravel of the path as we walk away from the house. He is silent for a minute, two minutes. Just our shoes on the gravel, the rhythmic *chunk-chunk* of the pitchfork on the path.

I am about to say something, try something out, when he starts.

"You and I will walk abreast to where the path bends, just there," he says. "It continues on there, about a quarter mile to the left, back down to the county road, to our old farm stand. At the bend I will turn to the right, go on along the property line, back around to the house. You will continue on."

The same words he used when we were together in the rainstorm, when he was pushing me forward. *You will continue on.* Same steady tone, somber and uninflected. He doesn't look at me while he's speaking, just keeps moving, moving fast for as old as he is, long strides with the pitchfork, fast for an old man. As for me, I'm doing my best, hobbling a bit, wincing with my injuries, but I keep up as well as I can—noticing in the meantime, despite all my physical discomforts and the anxiousness of this situation, that the Amish farm in late-day rain-streaked sunlight is the most beautiful thing I have ever seen: green fields, white fences, yellow corn. A flock of healthy sheep gamboling in small circles in their penned lea.

"Your dog," the man says gruffly, pointing, and there is Houdini, huddled like a phantom behind a shed, staring out. Poor confused sick dog. He sees me, and holds up his head to look me over with watery eyes. He starts to come and then scuttles back behind the little wooden building. I know how he feels. I'm not ready to go—I can't.

"Mr. Miller, can I just ask you a couple of quick questions?"

He doesn't answer. Walks faster. I nearly drop my blue notebook into the dirt as I fumble it out of my pocket. "Can you confirm that you did a construction job for a group of strangers, at the police station in Rotary?"

He keeps his eyes forward, but I can see it—a wave of surprise, of confirmation, rushing over his features and then away again.

I press on. "What did you do there, Mr. Miller? You did some concrete work up there?"

A sidelong glance and that's it. We're running out of road here. Running out of time.

"Mr. Miller?"

"I will tell my people you decided to return," he says. "You are overcome with grief for those you love and have decided to take your chances with the plague."

I scowl. I limp to keep up with him. No, I'm thinking. *No.*

Whatever else is going on here, I have not come this far merely to continue on now, to limp back down to the vegetable stand and my abandoned bike, back where I started.

"I'll tell them," I say. "I'll sneak back in and tell them."

Now he answers—now he answers right away. "You won't. You can't."

"Of course I can."

"I've made it impossible."

"How?"

He stops talking, just shakes his head, but this is good. This is what we need. All you need is a conversation. To work toward the information you need, to get what you want from a suspect or a witness—all you need is a conversation to begin, and then you shape it, push it.

"Mr. Miller? How are you doing it?"

Just a conversation. That's police work, that's half of it right there. I wheel back, change tack, try again. "How did it start?"

We're at a line of fencing. I stop, lean back on a post, as if to catch my breath, and he stops too. "No more about concrete," I say, raise my hands in mock surrender. "I promise."

"It was a Sunday," he says, and my heart glows. A conversation. That's half of it, right there. He's talking, I listen while he talks. "Church was at Zachary Weaver's. One or two men will go early and help to prepare the service. The others come along later. I was there early, on this day. At the Weavers' all was in an uproar. Someone had heard a radio broadcast. There was—lamentation. Distress." He shakes his head and looks at the ground. "And I could tell, d'you see?

I knew in the crack of an instant what I would need to do. I could see it in their eyes, these people, the change that would be wrought on them. It was already happening, d'you see?"

He doesn't wait for an answer. I don't interrupt.

"I went out on the porch and I saw my family walking to the house from our house and I made this decision in the crack of a moment, just like that. I just—I waved with my hand—like this—I waved—" He stops on the path and raises a hand, pushing at the air: go back, stop, turn around. "I walked out of Zachary Weaver's and I walked my family back to our home and I gave them all of that. The story you've heard."

"The illness," I say. "Pandemic."

"Yes."

He says it low, the one word *yes*, down into his beard, and for the first time since we've met I can read something other than grave self-seriousness on his face—a wash of grief and self-recrimination.

"The plague. The illness astride the land." His face darkens further. He hates his lie. It eats at him, I can see it. "I gathered my people to me and I told them that the situation was severe and that we must remain isolated, even from our friends and from our church. And I said it will be a hard time, but we have God and with God's grace we will survive."

And on he goes, off and running, a steady stream of low syllables. As if now that he's given himself leave to tell me some part of his story he feels compelled to tell all of it. As if part of him has been waiting lo these many months for someone to tell this story to, someone to share the burden of his accomplishments. He has been on a desert island alone with his desperate act of conscience, wrestling with his awful decision and the work it has required of him, in exile in his own home, alone through the hard months. The only people he has had to speak with don't speak English.

He recounts gathering his people all around the family table, asking for and receiving solemn promises from everyone, from the eldest to the very young, to remain within the safety of their own land until the sickness should pass. He describes how God provided him assistance, in the form of a ragged starving troop of CIs, who had made it somehow from their Asian homelands to Newfoundland, and from Newfoundland down to this pocket of midwestern America. They understood each other well enough to make arrangements, a trade—Atlee provides shelter in tents and lean-tos in a barren field on the far side of State Road 4, and in exchange they provide labor and loyalty and discretion. They work under him, they share in the spoils, they walk the perimeter of Joy Farms at night, unseen guardians.

It is a precarious arrangement. He knows that. Eventually, one of his children or one of his children's children will break the promise, wander off the farm and discover the truth. Or someone from the outside world, a burglar or a madman or a refugee, will smash through the fencing into the private world.

"It cannot last forever," Atlee says. "But it does not have to. Just a few more days."

We're getting close now, close to that bend in the road. The sun is halfway along its slow tumble down from noon to night, another day being burned down, sloughed away.

"These are hard times, sir," I say. "We've all had to make hard choices. God will forgive you."

He stares hard at the ground for a cold second and when he looks up I am expecting anger—how dare I speak for God, how can I?—but instead he is crying, his old lined face dissolved into childlike grief. And he says in a hollow voice, "Do you think so?" Steps toward me and grabs at my shirt front. "Do you think that it's true?"

"Yes," I say, "of course," and he envelops me in his grip and weeps into my shoulder. I don't know how to handle this, I really don't.

"Because I feel that it must be true, that God meant for it to be me. I was at the Weavers' before church, but it might have been one of the children at the school. It might have been one of the little ones who came back from town with this awful information. But it fell to me, to know, because I was the one who could keep them from it, to keep them in grace."

He pulls away from me, looks urgently into my eyes. "You understand that we don't drive automobiles because they might bring us closer to sin. No cars, no computers, no phones. Distractions from the faith! But this thing—this thing that comes across the sky. It would have happened like that." He snaps his fingers. "We would have fallen into grief, and from grief into sin. All of us. All of them."

He shakes his pitchfork back toward the farmhouse, his family, his charge.

"The danger to this world is not what matters, do you see that? Do you see? This world is temporary—it has always been temporary." He is reaching some sort of pitch, shaking with righteousness and pain. "God meant for me to protect them. For all the sin to be my sin.

Don't you see that He meant it for me?" Again, with fervor: "Don't you think that's what He meant?"

He is not speaking rhetorically, he needs an answer, and I bite back my first impulse, which is to say I have no idea what God meant, any more than you do, and then to go on, to point out the narcissism skulking in the shadows of his revelation, in this performance of humility: *I did what I did because I am burdened with understanding the intentions of the unseen hand.*

I don't say any of this. There would be no reason to do so, from the perspective of my ongoing investigation, no reason to upset the apple cart of this man's intricate belief system, to pull away at the world that he has built. I step closer and pat him on the back, sort of, feeling nothing through my bandaged hand and the rough thickness of his broadcloth coat. I wait for my galloping mind to find the smart thing to say. We've come now to the bend in the road, and it is the old man's intention now that I continue on, and if I do I leave behind my last chance of finding her, of laying eyes on Nico before the end.

"I'm sorry, my friend," he says. "I am sorry." His affect has changed again, he is chastened now, becalmed, tilting his head down toward the dirt. "You would not go, you wouldn't leave, and I felt I had no other choice."

"It's all right." I take his hands. I hold them between my own. "I was safe all along. I was not in danger."

Miller wipes his eyes with his big knuckles, pulls himself up to full height. "What do you mean?"

I feel, deep down beneath my injuries and exhaustion, a quicksilver glinting of joy. I've got him. I push it. I keep going. "I was meant to escape from that barn. God wanted me to have your help in finding my sister. I have traveled the country cloaked in his protection. I was never in danger."

He looks down for a moment, closes his eyes and murmurs. More prayer. So much prayer. Then he looks up at me. "Do you have a picture of her?"

* * *

She was there. In Rotary, at the police station. This was four days ago. Wednesday, September 26; Wednesday, the day before Cortez and I arrived. My stomach tightens. I need to know he's sure of the date, and he is, Mr. Miller has been keeping careful track of the time—careful track of each of his odd-job employments and the goods he receives for them—careful track of everything. He remembers the work at the Rotary PD, and he recognizes Nico's face right away.

I ask him to slow down. I ask him to start at the beginning. I take out my notebook and I tell him I need the whole day—would he mind going slowly and giving me the entire day?

Atlee had gone out that morning as he goes out every day, leaving his people with their usual strict admonitions to remain on the property. In Pike, between here and Rotary, he met a young man with a long face and a nervous expression, who gave his name simply as "Tick." The man promised him a crate of packaged meals in exchange for a small job of work at the Rotary police station.

"What do you mean, packaged meals?"

"Army food," says Atlee. "He called it something."

"MREs?" I say.

He nods. "That sounds right. Yes, MREs."

I write it down, *army surplus rations . . . Army? . . . long-faced man, "Tick"? . . .* and motion for him to go on. Atlee agreed to take the job and he and Tick traveled together to the Rotary station, arriving at approximately 2:30. He went alone because it was a simple job that Tick described: sealing a stairhead with a slab of concrete that had been custom-built for the purpose.

When they got to Rotary, Tick told Atlee to wait, said it shouldn't be more than fifteen or twenty minutes, and Atlee said that sounded okay, although he wasn't terribly pleased about standing around. He had other things he needed to be doing, there are always other things to do. But he waited, stood with crossed arms just inside the door of the police station, trying to stay out of the rain, and out of the way of a group of young men and women moving boxes and bags from the lawn down a flight of metal stairs into a basement.

Besides Tick, Atlee communicated directly with only one of them, a man who appeared to be the leader: a short stocky man, older than the others, with bushy hair and dark brown eyes behind horn-rimmed glasses.

"Did you get this man's name?"

"Astronaut."

"His name was Astronaut?"

"I might guess it wasn't. But that's what they called him."

I write it down. *Astronaut.* Two circles around it and a question mark.

This man Astronaut was quietly but unquestionably in charge,

Atlee says, giving the orders and keeping the group on task as they rolled up sleeping bags and zipped up duffels, stacked boxes of food and jugs of water and tromped up and down the staircase. There were boxes, too, big square shipping crates that looked heavy, that had to be carried by two people moving slowly as they descended the steps.

The contents of the boxes, Atlee doesn't know. My mind flies out in all directions. A machine saw—guns, ammunition—fuel—computer equipment—building materials—

I have arrived at the penultimate page of my slim blue notebook. I steady my hands. I am picturing these people: nervous, strange-looking Tick, Astronaut with the eyeglasses and the bushy hair. The kids, college-age kids like Nico, marching up and down the metal stairs like ants, hauling their food and their water and whatever was in those crates.

Atlee guesses there were fourteen people in this group: eight women and six men. I ask him what they looked like and he shrugs and says "they looked like people," and it occurs to me that it may be the same for Amish people looking at us as us at them: do we in our nonblack clothes and our ungodly accessories and haircuts, do we all look the same? I press him, though, get what details he recalls. There was a kid with bright blue sneakers, he remembers that, a tall kid, heavyset. One woman he remembers particularly, African American, unusually thin. I describe the sleeping girl, Lily, and he doesn't remember seeing any Asian women, but he can't say for sure. I describe Jordan, Nico's pal from UNH. Just describing him brings up a boiling of anger in my gut; I picture him, sneering, a shape-shifter, hiding layers of secrets beneath sunglasses and a smirk.

But Atlee doesn't recognize the description; no one he recalls as particularly short, no one in sunglasses.

But one person—one person he remembers distinctly. I still have the picture out—the ratty black T-shirt, stubborn expression, the studiedly unhip glasses—and I ask him to look again and he does, he looks again, nods again.

"Yes."

"You're absolutely sure?"

"Yes."

"This woman, she was in the group?"

"I saw her," says Atlee, "and I heard her speak."

After he had waited for over an hour for the group to be done with their packing and moving, Atlee was becoming increasingly impatient to do his job and be done with it. On the way there, he had noted a barn on Police Station Road, between the station and the town, and he was intending to stop there on his way home and sift it for what might be useful—animal feed, maybe, or tools, or propane. But now it was approaching four o'clock and his slowpoke clients were still moving their things up and down the stairs, and he was running out of daylight.

So Atlee goes to ask Astronaut how much longer and finds him, in a hallway outside the garage, talking to a girl.

"It was her," he tells me, pointing to the picture. "Your girl."

They were speaking, Nico and Astronaut, in hushed voices, at the end of the long hallway that cuts through the police station. Both of them were smoking cigarettes and they were arguing.

"Wait," I manage. "Arguing about what?"

"I do not know."

"How do you know it was an argument?"

Atlee smiles slightly. "We are a gentle people. But I do know what an argument sounds like."

"What were they arguing about?" I can barely hear my own words, my heart is beating so loud; blood is rushing into my head like cold water in a cavern. I feel like I am there—coming upon them, huddled together in conversation in that narrow corridor. Was it already stained with blood, with two overlapping trails leading into and out of the kitchenette?

"I cannot say what their subject was, but I could tell that the girl was the angrier of the two. Shaking her head. Poking the man in the chest, like this, with one finger. The man Astronaut, he says that the situation is what the situation is. The girl says, I disagree."

I let out a gasp of laughter. Atlee looks at me, perplexed. Of *course* she said that. That's my sister, that's Nico, stubbornly rejecting the most uncontroversial statement of plain truth—*The situation is what the situation is. I disagree.*—that's Nico, up and down and all around the town. I can *see* her saying that. I can hear her. I'm so close to her right now. I feel so close.

"And—okay. Okay, what else did they say?"

Nothing, says Atlee, and shakes his head. "I cleared my throat so they would see me standing there. I had been told half an hour, and now had been waiting three times as long. The man apologized. He was very polite. Very soft in his manner. He asked if I could come back at five thirty. He assured me that by that time they would have completed their move down below, and the concrete piece would be waiting for me to shift into place."

"And that's what happened?"

"Yes. I went and searched that barn as I had intended, and returned at the appointed time."

"At half past five."

"Yes."

"And they were all gone and the concrete floor piece was waiting?"

"Yes. Along with the food I had been promised. What you called them."

"MREs," I say absently, and chew for a moment on my lip. "You didn't pour the concrete?"

"No," he says. "It was built when I got there."

I don't write any of this down, I have run out of paper, but I think I will remember. The timelines, the details. I'll remember. "And so by five thirty all of them were gone?"

"Yes."

"They had gone under?"

"Well. I don't know. But they were gone."

And that's it, end of story, end of the day of September 26. Atlee and I stand together in thoughtful silence, leaning on a fence in the darkness at the far edge of Joy Farms.

After a last moment of standing side by side, Atlee turns away from the fence and wordlessly hands me the one thing that was missing from my pockets, my department-issue pistol. He has no more information to give me, but there is one thing I still need. I describe my request and he readily accedes—tells me where I have to go and whom to talk to. He takes my notebook and writes on the back of it. I bend my head gratefully. I feel genuine sadness for this old man, the mantle he has laid on himself, the Herculean task of making believe that the world is still more or less what it has been. He has acted like a Secret Service agent leaping in slow motion, hurling himself in the path of the information.

As I step at last off the fence and begin to say goodbye, Atlee Miller cuts me off, holds up his pitchfork at shoulder level.

"You said, I think, that this girl is your sister."

"Yes."

He looks me over again, seeming to decide something. "The man, Astronaut. Mild, as I said. Polite. But on his belt, a workingman's belt, he wore a long-barrel pistol, and a sawtooth buck knife, and a claw hammer."

Atlee's expression is set and somber. A chill drifts down over me like snow.

"He never took off the belt, never used it. But there it was. This is what I noticed about him, this man, the leader of this group," he says. "A quiet man, but with one hand always on this belt."

* * *

I see Houdini on my way out, still in that muddy spot he picked out behind the shed. Wallowing, practically inert, head tilted, asleep. A couple of the Amish kids are nearby, playing jacks on a patch of hard dirt. Houdini will like that, when he wakes up, he'll like to hear them laughing. It happens the same way Atlee described it, in the crack of a moment—I don't call to the dog. I don't even get close enough to wake him. I move quietly past with my head down, looking back once and then moving on.

It isn't easy, because he's a good dog and he has been good to me and I love him, but I leave him behind in this big green place that smells like animals and grass, among these people who will take care of him into a good old age, at least as far as either party knows.

* * *

"Wait, please."

A girl's voice, just loud enough to be heard. I stop and turn around and there's Ruthie, the one I caught cheating on the blessing, with the big blue eyes and the plaited strawberry blonde hair. One of the oldest of the giggling Amish girls, but she's not giggling now. Grave-faced, cheeks flushed from running, her plain black dress dusty at the hem. She has caught me at the crook in the path, where the farm turns into the road. Staring at me, intent, her anxious fingers reaching for my sleeve.

"Please. I have to ask you." She glances once nervously back at the house. I almost say "Ask me what?" but it would just be buying time. I know exactly what she means as soon as she says it.

The radio, up there in the barn. An innocent child alone in the moontime darkness of the loft, listening to forbidden music and enjoying a rare breath of independence, a respite from chores and sibling responsibilities, when she hears the baffling news, and at first she is confused, and then it slowly sinks in, what it means, what all of it means.

Pretending since then. Putting it on. Poor young Ruthie knows about Maia, just like her grandfather she knows, but she has not told him. Not wanting him to know that she knows, not wanting him to know that she knows that he knows. Hide-and-seek at the end of the world.

But here she is. Standing and waiting for me. Her fingers clutching at me. "How much longer?"

"Ruth," I say. "I'm sorry."

She tightens her grip on my sleeve. "How much *longer*?"

I could give her a reprieve: there's a plan in motion, actually. Department of Defense Space Command, they figured something out. A standoff burst, a nuclear detonation at one object radius from the asteroid, releasing sufficient high-energy X-rays to vaporize some portion of its surface . . . everything is going to be *fine*.

But I can't do that, so I just say it as quickly as I can, tearing off the Band-Aid, "Three days," and she breathes sharply and nods bravely but stumbles forward into my arms. I catch her and hold her small body to my chest and kiss her gently on the top of the head.

The voice of Cortez, singsong in my ear. *Everything reminds you of your sister.*

"I'm so sorry," I tell her. "I'm really, really sorry."

It's just words, though. Just a bunch of tiny little words.

PART FOUR

Go On and Get to Work

Monday, October 1

Right ascension 16 49 50.3
Declination -75 08 48
Elongation 81.1
Delta 0.142 AU

Everything is exactly as it was.

The headquarters of the Rotary Police Department is like a small gray ship docked in the gloom. The driveway a rough horseshoe of gravel. Two flagpoles, two beleaguered flags. I approach in sunrise silence, work shoes crunching on the gravel, like a mountain man returned to civilization after a long wilderness exile, only civilization is gone. It's just the one dull municipal building, planted like a ruin in the center of an overgrown lawn. It's raining again. It rained on and off all night.

I slept again for five hours in the middle of the night on the side of the road, at my same YOU ARE HERE rest stop, my coat jacket folded neatly for a pillow, my police-department pistol in the crook of my arm.

Now it's morning and as I step off the road onto the grass I can sense them, feel them—I can practically hear them down there under my feet, nosing around in their underground lair, the basement warren they dug down into and took over, the maze they've occupied. My mind has built mythologies around them all, cloaked their names in malevolent auras. Tick, long-faced and bizarre. The very thin black girl, moody and cruel. Astronaut with his bushy black hair and his belt of weapons. All of them are listed now in black pen in my blue notebook. Suspects. Witnesses, though to what I am not yet sure. They're all down there, scuttling around like spiders, and they've got my sister.

It's Monday now. Monday morning; 9:17, according to the Casio. Two days to go. I'm almost to the door of the station when there's a sudden sharp scrape from just above me. The roof. I jump back from the door, draw the gun, and shout "Police!"

Old habit. Can't help it. My heart beats. Silence—ten seconds—twenty—me stepping slowly backward, one big step at a time, trying to get to a place where I can see what's up there.

Then the noise again, a scrape and then a rustle, and then new silence.

I try again, louder. "If there is someone up there, show yourself immediately." What do I say then? *I've got a gun*. Everybody's got a stupid gun.

"Police," I say, one more time, and a hail of rocks and loose dirt flies out of the sky onto my face and my head. Tiny pebbles bounce off my scalp, dust fills my eyes.

I grunt, spitting debris out of my mouth, and look up.

"Oh, no! Policeman!" It's Cortez, just his face, big and ugly and leering, jutting out over the lip of the building. "I didn't see you there!"

He cackles while I lower my gun. I clear my throat and hawk a thick clod of dirty spit out onto the lawn. A nasty trick, childish, somehow out of character for the man. All I can see of Cortez is his upper half. He's lying down flat on the roof of the building, his torso extended over the edge, his big hands dangling down. His right hand is open, showing the palm, where he just let go of the dirt and rocks. His other hand is a tightly clenched fist. Behind him the sky is a fabric of gloomy gray clouds.

"What are you doing up there?"

Cortez shrugs. "Killing time. Hanging around. Investigating. I found solar panels up here, by the by. Hooked up to battery chargers. Whatever your sister and her playmates have got down there, it's all charged up."

I nod, combing grit out of my mustache with my fingertips, recalling Atlee's description of heavy crates, tromped down the stairs one at a time. What's in the crates? And then that question provokes the other, the question I can't answer and can't shake: Where'd they get the helicopter?

I swat it away, set my jaw against it. Stay on target.

"Cortez, can you come down from there? We've got to get to work."

He stays where he is, props his face up on one hand, like he's lolling on a summer lawn. "Cortez, they're down there. I talked to the man who dropped in that wedge. What it sounds like is this was the backup plan, this was plan B. They realized that all this stuff about the scientist and the standoff burst was a fairy tale, and they went to ground."

"Oh," he says. "Fascinating."

Cortez opens up his other hand and tosses a fresh rain of rocks and dirt onto my face. A small sharp shard catches in the corner of my eye.

"Hey," is all I have time to say before Cortez launches himself off the roof, his whole body all at once, flying down with arms extended, landing on top of me like a giant bat. He grabs the back of my hair and twists my head around and shoves my face into the muddy ground. Cortez's arms are strong, he's always been much stronger than he looks, he's a tightly twisted coil. I thrash around, lift my mouth from the ground to say "Stop it," and he bears down, a knee planted in my back. I don't know what's happening, this is somewhere between childish play-wrestling and him actually trying to hurt me right now, trying to break my back.

"I also had my bucket up there," hisses Cortez, "the bucket I've been pissing in. I was going to dump it on your stupid fucking cop head, but this is better." He twists my neck hard to one side, crams my face deeper into the mud. "More intimate."

I'm lying here sputtering and wondering in what year of my theoretical future police career I would develop the skill to occasionally be the one who surprises the guy, instead of being the guy who gets surprised. In Next Time Around at Abigail's mercy, her festooned with weaponry like a Christmas tree. Atlee frog-marching me through the woods. The unseen man in Rotary, behind his concrete blast wall, the nose of his machine gun. It's like a joke, I'm like a cartoon character. Everybody gets the drop on Detective

Henry Palace!

"I thought we were friends," Cortez growls. "Aren't we friends?"

"Yes."

I have managed somehow to wriggle around onto my back and face him, but now he's clutching my face with his hand, ropy fingers spread out across my jaw and cheeks like a hockey mask. Mud and grit still thick in my throat.

"Cortez—" I manage, through his fingers, and he tightens his grip.

"I thought that we were *partners*."

Suddenly I get it. What he's talking about. "I'm sorry," I say.

The girl, the cell, the key. It all seems so long ago: that flash decision, locking her up and hurling the key in there. The intervening days have been busy ones.

"I am, Cortez," I say. His eyes are angry slits, holes cut from a mask. "I'm sorry."

"You were just doing what you thought was right, is that it?" I nod, as much as I can with his fingers like tentacles wrapped tightly around my face. He tightens them. "You always do what you think is right. That's your deal with yourself. Right?"

"Yes." My voice comes out muffled and distorted. "That's right."

"Ech. *Policeman*."

He spits the word like a curse, an insult—*Policeman*—but then all at once he lets me loose and stands up laughing, a bully's loud victorious laugh. He turns away because he thinks the conversation is over, but it's not over, and I get up on all fours and launch myself like a wrestler at his knees and bring him down, I topple him like a tree and I'm on top of Cortez now, just like that, and throw a rabbit punch across his face.

"Ow," he says. "Fuck."

"How did you know?" I say. Gathering up the front of his dirty T-shirt. My hand hurts from hitting him, the palm burns and screams fire, folded tightly inside my fist.

"How did I know what?" But he's grinning, licking the droplet of blood that's sprung up on his lower lip. He knows what I mean.

"How did you know that I locked the cell door?" He leers. I lean in. "How?"

The grin widens, showing all his crooked teeth, before abruptly disappearing. His face becomes sincere—confessional. I'm still on top of him, pinning him. "I got lonely," he says. "I have been so lonely. And time is running out, you know?" His voice lowers to a ghoulish whisper. His eyes are frozen pools. "I thought I would just go and have a big time. Her and me." He licks his lips. "You would have done the same thing."

"No."

"Yes, Henry boy. Lonely boy. Look into your heart."

"No," I say, and I pull my face away but he curls his head up toward me and whispers, right in my ear. "Hey. Idiot. She's awake."

I let go of Cortez and leap to my feet and run. Oh, God. Oh, no. He's laughing on the ground, dying laughing as I barrel toward the entrance, laughing and yelling at my back. "She's been up since last night. She woke me up screeching but she won't let me in!" His voice gleeful, rich with delight, me grabbing the handle and yanking open the door. "She's pretty upset, Henry, old boy. Pretty upset." He's reveling in my distress, hollering after me as I run. "I can't believe you hit me!"

* * *

Lily is standing against the back wall of the cell, shivering, with her arms wrapped around her body, holding herself tight. The umbilical stub of the IV line dangles from her forearm where she tore it free. She has also torn the package of gauze off her throat, and her wound is raw and pink and glistening like grotesque alien jewelry.

"Who are you?" she says fiercely, and I say, "My name is Henry. I'm a policeman," and she howls, "What did you *do* to me? What did you do?"

"Nothing," I say. "Nothing."

She stares at me, fearful and defiant, like she's a sick animal and I'm here to put her down. She points with a trembling finger at the IV bag hung from the ceiling behind me. "What is that?"

"Saline solution, that's all. Ninety percent sodium chloride," I say, and then when I clock the disbelieving horror in her eyes I say, "*Water*, Lily, it's salt water, to rehydrate you. You needed fluids."

"Lily?"

"Oh, right, I . . ." Why am I calling her that? Where did we get that name? I can't remember. It doesn't matter. She's gaping at me. Baffled, distraught. My fingers are white where I'm gripping the bars.

"I peed," she says suddenly.

"Hey, that's great," I say. "Good for you." Like I'm talking to a baby, just saying words. "That means you're getting better." Trying to keep calm; keep her calm. "I put you in here, okay? You were asleep. But you're safe. You're fine. You're going to be *just fine*."

It's not true—she knows it's not true—everything is not going to be just fine—it's not so. Of course not. She's deathly pale, shivering violently, her face a piteous mixture of fear and wonder.

"What happened?"

"I'm not sure," I say. "I'm trying to find out."

"Where am I?" She licks her dry lips and looks around. I don't know where to start. *You're in the police station. You're in the Muskingum River Watershed. You're on Earth.* I don't know how much she knows. I wonder what I look like. I wish I had shaved. I wish I were smaller. I smell like dirt and fire.

"You're upstairs," I say finally.

"Where are the others?"

The back of my neck tingles. The others. Tick and Astronaut and the black girl and the kid with the bright blue sneakers.

"I don't know where they are."

"Who are you?"

"My name is Henry Palace."

"Henry," she whispers, and then, "Palace," and she looks at me, her eyes widening as they travel over my face.

"Henry, Henry," she says, and then she stares right at me, right into my eyes. "Do you have a sister?"

* * *

It's the same as the last time: I chased the dog and Cortez chased me, the three of us chasing toward the girl's body in the clearing, but now it's just me chasing Lily, which is not her name, cracking branches and brush beneath me, my flat feet thumping on the soil, brambles tearing at my pant legs like vengeful spirits trying to catch me and make me fall. Same as last time—same route—down a westward slope away from the police station, along the line of the small creek—but then Lily breaks left and I follow her, she crosses a small swinging rope bridge, and I follow and follow.

Hide-and-seek. Cutting through the woods. It's raining. My heart is galloping in my chest, leaping out ahead of me.

This is fine, I think crazily, this long moment of just running. The part before we get there, wherever we're going. My pulse is an ocean roar in my ears. The sun is a pale yellow circle through a thickness of rain clouds. Let's just run forever. Because I can feel it, oh man I can feel it—I know what's coming.

Lily stops abruptly at a low line of bushes, and her back stiffens, her head turns slightly to the left and then down, her whole body flinching as she sees whatever it is that she is seeing. I know what it is, though, I already know. Tightness in my chest like someone has tied it off with a belt. A burning in my lungs from running. I already know.

I move in slow motion. Past Lily's stationary form, through a low layer of brush into a little meadow, an opening in the trees.

There's a body in the center of the clearing. I stumble forward over tree roots, tripping over my stupid feet. I pitch forward, right myself, and then crouch, panting, beside the body.

It's her, I know it's her. She's facedown but it's her.

Lily is at the perimeter behind me, moaning. I turn over the body and it's just *her*, I don't get even an instant of uncertainty, not the slightest momentary reprieve: the face is immediately and unquestionably Nico's face. Jeans, long-sleeve T-shirt, tan sandals like the ones Lily is wearing. She fought back, too, before she was slain: bruising below the eye, scratches on her cheeks and forehead, a thin rusted trickle of blood under her nose. Bar fight wounds, nothing serious, except then you look down just a little bit and there's her throat—torn open, ugly, pink and red and black—but I go ahead and I ignore all of that, I do, I go ahead and I take her pulse—it's ridiculous, she's cold and waxen, but I place two fingers on the soft hollow area just below the lower jawbone, just above the brutal red line of her wound, I put my fingers in place and watch a minute go by on the Casio and there's no pulse because she's dead.

Her face tilts gently to one side, and her eyes are closed, as if in sleep. She's at peace, they would say that, people always say things like that, but it's an inaccurate statement—thoughts are thundering around in my head, grief is choking its way up my throat—she's not at peace, she's dead, she was at peace when she was laughing at something clever someone said, she was at peace when she was smoking a cigarette, listening to Sonic Youth. She liked all that '80s and '90s stuff, the college-radio acts. Hüsker Dü, the Pixies. That smart-ass Replacements song about the flight attendant.

There's dirt on her cheeks. I wipe it away with my thumb. A few strands of hair are matted across her forehead like delicate fractures. Her whole life, Nico was so pretty and always trying to pretend she wasn't. So pretty, and so annoyed about it.

I look up at the sky, up at the wavering gray sun and then past it, imagining I can see $2011GV_1$ in its current location. It's close now, a couple million miles now, our nearest neighbor. They say that for the last couple of nights you'll be able to see it with the naked eye, a new star, a gold pin in the black heavens. They say that just before impact the sky will brighten ferociously, like the sun has burst from its own skin, and then we will feel it, even on the far side of the Earth we will *feel* it, the whole world will quaver from the blow. They say that sufficient debris will be ejected from the impact site to fill Earth's atmosphere in a matter of hours.

I stand up, stumble away, and then I grab my forehead with both hands and slowly claw my fingers down my face: dig into my eyes, gouge my cheeks, burrow my fingers through my ridiculous policeman's mustache, disfigure my lips and my mouth, tear angry furrows into my chin. Birds are chattering to each other in a nearby tree. Lily, the girl, whatever her name is, she's still on the outskirts of the clearing, sobbing wordlessly, a dissonant ghostly moan.

Go on now, Detective, urges Detective Culverson, comforting but firm. *Go on and get to work.*

I turn back around and step close again, give myself a push and look at the body like any other body, the crime scene like any other crime scene.

Her throat is cut, the same as Lily's. Her face is covered with scratches and slight bruising, the same as Lily's. And her hair: a hunk is missing from the back, from just above the nape of the neck. She's had bad haircuts in recent years—punkish, short, choppy—so it's hard to tell. But I think it was hacked off. I shake my head, run my hand through my own short hair. I demand a summary of findings and it comes back in the voice of Dr. Alice Fenton, chief medical examiner of the state of New Hampshire, another old acquaintance: *We have a Caucasian female, twenty-one years old, signs of struggle including incised wounds to the fingers, palms, and forearms; cause of death is massive blood loss from traumatic laceration to the structures of the throat, inflicted with a knife or other sharp object wielded by a determined assailant.*

I bite my lip. I look at her face, her closed eyes. What else?

This clearing is smaller than the one where we found the first victim, the one who survived. The ravine where we found her was neat and circular, encircled by pines. This place is rougher around its edges, smaller and more irregular, surrounded not by forest trees but low ugly bushes, rough with pricklers and brambles.

The same evidentiary challenges, here, though, the same unuseful ground, thick with mud. Footprinting a lost cause.

I stand up again. My head spins with stars. I walk a tight circle. What else?

Slow down, Palace, says Detective Culverson, *slow down*, says Officer McConnell, and I tell my ghosts to hush up now, tell them to be still a minute because I can't slow down, I won't—there's no *time.*

Lily is still on the edge of the field, moaning and shaking.

"Hey," I say to her. Walking over quickly. "Hey. Are you okay?"

She shakes her head and wipes at her mouth with the back of one sleeve. "No," she whispers, barely moving her mouth. I step forward, closer, so I can hear. She says, "I don't know what happened."

"What do you mean, you don't know?"

"I remember running. Through the woods."

"From what?"

"Just—that's all I remember. Running."

"From who?"

She starts to talk but she can't talk, no words come out, her mouth hangs open and her jaw quivers.

"From *who*, Lily?"

"I don't *remember*." Her hands come up in front of her mouth. "I had to. No choice. I had to. It was just . . . run." The words escape one by one from behind the barrier of her hands, each little syllable encased in its own small bubble. "Run . . . run . . . run . . ."

I ask her again—from who—from what—why were you running, but she is done, she has stopped cold, stopped like a clock. Her hands come down, away from her frozen mouth, and her face is pure blank, staring forward. I peer into her eyes like narrow windows, as though if I look hard enough I can see through them and into the darkened theater of her mind, watch whatever happened to my sister unspooling inside Lily's eyes.

Lily's not her name. I still don't know her name. I have to learn her name.

I have to learn everything.

Attacker finds two girls in the kitchenette.

Corners them both and slashes victim one. Assuming she's dead, he chases the other one, victim number two, chases her out into the woods. And I can't help it, I'm thinking of good ole Billy, back at the RV, Billy draped in his bloody apron, holding a doomed chicken by the neck.

Meanwhile victim number one is hurt but alive and she stumbles to her feet and out of there, down the hall, trailing blood.

Perpetrator has more success with victim number two. He catches up with her out here, in this field; he slashes her throat down to the windpipe and she dies for real. Victim number one, meanwhile, is stumbling around until she collapses in another clearing in these blood-soaked woods.

Killer stalks back, panting, knife dripping blood, back down the hall to the kitchenette, and then—disappears.

The basement. I have to get down to that basement.

I turn to go back, find Cortez, get back to work, but then I stop.

Entrances and exits, murmurs Culverson. *Finish the scene.*

He's right, except with a shock of clarity I am aware that it's not he who is right, it's me, *I'm* the one who is recalling that it's a rookie move to clear a crime scene without giving a thought to entrances and exits. It's him I'm hearing, but it's really me—anytime I hear a voice telling me to do something, Detective Culverson's mild voice, or my mom's or my dad's or Fenton's or Trish McConnell's. At a certain point you have to concede to yourself that it's just you out here.

I walk the perimeter of the crime scene now, slowly, in the rain. I'm looking for a broken spot in the bushes where the victim or the killer crashed in, looking for evidence of a third party, and what I find instead, lying there innocuously beside a shrub on the far end of the clearing, is a backpack with the Batman logo on it.

I gaze wonderingly at the bag for a couple seconds, and then kick away the dirt and bend to lift it. It is instantly familiar, even comforting, the weight of it, the feel of the straps. It's *my* backpack, from when I was a kid. Fourth grade, fifth grade. Obviously Nico borrowed it from me at some point, obviously she was using it out here, taking it wherever she was going, but in my grief and confusion it is a baffling and magical sight: an object has been stuffed into a time machine at the beginning of my nine-year-old summer and popped out here in the woods on the day and time I found my sister dead. I lift it gingerly to my nose, as if the bag might still smell like eraser dust, bologna sandwiches, scratch-and-sniff.

It doesn't. It smells like dirt and the woods. It is bulky at the top but light, bulging irregularly. I tug the zipper and out tumble bags and bags of popcorn and chips and candy: Lay's and Cheetos and Kit Kats and granola bars.

"I knew it," I tell Nico. I steal a peek at the body, her body, shaking my head. "I knew it was you."

She took the full contents of that vending machine is what it seems like, even the crappy little items that no one ever wants, the Necco wafers and mints and thin packs of Wrigley's. I can picture her snaking her thin arms up the inside of the machine, again and again, fashioning a coat hanger into a hook to make sure she got it all. The old trick. *You're welcome, fatties!*

Buried beneath all the candy and chips is the rest of Nico's belongings. Shorts and shirts. A couple of handguns, a box of bullets secured with a scrap of Scotch tape. A pair of walkie-talkies—not just one, the pair. Underpants and bras. *Animal Farm*. A rain jacket, wrapped up tightly and secured with a rubber band. A red plastic flashlight, which I flick on and off. The bottom of the ancient Batman backpack is lined with layers and layers of duct tape to keep it from opening up and everything falling out.

I wipe tears from my eyes with the back of my hand.

She was on her way out.

The rest of this ridiculous club had at long last given up their foundational ridiculous idea, accepted with only a week left that this rogue military scientist was dead or still in jail or otherwise a no-show. Godot wasn't coming after all.

But not Nico. Not my stiff-spined little sister. She wouldn't accept the obvious.

The situation is what it is, said Astronaut, and she said, *I disagree.*

Even when the rest of them were ready to go to the backup plan, to slip underground and seal themselves in and cover their ears, my headstrong incorrigible younger sister was slipping out with a backpack full of junk food, bound for a military facility four hundred miles away, to track the infamous Hans-Michael Parry like Sasquatch, pin him and bring him to heel.

She was off to save the world all by her goddamn self, if that's what she had to do.

I let myself laugh, just the tiniest bit, but not for long, because her plan didn't work, because someone didn't want her to go. Someone followed her out, her and Lily, and cut their throats and left them to die.

As I shrug the Batman backpack onto my shoulder I find one last piece of evidence, just beside her body, poking up out of the mud. A slim stick of molded black plastic, curved at one end and jagged at the other as if snapped off.

It's the stem of a pair of sunglasses. I tug it out of the mud. I hold it for a long time in my palm and then I tuck it carefully in my pocket. The rain trickles down my face.

I don't know anything yet, not really, I still have almost everything to learn about what happened to Nico.

But this, this piece of plastic, I know what *this* means.

* * *

"Acceptance of loss is not a destination—it's a journey."

This was explained to me by a specially trained grief counselor, how recovering from the unexpected death of a loved one "is not a discrete event that happens at a specific moment in time," but rather a "process" that unfolds over all the slow years of a lifetime. I met with parades of such counselors in my teenage years, variously competent representatives of the healing community: bereavement experts, therapists, child psychologists. My grandfather would bring me and sit with open impatience in the waiting room, working the crossword, an American Spirit behind his ear waiting to be lit. His skepticism casting a distinct pall over all efforts to make me well.

"One must have time to heal," these experts were always announcing. My parents were dead; both of them. A part of me had been gouged out. "Healing will happen, in time."

There's no time, now, obviously. I won't heal. That won't happen.

I gather Nico up into my arms and hug her tight to walk her through the woods, back to the station. "Okay," I say gently to Lily, to the girl, whatever her name is. "Okay, come on now."

Wednesday, August 22

Right ascension 18 26 55.9
Declination -70 52 35
Elongation 112.7
Delta 0.618 AU

"So it's a group home."

"Yes. No. Well—group home makes it sound like it's for criminals or drug addicts," I say. "This is for policemen."

Abigail is skeptical. She chews it over for a minute, her eyes darting where they peek out over her allergy mask. She still isn't entirely convinced, but she seems to have backed off the idea of me putting a bullet in her head. I think we're done with that.

"What if they all hate me?"

"No one is going to hate you."

I evaluate the statement as I say it. Some of them will hate her. Officer Carstairs will hate her because she's not a cop; Officer Melwyn will hate her because she comes from me, and I've been nagging him about leaving the porch lantern on all night. Officer Katz will like her because she's young and good-looking. Most will not hate her, but they will be wary of her because she's an outsider, and because she's self-evidently crazy—but most people are crazy at this point, one way or another.

"You'll do just fine," I tell her. "There will be space for you, because I'm leaving. The Night Bird will work out the details."

"The Night Bird?"

"She's great. You'll see."

At last Abigail gets up and flaps open a giant black Hefty garbage bag and starts throwing things inside, clothes and guns and books and hairbrush and bedroll. She unclips her various armaments, leaving only the calf-sheath pistol and packing everything else in a rolling suitcase.

While she's packing I flip through the forty- or fifty-page document that Abigail handed me along with the map to Rotary, Ohio, which came out of a false-bottom suitcase and is marked TOP SECRET with a red stamp, just like in the movies. My eyes skim dense paragraphs, bristling with impenetrable details and the Greek letters of complex equations: optimal orbital distance, relationship of impact velocity (km/s) to kinetic-energy release (GJ), relationship of energy yield (kt) to mass velocity and initial density, target center versus mass-motion center.

Second to last page: CONCLUSIONS. Last page: PROTOCOL. I can't make sense of any of it.

On the blank back page of the TOP SECRET document I jot down the timeline I've managed to get out of Abigail, structuring the narrative. In mid-July, Jordan tells Abigail that Hans-Michael Parry, a.k.a. Resolution, has been located in Gary, Indiana; he tells her that soon the various "teams" will be gathering in Ohio, at the police station in a small town called Rotary. But then, sometime after July 21—after Jordan has put Nico on that helicopter, her and one other girl flying off from Butler Field at UNH—he tells Abigail they've got new instructions. Jordan and Abigail are to stay put in Concord because their designation has been changed to "backup team."

And then, abruptly on the morning of August 13, Jordan disappears. No signs of foul play, but neither does he leave a note or any new instructions. He's just "gone," Abigail says, whether to Rotary or off on some new adventure she has no idea.

He's just *gone*, and she's been sitting here alone since then, staring into the corners, feeling the Earth's rotation in her inner ear and choking on cosmic dust.

Now she seems more clear-eyed, calmer, as if simply having somewhere definite to go has allowed her to walk steady in her uneven world. She walks to the door of the store and doesn't look back.

On the way out, on the top shelf of a dresser, is a pair of Ray-Ban sunglasses. I've seen them before—the same ugly pair Jordan was wearing the first time I met him, at UNH.

I lift them, turn them idly between my fingers. "Jordan forgot his sunglasses," I say.

"Those things?" says Abigail, and snorts. "Are you kidding me? He's got a million of those fucking things."

PART FIVE

Isis

Monday, October 1

Right ascension 16 49 50.3
Declination -75 08 48
Elongation 81.1
Delta 0.142 AU

1.

"I made coffee. Would you care for a cup of coffee?"

"No."

"Are you sure? It's not gourmet or anything, but it's coffee. It's something."

"No, thank you." The girl looks up, looks at me quickly, a frightened bird, and then quickly down again. "Do you have tea?"

"Oh, shoot," I say, "no. I'm so sorry. Just coffee."

Lily doesn't say anything else. She's sitting on the edge of the thin mattress in the holding cell, staring at her hands folded in her lap. The politeness and patience I am showing her, the composed and even casual demeanor, is all artifice, a strategy designed to achieve a goal. The feeling I have inside is of having been exploded—like all of the things that for so long have defined me, all of my habits and memories and idiosyncrasies, everything that I have built up around whatever core there is of me, all of it has turned out to be plaster, and now it has been blown up and I am watching the powder drift in the atmosphere and settle slowly on the ground. The question now is whether there is or ever was anything underneath all of that, or was I always papier-mâché, a dragon head in a parade, all exterior adornment and nothing inside. I think there is something that remains, a hard warm stone like you find glowing on the ground after a fire. But I'm not sure. I don't know.

I am leaning against the back wall of the holding room, on the good-guy side of the bars, sipping from my thermos with exaggerated calm. From down the hall, in the garage, there is an occasional rattling blast of sound, Cortez grinding away at that concrete wedge with a diesel-fuel jackhammer. My sister's body is in the dispatch room, wrapped in a wrinkled blue tarp.

"So why don't we start by getting your name straight," I say. "It's not Lily, that much I know." I laugh a little, and it sounds hollow, so I stop.

The girl watches her hands. The jackhammer sounds again, growling from down the hall. So far the interrogation is going poorly.

"I wish that I could leave you alone," I say, "I really do." I talk slow, as slow as I can force myself to talk. "You've been through a lot."

"I have?" She looks up, genuinely asking, and then her finger runs along her throat, where she has allowed me to reapply the bandage. "I guess I have."

Mental pictures in strobe-light flash: Two girls, crazy with fear. Tan sandals slipping on leaves. Heavy footsteps crashing through the woods behind them. Nico, facedown, blood flooding from her neck. I blink, clear my throat. Talk very, very slowly. "Your mind is processing trauma. It's hard. The thing is, though, we're in a tough spot, so to speak, just in terms of time."

She nods some more, her small head nervously bobbling up and down, her hands twitching in her lap. "Actually," she says softly. "Can I—you said, about time . . ." She peeks up at me, and then down. "How much longer?"

"Oh," I say. "Sure." She doesn't know how long she was unconscious. She doesn't know. "It's Monday morning, October 1," I tell her. "There are two more days."

"Okay," she says. "Okay." She licks her dry lips nervously, pushes one stray lock of black hair behind one small ear, a simple gesture redolent of who she is, a girl in her late teens or early twenties, a kid who got lost in something terrible and strange.

"So I'm really . . ." I smile one more time, try to make the smile look human. "I'm really wanting to figure out what happened."

"But I don't know," she says. "I don't remember. It's all like this—I don't know." Glances up at me, scared, touches the thick gauze on her neck. "It's all black."

"Not everything, though, right?"

She shakes her head, barely, a tiny motion.

"Not your whole life?"

"No," she manages, glancing up. "Not my whole life."

"Okay, then. So we'll start with what you do remember, okay?"

"Okay," she whispers.

It's not okay. It's really not. What I want to do and what I would do if it would work is lift her and shake her by the feet until the facts come flying out like coins from her pockets. But this is how the process works. It works slowly. It's impossible to tell at this point what portion of her not remembering stems from literal amnesia, what portion from the atavistic fear of reliving whatever horrors she has encountered. The necessary tactic in either case is bound to be patience, small steady movement through the fog, toward the truth. You build trust: Here are the things we both know. Here are the things we are going to talk about. You coach. You coax. It can be hours. *Days.*

I slip through the bars onto her side of the room and place my coffee cup carefully on the floor and take a knee like I'm going to propose.

"You had this bracelet in your pocket, with the charms," I say. "The lilies. So that's why we called you Lily." She lifts it hesitantly from my hand and then presses it in her palm, folds her fingers around it tightly.

"My parents gave it to me."

"A-ha."

"When I was little."

"Gotcha. Nice. But, so—what *is* your name?"

She says something, in the back of her throat, too soft for me to hear.

"I'm sorry?"

"Tapestry."

"Tapestry?"

She nods. Sniffs a little, wipes a tear from the corner of her eye. I feel a dim glow of knowledge in the darkness between us, the first teardrop bulb glowing on in a string of Christmas lights.

"And is Tapestry a nickname?" I say. "A code name?"

"Yeah." She looks up and gives a watery smile. "Both, sort of. We all have them."

"A-ha."

They all have them. Tapestry. Tick. Astronaut. Does Jordan have one of these nickname/code names, I wonder? Does Abigail? Tapestry's black eye, I notice, is at the bare beginnings of the healing process, fading from dark purple to a soft bruised pink. She is—what? Nineteen? Twenty maybe. She's like a hummingbird, this girl. She sort of reminds me of a hummingbird.

"Did Astronaut assign you the code names? Astronaut is—"

The end of the question is "the leader, right?" but before I can get there she inhales sharply and her eyelids drop shut like window blinds.

"Whoa," I say, standing up. I take a half step forward. "Hello?"

She sits in her silence. I can see, or imagine that I can see, her eyes moving behind the lids, like dancers behind a curtain. Slow, Detective, slower. Build trust. Have a conversation. This is all covered extensively in the literature. In the FBI's standard witness-engagement guidelines; in Farley and Leonard, *Criminal Investigation*. I can picture the books on the shelf in my house, the neat line of their spines. My house, in Concord, that burned down. Suddenly, from down the hall, there is a determined thirty-second burst of jackhammering, *ka-da-thunk, ka-da-thunk, ka-da-thunk,* followed by a loud backfire, and then Cortez's exasperated hollering. "Oh, fucker! Fuck me sideways! Fuck!" and the girl looks up, surprised, and bursts out laughing, and I grab the moment, giggle also, lean in, shake my head with amusement.

"Oh, hey," I say, sighing. "My name is Henry. Did I tell you that already?"

"You did. Yes. Henry Palace. My real name is Jean," she says. "And I think—" She looks up at me, rubs her bloodshot eyes. "Actually, could I have—is there any water? Is that okay?"

"Of course, Jean," I say. "Of course it's okay."

* * *

The jackhammer is the property of Atlee Miller. It was hidden in the fruit-and-vegetable stand, as it turns out, where the farm lines up against the highway. The piece of light machinery was stashed there along with a range of other specialty equipment, the existence of which would raise uncomfortable questions among his family: like sophisticated radio equipment, for example, like heavy artillery. These items were under the guard of a solemn young man named Bishal, with whom I had a quick, tense exchange before I said the password Atlee had provided me and produced my notebook with his signature on it.

The jackhammer is "an old dog," Atlee warned, but he also assured me it worked with some coaxing. He did not say that the best coaxing involves shouting "fuck me sideways" when it stalls, but I trust Cortez knows what he's doing, digging away in there. The two of us proceeding along parallel tracks in our investigation, our earlier altercation behind us. Both of us drilling down—he into the dense resistance of the stone and I into this poor kid's damaged psyche.

Jean starts talking and talks for a while, sometimes in long jags but mostly in quick anxious bursts, frequently stopping and restarting, choking off sentences midway through, as if afraid of saying too much, saying something wrong. Bits and pieces. In her manner and appearance she is nothing like Nico—shy and hesitant where my sister was bold and direct—but sometimes, just the fact of her, her being a college-age kid who got sucked into this end-times looking-glass world, she reminds me so much of my sister that I have to stop talking for a second and hold onto my mouth or risk collapsing onto the ground.

"I was at Michigan," Jean tells me, clutching the paper cup of warm water. "The university? That's where I'm from. From Michigan. My parents are from Taiwan. My last name is Wong. They wanted me to come home. When the—when it started. Home to Michigan, I mean. Not Taiwan. They told me to leave school and come home and pray. We're Catholic. I was born in Lansing."

I'm not writing any of this down. My notebook is full, and anyway it's better not to write, not to draw her attention any further to the fact that this is not just a regular conversation. I listen because I have to, to show empathy and build trust, but I do not care at all about her lineage, her faith and family. I am a question mark aimed at an answer.

"I didn't want to, though, to just—just go *home*. Pray. I wanted to—" She shrugs, bites her lip. "I don't know."

In mid-January the University of Michigan wrapped up its existence with a final gathering of the community on the main quad to sing the fight song and raise a toast in Latin. But Jean

Wong remained on campus through the early spring, hanging around, at loose ends. As little as she was interested in huddling in a church with her parents and reciting psalms in Mandarin, she was equally repulsed by the last-months options being explored by her former classmates: all the drum circles and "sexperimentation," the semiorganized bus caravan heading south to the Gulf of Mexico, with pillowcases full of dope and breakfast cereal looted from the student center cafeteria. She was mainly angry, she says, and confused.

"I wanted to—I don't know."

I speak softly. "You wanted to *do* something about it."

"Yes." She looks up, and then repeats the phrase mockingly. "Do something about it. So stupid. Now, I mean. In retrospect."

For a while, Jean wanders around Ann Arbor. She is briefly signed up for a mission to the Arctic, being touted by an energetic young entrepreneur who claims the world's polarity can be shifted with the right combination of magnets. When that falls apart she moves in with strangers who are starting a cooperative "pickling and canning society," to lay in huge quantities of preserved produce for the aftermath. But none of this feels quite real, nothing feels useful. Finally Jean finds herself at a house party slash political gathering in the basement of a Pattengill townhouse, drinking bathtub wine from a red plastic cup, listening to a man standing on a coffee table explain how the whole thing is a "con job" and a "frame-up" and how the government could "stop it like *that* if it wanted to."

Jean snaps her fingers like the man on the coffee table snapped his fingers, and in my mind I am watching Nico snap her fingers, trying to sell me the same story. I experience a melancholy roll of feeling, sensing her presence in the room with us, her emphatic intonations, knowing that really she is dead down the hallway, in Dispatch, rolled up in a tarp.

The guy on the coffee table at the Pattengill party was a young man with "crazy curly hair" and bright blue shoes. He wore some kind of cape covered in glittering yellow stars. He was called Delighted—just the one name, says Jean quietly. Like Madonna. Or Bono.

"We kept talking to him after the party. Me and this girl Alice, I had met her doing the other thing. That pickling thing. We ended up—actually, we ended up moving in with him. Me and her and some others." She bites her lip, and I don't ask if Astronaut was one of the other people, he of the calm demeanor and the tools on his belt, because I don't want her eyes to slam shut again.

I guide her instead into a description of the sorts of activities that she and her new housemates got up to: throwing more parties, giving more speeches, printing pamphlets to convince more people that the government was playing false about the asteroid threat. That's as much as Jean will say, but presumably this upper-midwestern branch then progressed to the same second-order mischief as Nico and her pals in New England: committing street-corner vandalism; amassing small arms and hauling them around in duffel bags; eventually escalating to targeted trespassing on military bases, like the escapade that got Nico's husband, Derek, pinched at the New Hampshire National Guard station.

The one thing that troubles me is the geographic reach of

the organization. When Nico told me that there was a "Midwest branch" of this collective, I wrote it off as more tough talk, more BS; Nico having been fooled or trying to fool me. But here's Jean confirming she was recruited into this gang at a basement house party at the University of Michigan, many months and miles away from when Nico came in, in central New Hampshire. It's another aspect of this thing that speaks to a certain level of capability, a scale of operations that sits uneasily with my mental picture of Nico and some goofball pals playing at revolution in a Concord vintage store.

I don't know what to do with this kind of information. I don't know where to put it.

"Jean," I say abruptly, "we need to skip ahead."

"What?"

"Eventually a plan emerged, to track down a former United States Space Command scientist named Hans-Michael Parry, who claimed to be in possession of a plan to blow the asteroid off course. Right?"

"Right," she says, startled. I press on. "Your group or an affiliated group was going to find Parry and free him, get him to England where he could orchestrate a standoff burst. Right?"

A stunned pause, then a quiet "Right." She brings her pinky finger up to the corner of her mouth and gnaws at the nail, like a nervous child.

"And then he was found, right? In Gary, Indiana? And everyone was going meet down here in Rotary and await his arrival."

"It was all so *stupid*." This is the second time she's said it, and now her eyes are flashing anger at all of this stupidity. "We sat here.

Waiting and waiting, just—*waiting*."

She stops there, and I watch her hand rise mechanically back to her neck, her wound, her fingers twitching along the edges of the bandage. It's like she senses it, that we are getting nearer to the heart of this conversation, to the events of Wednesday, September 26—the mud, the knives, the violence in the woods beside the station—and the nearness of it draws her and repels her, like a black hole.

I force myself to go nice and slow, get there in time. I ask her about the people she was here with, and she does, debuting more silly code names: there was not only Delighted, there was Alice, who at some point became Sailor; there was "this real smiley kid, very young, called Kingfisher." There was a girl named Surprise and a man called Little Man, who was "super big, actually," so that was kind of a joke. Ha-ha. They all came down via a long zigzagging van ride from Michigan, detouring to pick up a couple of people in Kalamazoo, detouring again for a ton of packing crates from a warehouse in Wauseon, west of Toledo.

I lean forward.

"And what was in those crates?"

"I don't know, actually. I didn't—I never saw. He said—no peeking."

"Who did?"

No answer. She really won't say his name; she won't even let herself think it. I watch it appear and linger on her face, again, her palpable terror of this man, this leader. "Never mind," I say, "go on," and she does. She and her bunch were joined by the other group, the group that included Nico, in late July. People came and went. As she describes the atmosphere on the lawn of the police station these last couple months, awaiting this elusive scientist, Jean's face brightens, her body visibly unclenches. It's like she's talking about a garden party, like some sort of asteroid-conspiracy day camp: everybody hanging out, smoking, cooking hot dogs, flirting.

One guy in particular, she says offhandedly, was "totally in love" with Nico.

"Oh," I say, suddenly changing my mind, suddenly wishing I had my notebook, some notebook, something. "What guy?"

"Tick," she says.

"Tick." Strange looking. Nervous disposition. "Did she reciprocate?"

"Ugh. No." Jean makes a face, breathes out a tiny gale of fluttery sorority-sister laughter. "No interest. He looked like a—a horse, really. Plus he was sort of with this other girl, Valentine. But he would always make these jokes about Nico."

"Valentine?"

"That's her code name. Whatever. She's so pretty. Black girl, really tall."

Atlee saw her. I know of her already, and now I can put a name on the description. It's so odd, to start to feel like I know these people, this world, the last one my sister lived in before she died.

"What kind of jokes did Tick make?"

"Oh, my God. I mean. Adam and Eve? Like, you know. If the plan didn't work. If we had to go under. He and Nico were going to be like Adam and Eve. It was—gross."

"Gross," I say. I squeeze my eyes shut to capture the information, keep everything on file. "Hey, here's a question for you. Did Nico have one of these code names?"

"Oh," says Jean, and laughs. "She didn't use it much. She thought the whole thing was sort of stupid. But her code name was Isis."

"Isis?" My eyes pop open. "Like the Bob Dylan song?"

"Oh. I don't know. Is that where it's from?"

"Yeah," I say. "Yeah, that's where it's from."

I savor this small pleasant factoid for a moment, half a moment, before we press on into the hard part of this. It's going to get rough now, but it has to. Time is passing. There is nowhere else to go in this conversation but forward.

"So, Jean," I say. "So Hans-Michael Parry never turned up. And a decision was made." I look her in the eyes. "Astronaut made a decision."

"I'm tired," says Jean. She sets down her cup so fast that it tips over and the water rolls out. "I'm ready to stop."

"No," I say, and she flinches. "You just listen. Listen. Parry never showed up. And once everyone realizes it's not happening, Astronaut makes the decision to relocate underground. To move everything downstairs. Jean?"

She opens her mouth to answer but the jackhammer abruptly roars down the hall, and her face constricts with fear and she closes her mouth just as the machine goes silent again.

"Jean? Was that his plan?"

"His plan," she says, and then she shudders, violent but slow, like a theatrical enactment of a shudder: her face and then her neck and then her back and then her torso, a wave of revulsion rolling down the length of her body. "His *plan*."

"Lily?"

"That's not my name," she says.

"Oh, God, Jean. I'm sorry."

"I didn't want her to go. I told her not to."

"What?"

"*Nico.* We're going down, we're making the last trips, and she goes, she goes, 'I'm taking off.'"

"To go get Parry on her own."

"Right," says Jean. "Yes."

"So this was what time?"

She looks up, confused. "What time?"

I know it's after Nico and Astronaut have their argument in the hallway, and it's before Atlee closes up the floor at 5:30. "Is this about five o'clock?"

"I don't know."

"Let's say it's five o'clock. She tells you she's leaving and you did what?"

"I mean, I told her it was insane." She shakes her head, and for an instant I see reflected in her eyes this incredulous exasperation that I myself have felt a thousand times, trying to tell Nico anything she doesn't want to hear. "Just—useless. I said, why would you want to leave for nothing and be alone, when we can all be together? At least that, you know? Be together."

"But she went anyway."

"She did. We brought everything down, and I didn't think she would really go, but then everyone was like—she's gone. She was gone."

"And you followed her?"

"I—" She stops; her brow furrows; her eyes well up with confusion. "I—did."

I stand up. "Jean? You followed her."

"Yes. I had to, see? I had to. She's my friend."

I'm leading her as far out into this memory as she'll go, I'm holding her hand and leading her out on the slippery rocks toward the dangerous water. "You had to stop her from leaving, but then there was someone else. Someone followed *you*. Jean?"

"I don't remember."

"Yes, you do, Jean. Yes, you do."

Her mouth drops open, and her eyes widen, and then she shakes her head again, she stares forward into the air between us. "I don't remember."

She does, she is seeing something—someone—I see it happening in her eyes. I lean forward and grab her but she wriggles back, rolls away. "Jean, keep talking. Jean, stay with me. You went to stop her but someone followed you guys."

But she's gone, she's done, she falls back on the bed and throws her hands up in front of her face, and I am saying, "Jean! Jean. Somebody surprised you outside the station. With a knife."

She shrieks a little, a sharp burst of air, and then she presses her hand across her lips. And I grab her again, clutch her by the shoulders and lift her, and my shell of dispassion, my phony policeman's calm, is melting off of me, burned off by heat: I can't stand this, I have to know.

"Someone chased you and attacked you with a knife, and they killed my sister."

She shakes her head violently, keeps her hand clapped over her mouth, like there's a demon in there, something trying to slip free and wreck the world.

"Was it Astronaut?"

Eyes squeezed shut tight, body shaking.

"Or was it a stranger? A short man, sunglasses? Baseball cap?"

She turns her body away from me, turns her back. I wish I could pull out a picture of him—lay it on the bed, Jordan smirking in his stupid Ray-Bans, see Jean's face see the picture. But it's too late, she's disappeared, she's gone, turning her mind away from whatever it is she is unwilling to see. Her hand is clamped over her mouth, her body has fallen over onto its side and she lies there on the thin mattress, mute, terrified, useless.

"Oh, come on," I say.

I kick the bed and it bounces with her in it.

"Oh, come on, come on, come on."

2.

"Isis," of course, is the second track on the 1976 album *Desire*, and for a brief period when I was about fifteen or sixteen it was my favorite Bob Dylan song. It was around that time Nico discovered a journal in which I had carefully recorded my top twenty Dylan numbers, each annotated with the year written and the performers on the track. Nico found something hysterical about the fastidiousness of this particular exercise, and she ran around the house, dying with laughter, tossing the notebook up and down to herself like a chimpanzee.

It's weird to think back now, to think about who I was then, to think that at any time "Isis" was my favorite Dylan song. Now it probably isn't even my favorite song on *Desire*. But there's no reason Nico would have known that, and I think it is at least possible, I think it is perhaps even likely, that she chose the code name because she knew at some point, somehow, I would find out about it. That she left it behind not as a marker, a follow-me bread crumb like the bent fork in the vending machine or the butt of the American Spirit, but rather as a kind of a gift. Or else she did it just because it made her laugh, because various aspects of my personality make her laugh, and that, also, at this point, is a kind of a gift.

I walk down the hall from the holding cell to Detective Irma Russel's little office, and I flip her heavy leather-bound log book to the back and tear out sixteen sheets and fold them over neatly to form a book, and then I spend a good half hour recording everything that Jean had to say before she shut down, blanked out, went dark. How she came to be in the group; the names and approximate ages and appearances of her pals and coconspirators; the way her face turned cloudy and wild at the mention of the name Astronaut. How she realized that Nico had taken off, how she ran to follow her . . .

When I'm done writing, when I've written up to the brick wall at the end of the story, I walk back down the hall to Dispatch so I can sit next to Nico. She would laugh at me for all of this. She would tell me to take a load off, go back and have more beer with the rednecks, eat more chicken.

I press the power button on the RadioCOMMAND and the room fills with prayer: a gospel choir singing about the promised land in lush layers of harmony, transmitting up to God and out over a 600 MHz band. I picture a church somewhere, barricaded doors, blackout shades over the windows, a hungry happy congregation singing and singing till the day arrives. Till the promised land. I press SCAN and find someone claiming to be the president of the

United States of America, proudly announcing that the whole thing was just a test of the resiliency of the American people, and—good news—we passed the test. It's okay now, though, folks. Everything is fine.

I change the station. I change it again. Flickering voices, bursts of static, "*DO NOT DRINK THE WATER IN THE MUSKINGUM RIVER WATERSHED*," and then a tipsy ecstatic teenager: "I don't know where y'all motherfuckers are at, but we all motherfuckers are in the Verizon store at the Crestview Hills Mall in Crestview Hills, Kentucky, bi-zatch! Anyone looking to par-tay get on fucking I-75 . . ."

It's foolish to keep listening to strangers. I should preserve the battery; I should preserve my time. I press the SCAN button just one more time, the last time, and find a quiet and urgent voice, and I have to move right up close to the speaker to hear it.

"I repeat, I am in my car and I am driving south on Highway 40, if you get this and you still love me, I will be in Norman by five tomorrow, that's tomorrow . . . I repeat, I'm in the car, I'm on the highway, and I love you. I, uh . . ."

The voice trails off into silence, the rush of highway wind. I wait a moment holding my breath and then I turn it off, just as the jackhammer starts up again at last, steady and sure from Cortez's end of the hall. He fixed it. He's got it.

It remains hard to fathom, hard to believe, that this is what the world has become. That this, of all possible worlds and times in which I could have been born, could have been a policeman, that this is the world and time that I got.

"We got ripped off, Nic," I walk back over to my sister, look again at her face, the savaged flesh of her neck. "We got ripped off."

I start to pull the tarp up over her head but then I stop, I just hold it there like a blanket.

It's the wound. It's her throat.

Maybe I didn't look hard enough out in the woods, maybe I was distracted or maybe it's that just now I've had the experience of sitting and staring at Jean for half an hour, watching her talk, looking at her throat. Out there in the woods, at first glance, it was clear to me that these two wounds were the same: two girls, throats slashed, victim one and victim two, wound one and wound two.

But it's not so. Nico's injury is worse—much worse. Which makes sense, of course, because she's dead and Jean isn't. I lean in close, trace the line of the assault with the tip of a finger. Looking closely I see it's not a cut but a mass of cuts, a cluster of overlapping lacerations, forming a rough V below the victim's chin, pointing down. With the other wound there was blood, there was the raw pinkness of the exposed muscle, but now here with this second victim it goes deeper than that—below all the blood of the jugular and the shredded layers of throat there is the shell color of bone, the off-white piping of the trachea. The depth of the wound and its messiness suggest that she was struggling, moving the whole time, trying to defend herself, get free from what was happening.

I blink back to Jean's wound, the one I was just staring at

while she stumbled through her story, a less messy wound—a single slash, suggesting little struggle or no struggle, contrary to the bruising and lacerations on her face.

So—then—so—I stand up, pace in a tight circle—so she fought back, Jean fights back but is captured and subdued. Let's say a pill or pills, let's say the assailant pushes something into her mouth, covers her nose with his hands and forces her to swallow.

No—stop—I stop, smack the wall with my hand, think faster, Palace, think better. We're in a fast-moving scenario here, victim two—Nico—is already sprinting off into the woods, I'm the killer and I've got to catch her, can't let her go. I hit her with something. Knock her down. Jean's in the dirt—unconscious?—gets her with one quick smooth slice to the throat and then I'm off and running after victim two, after Nico Palace tearing breathlessly in her sandals through the woods.

But I checked Jean's body, while she was asleep, when she was still Lily, I checked her scalp for blunt force trauma, surely I did.

She was, though, she was *still.* Pills or an injection or the blow of a hammer to the side of the head, she wasn't moving when she was cut and Nico was.

I find that I'm panting, pacing, horrified. It's out there, it's up there, the dark heart of the sky, coming in fast.

Focus Palace but I can't but I have to. Keep going.

Killer catches up to poor Nico in that second clearing, gets on top of her and pins her down, and she's terrified, she's awake, she's writhing, and he grabs her from behind and slashes her throat until it's open.

I am trembling, like I'm there, like I'm in the scene, like I'm cutting or being cut.

There's something else, too. I turn around, away from the window, look at her one more time, wiping tears out of my eyes, feeling my knife hand clenching and unclenching. There's something else.

Among the messiness and the gore of the wound there is something—I crouch—lean forward, take out my measuring tape, and murmuring apologies to Nico, after all that she has suffered, murmuring "holy moly" and then "holy shit," I peel back small portions of her lacerated skin, one-tenth of a centimeter at a time, and I keep discovering them—smaller cuts within the larger, lines as small as insect legs. I move my magnifying glass across the neck and confirm that these smaller cuts are regularly spaced at quarter-inch increments along the whole line of the wound.

Parallel superficial incisions on the upper and lower skin margin of the wound. Dr. Fenton would say that nothing is certain, that certainty is for schoolchildren and magicians, but that parallel superficial incisions on the upper and lower skin margin of the wound strongly indicate that the weapon used was a serrated blade.

I burst out of the dispatch room and run down the hallway, hands spread out to either side like an animal wingspan, fly down the corridor to the kitchen to confirm my snapshot memory of the knives on the rack behind the kitchen. Butcher's blade; paring knife; cleaver. Nonserrated.

Back in Dispatch I run it down for Nico, explain to her about her wound, the parallel superficial incisions and what they mean. I remind her, furthermore, that the only serrated blade I am aware of, in the context of this investigation, is the sawtooth buck knife noticed by Atlee Miller, hanging from Astronaut's belt.

"Policeman."

"Yeah."

"Are you okay?"

Cortez. Tentative expression, narrowed eyes. Looking at me like I'm not actually okay.

I clear my throat. "I'm fine. Did you crack it?"

"You don't look fine."

"I am. Did you get us down?"

He doesn't answer. He's looking at the tarp.

"Palace," he says. "Is that her?"

"Yeah," I say. "That's her."

I give it to him fast, the thumbnail sketch only. "The sleeping girl, whose name is Jean Wong, originally of Lansing, Michigan—her memory of the incident in question is very uneven, essentially empty, but she was able to lead me directly to a field in the woods where I located the body. Cause of death is a deep wound to the throat with a serrated blade. That's about—that's about what we've got. So."

I stop abruptly. I know exactly what I'm doing by talking this way, very rapidly in crisp and distinct policeman diction, I'm stringing words out around my grief like a perimeter, like caution tape.

Cortez nods, solemn, adjusts his ponytail. I wait for him to ask again if I'm okay, so I can tell him I am and we can move on.

"Death," he says instead. "It's the fucking worst."

"Did you get us down there?"

"Yeah. I did."

"Okay. Okay, great."

He backs out of the room rather than turning, and as I stand up I see that for some reason I took one of the knives with me, the blood-stained butcher's knife from the kitchenette. I'm holding the handle tight in my fist. I look at it for a second and then I slide it into my belt, on the inside, close to my thigh, like a huntsman.

3.

So the group goes underground but then Nico pulls a runner and Jean runs after her and Astronaut chases them both, catches them, kills them one by one.

This is last Wednesday, sometime after four thirty p.m., probably closer to five. Me and my dog and my goon rolled in about three o'clock on Thursday morning. Hours. A margin of hours. I can't forget that. I won't.

It's Astronaut, or it's Jordan and he's using Astronaut's knife.

Or it's Tick, or it's Valentine. Or it's none of the above.

Nine times out of ten, in the usual run of things, a person is murdered not by a stranger but by a friend or family member, a husband or wife. There are exceptions—my mother was one—and neither is this the normal run of things. We live now in a world of wolves, blue towns, red towns, people roaming the countryside in search of safety or love or cheap thrills. Nico and Jean may well have emerged from their society of rogues unharmed, only to be set upon by some monster roaming the landscape, someone who had always wanted to slash the throats of two girls and took his opportunity before disappearing, laughing, into the woods. Plenty of people wear sunglasses. Plenty of people carry serrated knives.

"Ready, Policeman?"

"Yeah," I say to Cortez. "I am."

We are standing beside each other, hands on our hips, staring down the metal stairwell that descends, as predicted, from the middle of the police station garage. The infamous wedge of concrete that had hidden it has been reduced to a pile of rubble, which Cortez has arranged on a tarp beside the resulting hole, a pyramid of uneven stones. He's sweating like crazy from his exertions, his T-shirt is soaked, his ponytail unkempt and sweat-matted, rolling down his back. Peering down into the darkness, licking his lips.

"Okay," he says. "Okay, okay, okay. We get down there, first challenge will be getting through the blast door."

"Blast door?"

"People build bunkers, this is what they do: they put in a toilet, a generator, and a blast door." He's fitting on a Rayovac headlamp, tightening the straps. "Plus, of course, I've been up here jackhammering for the better part of an hour."

"And nobody came up."

"Because they didn't hear."

"Through the blast door."

"Gold star for you, Policeman."

He hands me a second headlamp, and I loop the straps over

my ears and across my scalp, wincing as the Velcro of the fastener brushes the gash on my forehead. "You can't shoot through a blast door unless you've got a shoulder-mounted nuclear bomb, but you sure can pick the locks." His headlamp winks on. "Well. I can."

Cortez is talking fast, grinning like the devil, eyes flashing with excitement, ready to rock. There is a new intensity about the man, a thrill of having cracked the floor and a twitchy excitement about heading downstairs—almost as if this is his case and I'm the one tagging along to lend him a hand. He can't wait to see what's down there, what comes next. I'm feeling what he's feeling, too, I need to know, I have to, and when I stare down into the darkness of the stairwell, beyond the edge of my headlamp's halo I see Nico's face, eyes closed, the dark red savaged mess of her throat.

Cortez steps down first, heavy boot heel clanging on the top metal step, me coming one step behind. The narrow metal stairwell shivers under our heels.

"Hi."

A timid voice, from back the way we came. Jean is standing in the doorway that leads out of the garage back into the hallway. Cortez and I both stop at the same time and turn our heads, and our headlamps crisscross like prison-break spotlights on her small worried face.

"You're going down?"

"Yes," I say. "We are."

"You must be Jean," says Cortez. "It's so nice to meet you."

She shifts from one foot to the other in the doorway, shivering, holding herself tightly. She is wearing black pants and a red T-shirt

I gave her out of Nico's abandoned backpack, and over that one of my extra jackets, which hangs on her like a monk's robe. She hovers there, uneasy, like she wants to leave but can't. As if she is a ghost, captured in the gloomy corner of the garage, tethered by her curse to a given radius.

"Can I come?" she says.

"Why?"

"I just—I want to."

I step back up, out of the hole. "Do you remember something, Jean? Something you can tell us?"

"No," she says, shaking her head. "No. I don't." She crosses her arms, sniffs the thick gray air of the garage. "I just want to come."

"Well," I start, but at the same time Cortez says: "No." I look at him, and he shakes his head. "No way." Before I can marshal an argument, which I am not sure I have, Cortez is talking fast, stage-whispering his objections: "A, this girl is, tops, a hundred pounds; B, she's unarmed; and C, she's clearly not in a healthy place. If you gather my meaning. We don't need her."

"She's been down there. She can guide us."

"It's a hole in the ground," says Cortez. "I think we'll figure it out."

I look at Jean, who looks back at me pleadingly, wavering on her feet. She doesn't want to be alone, that's all. She's so pale standing there in the dim light that she is virtually transparent, like I might look away and look back and she'll be gone, she'll just slip out of existence.

"Policeman, listen," says Cortez, no longer bothering to whisper, his eyes fixed on the thin staircase leading down. "We're not going in there to play ping-pong in the rec room. This isn't all the set-up for a surprise party I planned for you."

He's right. I know he's right.

"Jean," I say softly.

"No, it's—" She turns away. "Fine. Okay."

"We'll be right back," I tell her, which probably isn't true, and "you'll be fine," and of course that's not true either.

"You can't save everybody, my boy," says Cortez, while I watch Jean wander from the garage and maybe back to the holding cell that has somehow become her home, or maybe she'll be darting off into the woods, taking her chances in the broken world until it's gone. Or maybe she's done, maybe she's had enough and when we come back we'll find her up here, hanging by a bedsheet, eyes bulging and lips blue like Peter Zell.

We go down. Down we go.

Cortez descends first and I follow him into the darkness. He's whistling, softly, "hi-ho, hi-ho," and I follow the sound of him whistling and the clang of his boot heels on the metal steps, my headlamp catching half-lit visions of his back and the backs of his shoes, until he reaches the bottom and stops and says, "Huh."

There is no blast door. We come off the last step onto a cement floor; cement walls; a long basement hallway. It's cold, noticeably so, an easy ten degrees colder than upstairs; cold and dark and utterly silent. The smells of old stone, of mold and standing water, and underneath that a more recent scent, an acridness like something burning somewhere nearby. As we look around the empty room our headlamps cut overlapping slices of yellow gloom from the darkness.

It's nothing. It's just plain nothing. It takes a moment or two for me to identify the feeling creeping up into my bones while I'm standing here, staring at this long empty quiet hallway. It's disappointment is what it is, a low cold disappointment, because some part of me had *wondered*. At some point without meaning to I had allowed some faint bubbles of hope to form and rise. Because of all of it—not just the damn helicopter, but all of it: the impressive geographic reach of this group, from New England to the Midwest; the Internet capacity, Jordan nonchalantly hacking an FBI database on a dial-up connection while the rest of the world is in rapid regression toward the Stone Age; those mysterious heavy crates Atlee Miller saw being trucked down here on Wednesday afternoon.

Some idiot part of me was expecting to find a hum of activity. A rogue government scientist in a white coat barking out orders. Last-minute preparations for launch. Beeping consoles and screens filled with maps, a world beneath the world, humming along, preparing for action. Something from James Bond, something from *Star Wars*. *Something.*

But it's nothing. Cold; darkness; a bad stink; spiderwebs and dirt. Under the staircase there's a cheap wooden door, hanging open to a tiny room: fuse boxes; mops; a black potbellied furnace, silent and rusted.

Where are the *people*? Where are my buddies Sailor and Tick and Delighted, where are the brilliant revolutionaries, vanguard of the future? Where have the spiders scuttled off to?

Cortez, for his part, seems unfazed. He turns to me in the

strange wavering light of the headlamps, and his spooky excited grin is still in place. His face looks chopped up and put back together.

"Who knows?" he says, reading my mind. "Maybe they went out for milk."

My eyes are slowly adjusting to the dimness. I look up and down the hallway.

"Okay," I say. "How do you want to do this?"

"We'll split up."

"What?

I turn back sharply to him and our two pools of light form together and I see that his eyes are wide and flashing. There's definitely something going on with him, I saw it up at the top of the steps, some new eagerness coming to life in his head, taking center stage.

"I'll go thisaway," he says, like the sheriff in a Western, pokes his thumb off into the darkness and starts moving.

"No," I say. "Wait. What? Cortez."

"Just holler. Just do Marco Polo. Don't worry."

Don't worry? "Cortez?"

This is insane. I stumble after him but he's moving fast, swallowed up in the surrounding darkness. He's got some plan, he's following some star that I can't see. A wash of panic rushes up from my stomach, a rush of fear, deep anxiety, as old as childhood. I don't want to be down here alone.

"Cortez?"

4.

I take big careful steps along the gray floor, my back pressed against the rough concrete, my light bobbling in front of me like I'm an anglerfish. My gun is in my right hand. Eyes seeking, trying to adjust. Walking through a shadowland, through a photographer's negative, shining the light. A few bulbs dangle bare and functionless from the ceiling, among a tangle of sagging, rusted pipes. A bare stone floor, uneven, cracked in long lines across the foundation. Spiderwebs and spiders.

The layout of the police station basement appears much like the layout upstairs, a single long hallway broken by doors. There are just fewer of the doors down here, spaced farther apart. It's like this world down here is the corpse version of the world upstairs, the decaying mirror image of what's above. Like the building died and was buried down here, underground.

Somewhere down the hall I hear the creak of a door, a

footstep: steel boot heel on concrete. Another footstep and then a quiet rustle of laughter.

I whisper sharply. "Cortez?"

No answer. Was that him? The door creaks again, or maybe a different door. I turn slow, 360 degrees, watch my semicircle of light bobble across the darkness, but it doesn't find him. What was he laughing at? What's funny? I don't know if he's still somewhere in the hallway, on the far end of it hidden in shadow, or if he's slipped through one of the doors.

There's a scratching sound, above my head, something small up there, tiny claws scrabbling over the rusted interiors of the pipes. I stand for a long moment, as if at attention, listening to the mouse or mole or whatever it is, feeling each of my heartbeats like a whoosh of air in a bellows, feeling a flush of fever in my face. Maybe it's a function of having lost so much weight—of being so tired—but I can, I can feel it, each individual heartbeat, every second passing.

All in all I'm counting only three doors, clustered together at the end of the hall. Two up ahead on my left, one just to my right. I shake my head, press my fingers into my eyelids. Three doors, three rooms. Doors and rooms. All I have to do down here is what I did up there, go down the line, search each room, clear each one, check them off, one at a time.

They're even labeled. The door directly next to me on the right says GENERAL STORE in big spray-painted letters, bright red. On the other side of the hall, the closer of the two doors says LADIES, same paint, same color. The one next to it should say

GENTLEMEN, but instead it has no words, just a graffiti depiction of male genitalia in bright blue paint. Sophomoric; charmless; bizarre in the context. This little masterpiece I presume to be what Cortez was laughing at, but it doesn't look like it's that room he chose to enter—it's the door marked GENERAL STORE that's slightly ajar. I peer through it and say, "Marco," and he doesn't answer and for a second I can see it vividly in my mind, Cortez in there, taken by surprise, his throat sliced open, red blood spilling out, writhing on the floor, blood spurting from the terrible wound.

"Polo," he says, indistinct and distant. I exhale.

I shake my head. Where are the people? Maybe one of these doors leads to another hallway, another exit; another staircase, leading farther down. Maybe they came down here and disappeared, dissolved into patches of dust or shadows.

The door marked LADIES is locked. I rattle the handle. Bedrooms? Women's bunks? I press the door with two flat hands, find it to be flimsy, just pine or pressboard. Eminently breakable, calling to be kicked down. I take a deep breath and prepare to kick in the door, and while I'm suspended there, between intention and action, another memory crowds in: my mother, a couple of years before she was murdered, she said this beautiful thing to me about how your life was a house that God had built for you, and He knew what was in each room but you didn't—and behind every door there was a discovery to be made, and some rooms were full of treasure and some with trash but all the rooms were of God's design—and at this point, these many years later, I have to wonder if it isn't more accurate to say that life is a series of trap doors, and you fall through them, one by one, tumbling down and down and down, one hole to the next.

I raise my gun up to chest height, like a real old-fashioned policeman, and kick open the door marked LADIES. It flies open and cracks against the wall, ricochets back against my shoulder and cracks into the wall a second time, and my light looks in on a room full of corpses.

* * *

It takes time. To get the whole picture, it takes some time. Investigating a pitch-black room with a headlamp, what you get is a mosaic picture, like shaking puzzle pieces one by one out of the box. You turn your head and suddenly the light fills with a man's face, scruffy beard, features slack, eyes staring straight ahead. Turn your head again, the light moves, and there's an arm in a dress shirt, sleeves rolled up, fingers curled, inches from the plastic Flintstones cup that's rolled away from the hand.

My light moves through the room, seeing one thing at a time.

In the center of the room there is a small square card table with cups and saucers on it. There are dead bodies seated around it as if for tea. A man with a long ugly face and a buzz cut, head back and to the side, like he's fallen asleep on the crosstown bus. One of his hands dangling down to his right, the other hand on the table, fingers interlaced with the fingers of the girl next to him. This is Tick, then, and the girl whose hand he is holding is

Valentine—African American, very dark skinned, long arms. She has fallen forward and her cheek is flat on the tabletop, a line of fluid running from the corner of her mouth like a spiderweb.

Two more people are at the table. Everyone has a cup. Four for tea.

Across from Tick is Delighted, handsome young fella, clean-cut, slumped backward, head lolling. In the cape that Jean mentioned. I crouch under the table and find his trademark bright blue sneakers. Next to Delighted is a girl with a wide face, round cheeks, curly hair—maybe that's Sailor, formerly Alice—her body turned slightly away from Delighted, as if upset with him or embarrassed by something he just said.

I shine my light into Sailor's cup: it looks like tea, it really does. I sniff at it but don't catch a scent. I don't touch anything. It's a crime scene.

I make my way from the center of the room out to the perimeter and find more corpses—many more. I am keeping it together, though, I'm doing fine. I'm shining my headlamp into each pair of eyes like an optometrist, examining each pair of dilated pupils.

I hold up wrists, take pulses, listen at chests. There is no sign of life in anybody. I'm in a wax museum.

Close to the door is a seated man, bearded chin resting on his thick barrel chest. Little Man. Remember? It's funny because he's so big. Ha-ha. Another corpse, a man I've heard no description of, shirtless with a muscle-man build and a scar on his cheek and a surfer's blond hair. Next to him, jutting out from under the table, are two feminine bare feet, crossed demurely, slim ankle over slim ankle. For some reason I think this is more likely to be Sailor than the girl at the table, or maybe it's someone else entirely, maybe it's one of the four girls—four if I'm doing the math right, four of Atlee Miller's estimated eight girls and six men—whose code names I never got. Whoever she is, she drank hers out of a thermos, the thermos is cupped in her lap with no top on, and I shine the headlamp down into it and catch a glimpse of the last few drops of dark liquid.

I go back to the table. The girl who is half eased away from Delighted, I've seen her face. I met her. Nico's friend. She was flying the helicopter.

I look at it again, the poison, shine my light into the cups and glasses and thermoses, confirming that they all drank the same draft, whatever it is. I will never know what it is. We're past all that now. *Send it to the lab, boys!* It was something bad for you. They all drank it and died.

There's even a note. It's on the wall, black and green graffiti letters on the concrete: ENOUGH OF THIS SHIT.

There are more bodies. A girl curled up over here like a sleeping cat, a dreadlocked blonde next to her, arms and legs splayed out at crazy angles. A woman of early middle age, arms crossed, cross-legged against the wall like she's doing yoga. What's funny is that I keep expecting to find Nico among this room full of suicides, even though I already *found* her, I found her in the woods, she's already dead.

The last body lies on the ground, in the back corner,

facedown. A man, a generation older than the rest. Thick dark hair. Dark brown eyes. Glasses, one lens cracked where his face hit the concrete when he slid off a folding chair. I stoop and shine the light right into his eyes. Astronaut. Mouth open, tongue sticking out, eyes wide open and staring at the door.

I reach down to check the famous belt but it's not on, so I get down on all fours and crawl around for a minute, trying to find it, and my hand comes down on the cold flat flesh of his hand, Astronaut's, and I lurch up out of my crouch and race for the door because this is a crime scene, for God's sake, I trip over Sailor's extended feet, or whoever's feet those are, and reach the hallway just in time to bend forward and vomit on the ground. Nothing in my stomach: black strings of coffee-colored bile, pooling at my feet in the light of the headlamp.

I straighten up and rub at my face with my shirtsleeve and try to think this through. Dead in that room are six women—Valentine, Sailor, and four more—and five men, Tick, Astronaut, Little Man, Delighted, and the stranger with the surfer hair.

This is what Nico was escaping from. This was the backup plan that sent the wave of atavistic revulsion shuddering down Jean's face.

Mass suicide I understand, group suicide has been a part of the landscape since the beginning of this, since $2011GV_1$ first made herself known. Spiritual pilgrims. Desperate seekers. More recently it's only rumors: 50,000 people all dead together at Citi Field. A tribe of native Peruvian people burying themselves to the neck in the desert, their suffering meant as some kind of sacrifice to the fearsome new god streaking across the sky. Stories that can't be true, that you hope aren't true. Supposedly there was a group that drowned themselves in a reservoir outside Dallas, their bodies bobbing to the surface for weeks, hastening the end of the northeast Texas water supply. Supposedly there are "Last Call" party boats operating 24/7 now in New Orleans, going out on Lake Pontchartrain with champagne and caviar and enough dynamite to blow a hole in the hull once everybody on board is good and wasted and ready to go.

So this here, then, in the Rotary P.D basement, this here is nothing. The plan to save the world gets scratched and *this* is the backup plan, one kind of craziness cross-fading into another. No one hunkering down to tough it out—it's bottoms up, it's ENOUGH OF THIS SHIT, it's everybody dead in the same grave underground. Except that Nico Palace—I'm standing in the dark, still waiting for my stomach to settle, I'm staring at nothing, at the black-on-black outline of the door across the hall, thinking of my sister—Nico Palace says thanks but no thanks. Nico says *I disagree*, the situation is not what the situation is. Nico who, drunk at age fourteen, informed me that our father had been a coward for hanging himself over grief for Mom, "a rat-shit coward," declines to raise a toast and gulp down a thermos full of death. She rejects plan B and heads out with her backpack full of candy on her Hail Mary bid to complete the mission and save the world.

And Jean follows to stop her, to convince her to take the easy way out, the quick way. *Why would you want to leave for nothing,* she tells her, *why would you want to leave for nothing and be alone, when we could all be together?*

She's telling her all that when someone else emerges from that underground lair, bursts up from the ground like a hand from the graveyard at the end of a horror movie, someone follows them and catches them. Assumes they're both slipping free from the plan and insists they both take part.

Someone. It's Astronaut, if Astronaut has time. I've got him talking to Nico in the hallway at 4:30, when the move downstairs isn't close to done. Benefit of the doubt, rapid motion after that, and it's 4:45 before everything is downstairs. So that means Astronaut is then running back up the stairs, hunting down Nico and Jean, chasing and killing them sequentially, and then running back *down* the stairs before the hole is sealed at 5:30.

I glance back over my shoulder into the room full of the dead. I'm going to go back in there. I am. In just a second I will. If the Astronaut scenario is hobbled by the timeline problem, that means anyone else currently dead in that room is also eliminated, and that leaves the sixth man.It was eight women and six men who came down here, and eight women minus Nico and Jean equals the six female corpses in the ladies' room, but six men minus *who* equals five dead men?

Is the answer Jordan? Jordan isn't in the room—Jordan's not dead from poison—where is Jordan?

But the other question, the main question really, the question that looms like a thundercloud over all of the others, is why—*why*—what sense did it make, whoever the killer was, why? What purpose did it serve at this late date for her to die like that, out there in a field, bleeding and gasping, what possible need could that have filled, to find those who'd slipped the suicide circle and bring them back and make them die? The word *why* a tenor bell clanging in my brain while I'm standing there with my back to the door, trying to get myself to go back in and take more evidence.

I can lift prints off of dead bodies with gunpowder and Scotch tape. And then if I can find the knife I can lift prints off of that too, either prove that Astronaut was the last person holding it or rule him out.

I'm close to this thing, I've almost got it, facts are crowding in around me and they just need to be sorted, sifted, thought through, pieced together. Stars in a distant sky, glimmering in and out of focus, almost in a constellation but not quite taking shape.

"Henry!"

Cortez's voice, sharp, excited. He found more bodies. He must be in the other room, the one with the anatomical graffiti. He found something.

"Don't touch anything," I shout, feeling along the wall for the doors. "It's a crime scene."

"A crime scene? Henry, Jesus, come quick."

His voice is coming from the third room, the room marked GENERAL STORE. I come out into the hallway, following my light, and I see his head poking out of the open door.

"Come in here," he hollers. "Oh, Policeman. You've got to see this."

5.

Cortez is standing in the center of the room, surrounded by packing crates stacked to the ceiling, rubbing his hands together. "Okay, man," he says. Manic. Juiced. "Okay, okay, okay."

"Cortez?"

"Yes, yes, yes."

I flash my light past him and around him and find the same dull contours of the rest of the basement: gray dusty walls, cracking concrete floors. The crates stand surrounded by piles of disorganized junk: sagging-sided cardboard boxes; a blue plastic packing bin filled with camping lanterns and kitchen matches. In the back, a rack of clothing: puffy coats and long johns and stocking caps. Two half-height steel filing cabinets, piled one on top of the other like decommissioned robots.

And Cortez in the middle of it all, his foot up on one of the packing crates like a conquistador, his face a mask of joy, eyes wide and full of promise. I aim my light at him and it's like he's glowing, all of that barely restrained intensity I sensed before is restrained no longer, it's beaming off of him in waves.

"Well?" he says.

I'm impatient, I'm confused. I want to get back to my bodies, get back to work.

"Cortez, what?"

"What, what? What do you think?"

"About what?"

"About *everything*."

"Everything *what*?"

He laughs. "Everything *everything*!"

We're Abbott and Costello all of a sudden, down here in the darkness. My mind is elsewhere. Where is that weapon? The infamous sawtooth buck knife. It occurs to me with a shudder of horror that I won't find it anywhere on that floor in the darkness, because the killer may have pitched it into the woods. But again why, always why—why throw away a knife when you're about to kill yourself—why hide evidence in a forest that's about to burn to ash? My mind is reeling with facts and suppositions, but Cortez grabs my arm and drags me over to one of the crates. He turns, squats, and slides the lid off and it clatters to the ground and he steps back dramatically.

I aim my headlamp inside the crate: it's full of macaroni and cheese. Dozens of boxes of it. A generic brand, not even a brand at all, just the cardboard boxes stamped MACARONI AND CHEESE.

Cortez waits behind me, breathing heavy, running his hands through his hair. I pull out a few of the boxes, toss them aside, wondering if it's under the mac and cheese—the gold bars, the guns, the bricks of refined uranium, whatever is supposed to be impressing me right now. But no, it's a crate full of pasta, bright orange boxes of uncooked pasta as far down as I can dig.

"Cortez—" I say, and he waves his arms and yells "Wait!" like a TV pitchman. "Wait, there's more!"

He's pulling the tops off more of the crates, wrenching them off like coffin lids, but it's more of the same, more nothing—more macaroni and cheese and then a crate full of spaghetti sauce, forty Costco-sized megajars of lumpy marinara. Stuffed ravioli, applesauce, foil-wrapped snack cakes . . . it's all nothing, boxes full of nothing, except it's more like a parody of nothing. It's like a joke you would play on someone who wanted to prepare for the end of the world. "Well," you would say, smirking behind your hand, "well, you're going to need pasta!"

But Cortez isn't laughing. He's looking back and forth between me and the boxes of junk food, as if waiting for me to drop and scream hallelujah.

"We found it," he says at last, smile widening, eyes practically pinwheeling.

"We found what?"

"A stash. A horde. We found *stuff*, Policeman. Weapons, too: Tasers and helmets and walkie-talkies. *Stuff.* And this here," he says, turning to kick another of the crates, "is full of satellite phones. All charged up. I knew these people had stuff down here."

I stare at him, baffled. This is his own mania, Cortez's very own brand of undiagnosed asteroid psychosis. Tasers? Helmets? Like we can sit underground with our helmets on and weather the collapse of civilization like a thunderstorm. Who does he think we're going to talk to on our satellite phones? But he goes on, wrenching the lid off a crate of bottled water and shouting "Ta-da!" like he's discovered King Tut.

"Five-gallon jugs," he says, yanking one out by the thin plastic handle. "There are twenty-four in this crate, and five of the crates so far are just water, just so far. A person ideally has three gallons a day, but it's really one and a half, just to *live*." His eyes reflecting the headlamp are buzzing and flickering like a computer, crunching the numbers. "Let's make it two gallons."

"Cortez."

He's not listening. He's done—he's gone off to wherever he is, he's jumped the rails. "Now, if we're these jokers, if there are fourteen of us—you said fourteen?"

"There were," I say. "They're dead."

"I know," he says, offhandedly, and goes back to his calculations, "if there are fourteen people that's a month, maybe. But for the two of us, Skinny Minny, for just the two of us . . ."

"How do you know they're dead?"

"Wait, wait," he says, dragging a cardboard box away from the wall and digging in, so keyed up he nearly pitches forward into it. "Look, water filtration tablets, at least a gross, so even once the jugs run out, we can unseal ourselves, get up to that creek, remember the creek?"

I do. I remember splashing through it, following Jean, desperate to get where she was leading me, not knowing yet but somehow knowing that it was Nico's body we were running to find. I am staring at Cortez, my confusion melting over into anger, because I don't care how many jugs of water are down here—I don't care about the other stuff, either, all the piles of boxes and bulging black trash bags.

"I know what you're thinking," he says suddenly, stopping in his frantic motion to take one big step closer to me and shine his headlamp bright into my eyes. "I know you. You can't see it because you don't know how to look, but I look around in this room and I see a room full of days. Days of life. And I don't know what it's going to be like out there, afterwards, but if days are invested wisely they can be turned into months, and months into years."

"Cortez, wait," I say, trying to focus, blocking his light with my hand. "How did you know they're dead?"

"Who?"

"The—the people, Cortez, the—"

"Oh, right, right. I found one in that room with the cock and balls on it. In a Barcalounger holding a cup of something. Slumped over with his feet up and eyes aced out." He does a quick pantomime of the vic, crossing his eyes and rolling out his tongue.

"Wait—"

"And when I heard you puking your guts down the hall, I figured you'd found the rest."

"Cortez, wait—the man you found—"

"Can opener!" he says, diving his hand into a bag and yanking it back out. His voice is getting louder and louder, buzzing and jumping. "Jackpot! That's really all you need, friend policeman, in our difficult modern times, is a good can opener." He tosses it toward me, and without thinking I open my hands to catch it. "This is what we came for."

"No." I seek his eyes in the darkness, desperate now to make him calm down, to make him hear me. "We came to find my sister."

"She's dead. Yes?"

"Yes, but she was—she's—we're not done. I mean, we came here to help her."

"*You* did."

I drop the can opener.

"What?"

"Oh, Policeman," he says. "Dear child."

Cortez—my goon—he snaps a match and lights a cigarette in the darkness. "I knew I wasn't going to spend the afterlife with a bunch of cops in the wilds of western Mass., no sir, that was not going to be a comfortable environment for a man like me when the going got rough. But I knew that there was a place like this at the end of your rainbow. As soon as you said that your sister rescued you in a helicopter, I said, well, gee, these people are loaded up. They have a safe place somewhere, full of stuff. Full of *days*. This down here, it isn't as good as I hoped, but it's not bad for the end-times. Not bad for the end-times at all."

He laughs like, what can you do? Laughs and spreads his palms as if revealing himself, Cortez the thief, as he is and always was, the person I always knew was there but never wanted to see. I am surprised, but why am I surprised? I decided at some point that he had made my road his road, given over to me the last two months of preimpact existence, because I was on my cockamamie hero's quest and required an able and agile sidekick—I reached that conclusion without thinking about it much and put the question aside. But everybody does everything for a reason. That's lesson number one of police work; it's lesson number one of life.

You would think I would have figured it out by now, that a person's outward presentation is just a trap waiting to be sprung.

"I'm so sorry about your kid sister," he says, and he means it, I can tell, but then he keeps going. "But Henry, the world is about to die. That's the one part of this that isn't a mystery. We solved it. The asteroid did it. And these people here have chosen to skip the part that comes next, so we're moving in. We're taking over the lease."

This conversation is killing me. I have to get out of here. I have to get back to those bodies, I have to see that other victim, I have to get back to work.

"Cortez, the other man you saw, what did he look like?"

He steps forward, cigarette dangling, but he doesn't answer.

"Cortez? What did he look like?"

He gathers up the front of my shirt and bounces me hard into the concrete wall. "Here is what is going to happen. We're going to seal ourselves in this room."

"No. No, Cortez, we can't do that."

He's whispering to me, cooing almost. "We seal ourselves in, and we don't pop the cork for six months. After that we make runs for water if and when we absolutely have to, but otherwise we relax in our new paradise until the spaghetti sauce runs dry."

"We won't survive the impact."

"We might."

"We won't."

"Somebody will."

"But I don't—I don't want to do that. I can't."

This is a solvable case. It's a crackable case. I have to crack it.

"Yes, you can. It's a room full of days, Henry. Share the days with me. Do you want the days or not?"

"Cortez, please," I say, "there are these bodies," I say, "and I can pull prints with Scotch tape and gunpowder"—and his expression softens into sadness, and I see at the very last minute that he's got one of the Tasers, he put one in his back pocket, and he jerks his arm toward me and the hot kiss of it shoots into me and I jerk and jolt and tumble to the ground.

PART SIX

Plan B

Tuesday, October 2

Right ascension 16 47 47.9
Declination -75 18 19
Elongation 80.4
Delta 0.034 AU

1.

"*DO NOT DRINK THE WATER IN THE MUSKINGUM RIVER WATERSHED.*"

Oh—

"*DO NOT DRINK THE WATER IN THE MUSKINGUM RIVER WATERSHED.*"

Oh no—

"*DO NOT DRINK THE WATER IN THE MUSKINGUM RIVER WATERSHED.*"

Oh God, oh no.

Cortez, please don't do this. Please don't have done this. I know so much—but not enough. I've almost got it but I don't have it yet.

But he did, he did it, it's done. I'm in the holding cell, I'm on the bad-guy side, behind the bars, on Lily's thin mattress. The sturdy Rotary Police Department RadioCOMMAND console is a few feet away, droning its endless warning about the Muskingum and its stupid toxic watershed. Cortez must have done it while I was still rolling in and out of consciousness, my head still buzzing, considerately dragged the RadioCOMMAND down the hall for me, and left me food, too, a pile of those MREs, along with four of the big jugs of water. I can see them when I turn my head, my neat pile of refreshments, squared off against the rear wall of the cell.

I bend forward on the thin cot and roll over onto my stomach and heave myself up to all fours. This is going to be fine. It is unquestionably a setback, yes, no question, but there has to be a solution, there has to be a way out, there must be and I am going to find it and be fine.

The radio squawks and hisses. "*DO NOT DRINK THE WATER IN THE MUSKINGUM RIVER WATERSHED.*" The rest of the recording, the part about the safe harbors, the first-aid stations, the drop-off/pick-up sites and the Buckeyes helping Buckeyes, has been edited out of the broadcast. Now it's just the warning about the water, on and on into infinity.

There is sunlight in the room, which means that it is daytime. The Casio says 12:45, so it's 12:45 in the afternoon but on what day?

I grind my fingertips into my eyes and grit my teeth. I don't know if I was ever actually unconscious, but I don't think so. I might have been. I experienced the shock and pain of the Taser, half an amp lighting up my abdomen, and then my arms and legs locked and shook and I was on the floor and my assailant, my friend, he bundled up my body in a tarp, and I was only flickeringly aware, my brain temporarily made into hash. I might have even struggled, might have even tried to lodge some sort of groaning protest—but at some point the struggle became impossible and I felt him drag me up the stairs and over the lip of the basement, and my mind slipped out from under me.

I breathe the dust of the small gray cell. I'm going to get out of here, of course. I'm locked in here at present but I obviously will not die in here. This bad situation, like all bad situations, will find its resolution.

I check the Casio again and it still says 12:45. It's broken. I don't know what time it is. Maia is out there streaking closer, and I'm locked in place. A hot bubble of panic rolls up from my lungs and I swallow it with difficulty, breathe and breathe. New spiderwebs have been knitted between the legs of the bed and the corners of the floor, to replace the ones we scraped away when first we made the room ready for Jean. For Lily, that was her name at the time. Lily—Tapestry—the sleeping girl.

She's not here. I don't know where Jean is. Cortez is down there. I'm up here. The ladies' room is full of corpses, the men's room has just one. Nico is gone. The dog's on the farm. I don't know what time it is—what day—

I lurch up out of the bed and my right foot stumbles into something on the ground that makes a wobbling hollow noise as it falls over. It's the carafe, from our rickety coffee-production operation. It's all here, carafe and pencil-sharpener grinder and hot plate and an approximate half share of our dwindling beans. Cortez betrayed me and attacked me and dragged me up here, exiled me and my intentions, and left me here in the jail cell with food and water and coffee and beans. He is way down there rubbing his hands together, flitting among his treasures, a dragon on his pile.

I stare at the beans, halfway up and halfway still lying down. Didn't I have a feeling that I would end up in here? Didn't I? I can't remember, but I think I did, I think I recall staring at poor sick Jean and imagining myself, unwell and declining in the same spot, poor sick me. Like it's all a loop, like time is just this bending, folded-over strip, eating its own tail.

I try to stand up again—I succeed—I'm up—I try the door, the door is locked.

Nico, I'm just—I'm trying to do it. I'm trying. Okay? I'm doing my best.

I bring my hands up to my face, the stubbled surfaces of my cheeks. I hate my face right now, this ungainly disorder, like an overgrown garden. Maybe I'm wrong, maybe there's plenty of time left. I've lost track of it. I'll rot in here. I'll piss in the corner. I'll get hungrier and hungrier. I'll count the hours. Man in a box.

I can see it on the wall opposite the cell: the hook just inside the door where the key ring used to hang.

This is a death that is worse than death, buried alive in a country jail cell, knowing a lot but not enough—what I have is the dark circle of the story like a rock and I need to keep it rolling forward and accreting mass like a snowball, I need for it to *grow.* What time is it, what day—maybe it's about to happen right now, right now: the boom, the flash in the sky, the rattling of the ground and then everything to come after, and in the chaos and fire the crime scene will be burned away and this police station will collapse in on itself and I'll be dead and no one will ever know what happened.

I scream full-throated and launch myself at the bars and grip them and shake them and still screaming I slam my hands open-palmed against them, again and again, because I have to get down there, I have to know, I have to see.

And then footsteps, coming down the hall. I shout and bang on the bars.

"Cortez? Cortez!"

"Who the fuck is Cortez?"

"What?"

The back wall of the cell explodes, showering dust down all around me. Then the dust is clearing slowly and Jordan is on the other side of the bars, holding a black semiautomatic pistol in one hand, holding the keys to the cell in the other hand, and he's staring at me and his eyes are burning and fierce. No sunglasses, no jaunty ball cap, no smug smile.

"Where is she?" he says, holding his gun straight up in the air. "Where's Nico?"

I edge backward in the cell. There's nowhere to hide. Just a bed and a toilet.

"She's dead," I tell him. "You know that she's dead."

He fires again, and the heat of the bullet rushes past me and the back wall explodes again, closer to my head, and I discover that I have thrown my hands up over my face, ducked and flinched. It won't end—that dumb animal instinct to live, to keep going. It doesn't end.

Jordan looks bad. I've only known him smiling; smirking; leering; taunting. That's how he lives in my mind, the punk kid lording it over me, hoarding his secrets in Concord. Now he looks like a composite photograph where they've aged the criminal so you can recognize him after years have passed. His young face is mossy with stubble, and he has a deep gash running down from one ear to the corner of his cheek. There's some manner of acute infected injury on his right leg, the cuff of his pants rolled up over a haphazardly bandaged wound, dripping around the edges with red and black and pus. He looks grief stricken and desperate. He looks how I feel.

"Where is she, Henry?"

"Stop asking me where she is."

He did it. He killed her. The clarity is like fire. Jordan steps toward me. I step toward him. It's like the bars are a mirror, and we're both the same guy, two images coming together.

"Where is she?"

He raises the gun and aims it at my heart. I feel again the stupid shivering need to live, to turn around and duck, but this time I stay put, I grind my heels into the floor, staring at his wrathful eyes. "She's dead," I tell him. "You killed her."

His face narrows with pretend confusion. "I just got here."

He points the gun at me, and now I do, I feel like, fine, that's fine, let me die here, let the bullet collide with my brain and be done with it, but first I need the rest of the story. "Why did you cut her throat?"

"Her—what?" he says.

"*Why?*"

I drop quickly, bring my knee down on the coffee carafe and bust the glass. Jordan is jerking the gun to follow my actions, Jordan is saying "stop that fucking moving—" but now I've got an uneven triangle of glass in my hand and I launch myself forward off the ground in an ungainly leap, find his stomach between the bars and stab him in the gut. "Hey—goddammit—" He looks down, horrified. It's a superficial wound, the glass dangles at a shallow angle, but there's blood coming out of him like crazy, a thick fast welling out of blood like oil, and my hand is darting for the key on its ring in his other hand. I'm a beat too slow, he flings the ring and the key out behind him, out the doorway and into the hallway.

I say "Damn it," and he says "You asshole," clutches a hand to his stomach and brings it up all bloody.

"Why did you kill her?"

I have to know. That's all I need is to know. I am dimly aware of the RadioCOMMAND still going, "*DO NOT DRINK THE WATER IN THE MUSKINGUM RIVER WATERSHED,*" and Jordan reaches for my throat between the bars, but his hand is all slick with the blood from his stomach and it slides off me. I move backward and spit at him. "I'm looking for her," he insists. "I came here to find her."

I slide a long hand between the bars and grab his leg, worm my forefinger under the bandage and jam it into the wound on his calf and he screeches and I jam it in more. A nasty trick, bad-guy wrestler move. Jordan writhes away from my hand, but I don't let go—I've got both of my hands wriggled through the bars now, one hand clamped onto him at midthigh, the other hand still gouging his infected wound. I'm behaving like a monster. He is screaming. I want answers. I need them.

"Stop screaming," I tell him, both arms extended as if through the holes in a puppet theater, holding him fast through the bars. "Talk. Tell me."

"What?" He says, choking out the word, gasping from pain. "What?"

"The truth."

"What truth?" Jordan gasps. I ease up slightly on my grip, give him a moment of relief, not wanting him to pass out. The information is more important. I have to know. He's heaving desperate breaths, clutching at his wound, both of us on the ground in the grime. I give him what I already know, build a bridge of common understanding, Farley and Leonard, *Criminal Investigation*, chapter 14.

"You abandoned your girlfriend in Concord. You and Abigail were supposed to stay but you left anyway. You made sure you were here on the big day, T-minus one week, when the whole group was supposed to go underground. How did you know that was the day?"

"I don't know anything. I told you."

"Liar. Killer. You were here at five on Wednesday the twenty-sixth because you knew that that's when they'd be going underground and you knew that Nico would leave. Maybe you told her—maybe you told her to leave, to meet you outside the station. And there she was. She had a backpack on. She was happy to see you."

I twist my finger, work it into the wound, and he writhes away, tries to, but I've got him tight, I'm clutching him to the bars, holding him in place.

"The other girl was an unwelcome surprise though, right?"

"What other girl?"

"So you had to kill her first, quick, knock her out and slash her throat and then chase Nico—"

"What the fuck—no—I came here to save her."

"Save her? To *save* her?"

Now I'm just twisting at his leg, now I'm trying to inflict as much pain on him as I can. I don't care if we both die here, locked in our improbable clench for however long is left. He can tell the truth or both of us can die.

"You slashed her throat, and you slashed that other girl's throat, and you left them. Why, Jordan? Why did you do that?"

"Is that what happened? Is that what happened to her?"

And then he throws his head back and slumps over on his side of the bars. I don't care, I keep at it, I have to hear him confirm it. I need that, and Nico does.

"Why did you kill her? Why? How does killing my sister fit into your stupid plan to save the world?"

There is a long pause. "*DO NOT DRINK THE WATER IN THE MUSKINGUM RIVER WATERSHED,*" the radio says, and then again. Jordan starts laughing. His eyes are rolled back in his head, and he gives off this weird cold laugh, a gurgling throaty chuckle.

"What?"

Nothing. Dead, dry laughter.

"What?"

"The plan. The plan, Stan. There's no plan. We made it up. It's not real. We made the whole thing up."

2.

Almost always, things are exactly as they appear. People are continually looking at the painful or boring parts of life with the half-hidden expectation that there is more going on beneath the surface, some deeper meaning that will eventually be unveiled; we're waiting for the saving grace, the shocking reveal. But almost always things just are what they are, almost always there's no glittering ore hidden under the dirt.

A massive asteroid really is coming and it will kill us all. That is a true fact, hard and cold and irreducible, a fact that can be neither diverted nor destroyed.

I was right, all along, in my pedantic obnoxious small-minded insistence that the truth was true—the simple brutal fact that I kept explaining to Nico, that I kept trying to use to corral her or cudgel her. I was always right and she was always wrong.

Jordan is explaining it all to me, running down the whole story, laying out the inside scoop on the great underground asteroid-diversion conspiracy, explaining in intricate detail how I was right and Nico was wrong, and I am experiencing no joy in having been proved right. It's actually the opposite, what I'm feeling, it's actually the black and bitter opposite of joy: this awful opportunity to say "I told you so" to someone who is already dead, to say "you were wrong" to my sister, who has already been sacrificed on the altar of what she was wrong about. I am wishing in retrospect that I *hadn't* told her so, that I had just let her alone, maybe even allowed her the pleasure of thinking for half a second that her brother and only living relative believed her. That I believed *in* her.

It wasn't just that the plan would never work, the standoff burst, the precisely orchestrated atomic recalibration of Maia's deadly course. The plan never existed. Its author, the rogue nuclear scientist Hans-Michael Parry, never existed either. They were pure suckers, the lot of them, Astronaut and Tick and Valentine and Sailor, Tapestry—even Isis. Suckers and saps. They were huddled together out here at the police station waiting for the arrival of a man who never was.

Now she's dead, so it doesn't matter. They came all this way for nothing, and now she's dead.

We're outside, between the flagpoles. It's a beautiful afternoon, cool and crisp and sunny. The first pleasant day since I got to Ohio. Jordan is running down the whole story and while he does I am clutching my face and tears are spilling out around my fingers.

* * *

Astronaut's real name is Anthony Wayne DeCarlo and he has no scientific training, no special understanding of astrophysics, no military background of any kind. He is, or was, a bank robber, a retailer and manufacturer of controlled substances, and a conman. At age nineteen DeCarlo drew a ten-year prison sentence in Colorado for boosting an SUV as a getaway vehicle when his older brother robbed an Aurora-area Bank of America. He was paroled after four years and three months, and six months after that he was arrested in a rented apartment in Arizona that he had turned into a laboratory/dispensary of designer narcotics. Five-year bid, out in two on good behavior. And so on, and so on. By the time he turned forty, which was the year before last, he was known to law enforcement in an impressive range of jurisdictions as a good-looking and silver-tongued bad guy, skilled in the manufacture of a variety of illicit substances—so much so that one of his aliases, the one he prided himself on, was "Big Pharma."

He would have spent a lot more time in jail, over the years, except he had a special knack for gathering acolytes and setting them up to do the dirty work—younger men and plenty of younger women, who frequently ended up serving prison sentences for carrying, for selling, all the stuff that otherwise he would have done himself. One parole officer lamented, somewhere in DeCarlo's thick case file, that he "would have made a great leader, had things gone another way."

And then they did, they really did, things went another way. The asteroid appeared, transforming the lives of thugs and drug dealers right along with policemen and actuaries and Amish patriarchs. By the time there was a ten percent chance that Maia would smash into the Earth, Anthony Wayne DeCarlo is living in a basement apartment in Medford, Mass., and he has become Astronaut: leader of a movement, weaver of conspiratorial webs, savior of humanity.

For a restless soul like DeCarlo, paranoid and insecure, Maia was the answer to a prayer he didn't even know he was praying; a basket in which to put a lifetime of inchoate antiauthoritarian energy. Suddenly he's on a soapbox in Boston Common, a charismatic voice for the government conspiracy line, a street-corner preacher with a fistful of dubious scientific "findings" and a handgun jammed in his back pocket. And he's attracting a new constellation of followers: young people, freaked out by death rolling across the sky, looking for something—anything—to do about it.

They fell for it. My sister fell for it. And it's not hard to see why, it's never been hard to understand. The alternative was to believe what her droning, lecturing, scolding cop brother kept telling her: We're in for it. There's no hope. The truth is true. The Astronauts of the world were selling a better story, much easier to swallow. The Man is setting us up. The fat cats and the big shots, brother, they *want* you to die.

Lies, lies—it's all lies!

It's around this point, late autumn last year, that the Federal Bureau of Investigation starts keeping tabs on Anthony Wayne DeCarlo, a.k.a. Astronaut. The FBI, like most federal agencies, is suffering from employee attrition, with agents leaving in droves on their various Bucket List adventures. For those still at their desks, a lot of the workload in the last year has been keeping an eye on creeps like DeCarlo, all the terrorists and psychopaths and run-of-the-mill criminal jackasses whom Maia has given a new lease on life, all of them talking big about last-ditch antigovernment violence, how they're going to reveal or disrupt the cover-up, whatever they claim is being covered up: the government made up the asteroid, the government is hiding the truth of the asteroid, the government built the asteroid. You name it.

Astronaut and his crew weren't even cracking the top thirty, in terms of threats worth worrying about, until a kid named Derek Skeve got caught breaking into the New Hampshire National Guard station. Under interrogation he admitted that he had been pressured into the dangerous mission by his new wife.

"It was Nico who sent him in there, see? She sacrificed him," says Jordan, whose name is not really Jordan. "It was demanded of her. To prove her loyalty to Astronaut, to the organization, the goals of the organization."

Jordan's name is really Agent Kessler; William P. Kessler Jr. My mind is filling with new information, filling up fast.

"DeCarlo loves to play these kinds of cruel games with his people: in group/out group dynamics, tests of loyalty," says Kessler. "He used to do it when he was running dope: needle scumbag number one into lowering the hatchet on scumbag number two, and he's your scumbag forever. He did the same tricks to build his new conspiracy group."

Agent Kessler is FBI. He was a trainee in the technical services division, he told me, rapidly promoted to field agent, just as I was rapidly promoted to detective when everybody else quit or disappeared. The Astronaut conspiracy was his first case—"still working on it, as a matter of fact," he says, staring up at the flagpole, at the ragged lawn of the Rotary police station.

It took ten minutes of good cop/bad cop for Skeve to start babbling about moon bases, and Kessler's team knew he was a patsy. But then they got ahold of one of Astronaut's other shed dupes and figured out what the man was really after: loose nukes. They decided to give them to him. Kessler made his debut as Jordan Wills, a smug wisecracking provocateur in cheap Ray-Bans.

"I showed up at the dude's house in the middle of the night," says Jordan. Kessler. "And I give him this whole crazy rap. I'm a former Navy midshipman. 'I've got this hidden trove of documents, about this scientist and his master plan. I heard about your group . . . you're the only ones who can help us. You're the only ones!'"

"And he bought it?"

"Oh, yes," says Kessler. "God, yes. We told him there were other teams, teams all over the country. We gave him the specific part that he and his buddies were supposed to play. And zoom. Off they go. Chasing the imaginary bombs in all the places I told them to look. Hither and thither, hither and yon. Kept them from killing anybody. Kept them from finding any *actual* bombs. Kept them spinning their wheels."

I listen. I nod. It's good—it's a good story. The kind of story that I like, the story of a well-conceived and well-executed law-enforcement operation, carried out by diligent operatives staying on the job to keep decent people safe even in the most difficult circumstances. A slow-play sting with a clear intention and a simple strategy: identify the membership of the organization, keep it busy, feed the fire of their lunatic hope. The story, though, it's hitting me in a tender place, it really is. I'm listening and periodically I'm reaching up to clutch my face while tears roll down and around my fingers.

Kessler and his fellow agents provided Astronaut with all the necessary window dressing to convince them they were involved in a real conspiracy. Internet access and communications equipment, official-looking NASA and Naval Intelligence documents. And of course the ultimate prop: an SH-60 Seahawk, a twin-engine medium-lift helicopter that one of Kessler's FBI associates was able to "borrow" from a Navy division that had just been recalled from peacekeeping operations, now moot, in the Horn of Africa.

All the stuff that made me wonder, in my dark moments, if I was wrong, if the truth was not the truth. It all looked real because it was supposed to look real.

"What about the document itself?" I ask him. I've still got it, it's in the wagon somewhere, fifty pages of gobbledygook and indecipherable math. "Where did the numbers come from? The whole—the plan?"

"The Internet." Jordan shrugs. "Public records. Someone might have pulled a file from NASA. The truth is, at a certain point it was like a game. How preposterous can we make the whole thing? How unlikely a scenario, how self-evidently unbelievable, and see if these people would still believe it. Turns out: pretty much all the way. People will believe pretty much any goddamn thing if they want to bad enough."

The endgame played out just as they had imagined it. Kessler in his role as Jordan lets Astronaut know that Parry has been located and set free—one fake person telling a conman about the location of another fake person—and that he, Jordan, is arranging his transportation to the Ohio location. It's Astronaut's responsibility to gather up everyone else, get to this abandoned police station near a municipal airfield, and wait.

"And he did it."

"Of course he did. By that time, he was sure that he really was going to save the world. He thought he was the drug-dealing robber who had turned into an action hero. But we were writing the script, and the script ended with them sitting in the middle of nowhere, not bothering anybody, waiting for someone who doesn't exist, until lights out."

* * *

We walk slowly through the woods, Kessler and I. To the small rutted field surrounded by bent trees. Patches of black-red blood are still evident in the muddy puddle where I found the body. He told me he wants to see the crime scene; take prints, do a sweep for evidence. I've explained that I did all of those things, but he said he'd like to do it himself.

He wants to see, so here we are, but he's not doing anything. Agent Kessler just stands at the edge of the clearing, looking at the ground.

Everything is clear except one thing, and even that is pretty clear.

"Jordan?"

"Kessler," he reminds me quietly, stepping into the clearing.

"Kessler. What happened? Why are you here?"

He squeezes his eyes shut and then opens them again.

"Kessler?"

He's crouching down on his heels, staring at the mud where Nico died. I need to hear him say it, though. I need to know everything. I have to.

"Kessler? Why did you come out here?"

He speaks slowly. His voice is choked, low.

"DeCarlo's a maniac. At heart. The file is spiked with bad acts. Sudden violence. He gets double-crossed or cheated, or when things go wrong . . . bad acts." The smug kid that I so hated is gone; the furious FBI agent on a mission is gone. Kessler is just a kid. A young guy with a heavy heart. "We knew he was capable of anything at the end, if he figured out that it was all bullshit—or even if he didn't figure it out. When he finally realized that the world was really going to die, that *he* was really going to die. The fucking narcissist. God knows what sort of horror show this thing might turn into." He drifts off, staring. "God knows."

I picture my sister facedown in the dirt. Of course I do. I can't help it. Facedown in the dirt, her open wound clotting with mud. *God knows.*

"I couldn't—" Kessler says, and then he breathes through his teeth, stamps his boot on the ground. He covers his face with his hand. "All the rest of 'em, fuck 'em. Stupid wild-eyed hippies, let 'em get what they deserve. Trying to steal a fucking bomb. But not—" He cries out again. He sinks slowly to his knees. "Not her."

I knew it. I guess I've known it since he came limping down the hallway to the cell.

"You—had feelings for her."

He laughs, a wet mucous weeping laugh. "Yeah. You man-child. You weirdo. I had feelings for her. I fucking *loved* her."

"But you could have saved her. You could have told her not to come, told her it was all a set-up."

"I did!" He looks at me, not angry but imploring. Desperate. Bereft. "I told her *everything*. That day in New Hampshire, out in Butler Field, waiting for the chopper to come and scoop her up, I told her that the whole thing was a set-up, that I was an FBI agent, that DeCarlo was a fraud and a psychopath. Capable of anything." He chokes out the nickname. "Big Pharma. I showed her my fucking badge." He trails off. "But . . ."

Damn it, Nico—damn it. "She didn't believe you."

Kessler nods, exhales. "It was too late. She was too deep into it. Into this fantasy world that I created my damn self. I said, you'll believe me when Parry never shows up. I said, promise me, if he doesn't show up in two weeks, you'll steal this fucking helicopter and come back home. I said, *promise me*." He is crying now, his face buried in his hands.

No way she promised. My sister has never promised anything.

"She never came back. I had to come. At a certain point, I just—I couldn't stop thinking about her—try and find her. I couldn't let her die out here—" and he says it, the exact words I was thinking ten minutes ago. "Couldn't let her die out here for nothing."

Neither one of us says what is obvious and true, that he was too late. That we were, both of us, too late.

Agent Kessler doesn't actually look for evidence. He doesn't take any prints. He just stares at the ground for a while, and then we turn around and slowly walk back together through the woods.

3.

Now it's my turn. I've got his story and now Agent Kessler wants mine.

We make our way back through the woods from the crime scene to the police station, stepping over brambles and then across the rope bridge, grunting with the exertion, two twentysomethings hamstrung by multiple injuries, walking slowly through the woods like old, old men. While we walk I run down the investigation in progress, piece by piece: I tell him about finding Jean in the woods, about the subsequent discovery of Nico's body, bearing a similar injury, similar in kind but not degree; I tell him about my eyewitness to Nico's argument with Astronaut an hour before her death. I talk and talk, and he interrupts on occasion with insightful or clarifying questions, and we fall into my old favorite rhythm of conversational police work—the laying out of a fact pattern, the straightening out of details in my own mind so they can be vetted by a fellow officer.

When we are back at the police station Kessler stops in Dispatch to examine Nico's body while I go back to the garage and walk slowly around the cratered wreck at the center of the floor. It looks like Cortez took the time to fill up the stairwell with as much rock as he could—all the stones that resulted from smashing out the wedge, plus more big chunks he jackhammered out from all over the garage floor. It's rutted and cratered in here, like the surface of the moon. At the edge of the pit is a loose end of rope, snaking out from the pile of rubble. I can picture my erstwhile sidekick after he left me in the jail cell: loading up the tarp with stones, pulling it down in his wake, collapsing the tunnel mouth behind him like the Red Sea crashing down behind Moses.

Cortez, putting up a KEEP OUT sign; Cortez, taking over the lease.

"No way on the suicide," says Kessler abruptly, coming into the room.

"What?"

He clears his throat. "The rest of them, sure. For the rest of them, I like it. They give up on Parry, maybe they realize they got punked. Maybe they even realize DeCarlo is a psycho. Life postimpact is going to be brutish and short. Bunker or no bunker. Poison becomes the good option."

Kessler's manner on all this is staccato, clipped, just the facts. He's doing exactly what I did after looking at what he was just looking at: Nico's frozen face, the red and black wreck of her throat.

He's wrapping up the pain of that in CAUTION tape, drowning it out in crime-stopper rhythms. I like it. I find it soothing.

"But Astronaut? No," he continues, shaking his head. "No way."

"You said he was a maniac," I say. "You told me: capable of anything."

"Right. But not that. Capable of talking other people into suicide, yes, but not himself. He's a world-class narcissist. Delusions of grandeur on an astronomical scale. Suicide doesn't fit the profile."

"It's a different world."

"Not that different."

"But I—" I glance down into the rubble pile. "I saw him. A middle-aged man with bushy black hair, horn-rim glasses, dark brown eyes."

Kessler scowls. "Where did you get that description?"

"Miller."

"Who?"

"This Amish guy. My witness. Was there another man in the group who might have matched that description?"

"Not likely," says Kessler. "Possible. We did our best to keep track, but people drifted in and drifted out. All I know is, in no scenario is Anthony DeCarlo a suicide."

I turn back to the rubble-choked stairhead. The idea of this, of my having made a wrong ID down there, of the man who killed my sister still being alive—it flickers in me like a pilot light. I bend down without thinking about it and roll an oblong stone from the top of the pile, and then another one.

"So you think he's down there?" I say to Kessler.

"Oh, I certainly hope so." He comes over and gets down on a knee to help me, grunting and lifting a stone. "Because I would very much like to kill him."

* * *

While Agent Kessler and I dig out the rubble from the stairhead, while we pull out boulders one by one and the muscle ache gathers in my shoulders and in my back, my mind flies out from my body and circles the globe, zooming over distant landscapes like a ghost in a fairy tale, wandering the world. Everywhere there are people praying, people reading to their children, people raising toasts or making love, desperately seeking pleasure or satisfaction in the last tissue-thin hours of existence. And here I am, here's Palace, knee-deep in a pit of stone beside a stranger, digging and digging, tunneling forward blindly like a mole into the next thing that comes.

When the path is clear we go down, the narrow metal stairwell shaking under us as it did before, me first and then Agent Kessler.

In the basement corridor I flick on the Eveready and shine it into the corners and everything is as it was: darkness and silence and cold. Concrete floor, concrete walls, weird chemical stink.

Kessler stumbles on something, sending pebbles scuttling and rolling. I turn and gesture for him to be silent, and he scowls and gestures for *me* to be silent—a pair of bedraggled law-enforcement professionals pulling rank on each other in a darkroom dumbshow.

I sniff the air. It's the same, everything is the same down here, but it's not the same; it feels different. The air has been unsettled somehow. The same darkness, with new shadows in it.

We move past the tiny furnace room and shine our flashlights over the three doors: ladies' room, general store, and then the door with the graffiti.

"The bodies?" says Agent Kessler. "Palace?"

"One sec," I murmur, my eyes fixed on the door of the general store, which is open, open at an angle of about twenty-five degrees. It's propped open, as a matter of fact, held in place by an empty box of macaroni and cheese, folded over into a wedge. I step toward the door, my gun raised. Cortez told me his intentions in no uncertain terms: to stay in that room for six months after boomsday before creeping out to assay the outside world. And yet there's the door, held purposefully ajar. The question is why, the question is always why.

"Cortez?" I say, letting my voice travel down toward the door. I step toward it. "Hey, Cortez?"

Kessler mouths something in the darkness. I lean closer and squint and he holds up his light and mouths it again, exaggerated: "Fuck him."

Right. He's right. Fuck him. I shine my light at the door marked LADIES, I nod to Kessler and he nods back and pushes in. I look back again at the general store, experiencing dark waves of anxiety, and then I walk in after Kessler.

"God," says Kessler, full voice. "For God's sake."

I walk past him, into the grim waxwork tableau. I breathe slowly, not letting it get to me, the rotting air and the corpses like mannequins, slumped against each other like melting candles. Valentine and Tick with their hands linked, Delighted in his sparkling cape. Sailor/Alice under the table, legs daintily crossed. All of them with hooded eyes, their cheeks frozen and pale, their mouths falling open as if wanting more to drink. Jordan moves through the room as I did before, getting fractured pieces of the whole horrible vision, muttering "Jesus Christ" to himself and shaking his head uneasily. A technical services trainee. A kid.

He shakes it off, though—quickly, quicker than me. Kessler starts ID'ing bodies as he finds them, calling out the code names I already know—Delighted and Tick and Valentine and Sailor under the table—and adding some I hadn't yet heard. "This is Athena," he says of the round-cheeked girl with her back half turned away from Delighted. "A veterinary assistant. From Buffalo. Delighted's name is Seymour Williams, by the way. He's a paralegal from Evanston. His father owned a clothing store."

The built blond guy with the scar on his face is Kingfisher. The other women are Atlantis, Permanent, and Firefly. The big man is Little Man, as I suspected.

"No Astronaut," says Kessler, and I say, "he's back over here," and I move in the darkness to find him and I find Cortez instead. He's rolled halfway over, his body hidden by the open door, his right arm awkwardly thrown over his torso, like he was rolled in here and dumped like an old carpet.

And his face—I shine the light—he's been shot in the face.

"Palace?"

I find my feet as conclusions tumble into my mind, quickly, a rush of realizations, like keys turning in a series of locks: Cortez was killed recently, in the past twenty-four hours, that's the first thing I think, so this is a new murder, so the killer is still alive—and Cortez blocked the stairs behind him so the killer is down here with us, the killer is close.

"*Palace?*"

I have my hand on Cortez's neck to make sure that he's dead, but he's definitely dead because of his face: he has been shot in the face with some sort of expanding projectile, a hollow round, causing an explosive blast wound, cratering his mouth and nose. Poor Cortez with his face blown off, dead of a gunshot wound in a room full of people who drank poison. It's like he was invited to the wrong party. It's funny. Cortez would find it funny.

"Palace, goddamnit," says Kessler, and I look up, startled.

"Kessler—"

"It's not him."

"What?"

"This. Here." He's a few feet away, in a squat like me, shining his light on a body, like me, the corpse of the man with the thick hair and the glasses. "This is the body you thought was Astronaut, is that correct?"

"It's not him?"

"No."

More realizations, tumbling into place. I pivot and look

where Kessler is looking, where his light makes an eerie halo around the face.

"You're sure?"

"I've seen the man," says Kessler. "I've talked to him."

"That's not him? Dark brown eyes—"

"Those eyes aren't dark brown."

"Of course they're not now, he's dead—"

"They're hazel."

"Well, they're not hazel."

"Palace, it's not *him*."

We are whispering, intensely, and then a gunshot explodes somewhere in the silence of the basement, and then somebody is screaming—maybe more than one person—and we race toward the door, the two of us, trap ourselves briefly in a Three Stooges moment, two abreast in the entranceway, and then we burst free and scramble, me first and then Kessler, across the wide empty furnace room toward the origin of the noise.

It's the men's room, the one with the graffiti, except now that door has been shot open and there are lights in here, and I can see them both as soon as I get in there, frozen in place across from each other in the tiny space. Jean with a handgun clenched between two hands, held out directly in front of her small body and aimed at his stomach: Astronaut, a.k.a. Anthony Wayne DeCarlo, a.k.a. Big Pharma, in a flapping-open terry-cloth bathrobe and nothing else, unconcerned about his paunchy nakedness, unconcerned about the woman with the gun, seemingly unconcerned about anything.

The room is the size of an apartment kitchen, lit up like a barroom with neon lights, crammed with paraphernalia for cooking drugs: empty vials, long twists of tubing, one Bunsen burner active and bubbling with something foul, another burner shut off.

In one of the raised hands he's got a gun of his own, the gun that killed Cortez—a big antique long-barrelled pistol that must be loaded with some sort of nasty homemade semijacketed rounds. The belt, I notice, is still on his pants, a pair of filthy Levi's crumpled in the corner. Only the clawhammer is still on the belt.

I say, "Everyone lower your weapons." Nobody lowers their weapons. I'm one step into the room, and Kessler is just behind me, breathing hard, holding his gun, trying to see around me into the room. Astronaut yawns, a long lazy lizard's yawn. Jean's body is twitching, shifting, oscillating. It's like her atomic structure has been unsettled, like she's a jet traveling too fast, breaking some sort of barrier, and we are watching her shake apart.

"Drop the guns." I try it again. "Drop them."

Jean keeps her eyes on Astronaut but responds to me, a murmured shush like we're at the library and I'm talking too loud. Astronaut laughs and winks at me, quick and reptilian. For someone who has been holed up smoking crack or meth or whatever he's cooking behind him on that elaborate works, he is cool as a cucumber, steady as she blows, hands still half raised as if by choice: I submit to your firearm's implied threat but I'm not going to make a big fucking deal about it.

The room reeks: hydrochlorides, ammonia, burnt salt. There is a background noise, a low *chug-chug* of the gas generator keeping the room alive with neon: beer-brand signs, a gaudy colored-glass Captain Morgan figurine, strings of Christmas lights. The armchair that Cortez saw, plus a piece of a sectional sofa and an ugly lamp, all crammed in here. It's like the man has re-created his natural habitat below the world, a scumbag terrarium.

I am jerking my head back and forth between the two of them, doing rapid calculations, understanding things in reverse order as they happened, unspooling the film backward. Cortez peeked in this room yesterday and saw a man with his eyes aced out and his legs kicked up and assumed that he was dead. But Astronaut wasn't dead, he was just riding the waves of whatever substance or combination of substances he's been riding the waves of for the past week. Cooking and consuming, steeping himself in fumes, happy as a clam in this one-room infuser of hot chemical smoke. At some point, though, he came back to life, took a turn around his subterranean dominions and found Cortez squatting among his mac and cheese and shot him in the face.

I have to keep my eyes in the present—the story is proceeding in front of me—the parts are still moving—Jean is stepping forward with her gun leveled, ready to kill DeCarlo—just as she wanted to do yesterday when she asked if she could come with us.

"You monster," she whispers, and he ignores her, replies cheerily: "You did it!" Like he's proud of her. Like she just bowled a perfect game. "You're back! I'm so *proud* of you, baby."

"No, you're not," she says to him.

"Sure I am, little sister."

"Stop."

"Okay, I'll stop," he says, and he smiles at her and licks his lips. "I'm stopping. But I'm so proud of you."

"You're a liar."

I look at him, smirking and naked. A liar is the very least of what he is. He killed them all. Not just Cortez, and not just Nico. There was no suicide pact—he poisoned the lot of them. It was his plan B. Just his.

Jean can't shoot him—she's working on it—she's gathering the nerve. DeCarlo moves his non-gun hand down casually to scratch his ass. Comfortable, easy in his skin, high out of his mind. I'm trying to get the details right, thinking as fast as I can. What is he proud of her for? It's a lie, she is calling him a liar, but what is the nature of the lie?

She's getting ready, charming monster or not, she's going to shoot him. He tried to kill her, and now she's going to shoot him and the rest of the answers will be dead.

"Jean," I say, but she doesn't even hear me.

"Look at me," Jean says to Astronaut, running her finger across the line of her scar, like I saw her do over and over during her interrogation. "*Look.*"

"You look beautiful, little sister," he says. "You look amazing."

"Look what you *made* me."

I glance behind me at Agent Kessler and I can tell that he's as confused as I am by this dialog, but I can also tell that he doesn't care, the details don't matter to him anymore. All he knows is that Astronaut killed Nico, whom he loved, and now he is bringing up his own weapon, trying to get around me to get his shot, even as I say "Jean," sharply, loudly, to draw her attention and keep her from pulling the trigger.

Everybody needs to hold on—everybody needs to just hold on. Because nothing yet has explained Nico. I have no explanation for why he chased down my sister and cut her throat and left her gasping, breathing blood, to die alone in the mud.

"Mr. DeCarlo," I say. "Why did you kill Nico Palace?"

"I don't know who that is."

"Why did you kill the girl you called Isis?"

"Sorry, man, it's not ringing a bell."

He snorts laughter, and Jean's eyes sharpen with anger, and I feel Kessler's wrathful breath behind me. Astronaut grins at the girl tauntingly, radiating wickedness, standing in his louche bathrobe in a tiny room full of people who want to kill him. I feel the gun in my hand, the knife in my belt, I feel the Earth itself screaming for the death of this man, poisoner and conman and thief, but I need nobody to die right now. I need stasis, I need time to stop until I can claw the last pieces of truth out of this acrid little room.

"Nico told you she disagreed with the decision to go underground, Mr. DeCarlo," I say. "She left. She posed no further threat to you, she was going to take no share of your space or your water or narcotics."

"Or pasta sauce," he says, giggling. "Don't forget about my pasta sauce."

"Mr. DeCarlo, why did you kill her?"

"Shit, man, it's a question for the philosophers," he says.

"Why does anyone kill anyone, right? Isn't that right, little sister?"

Jean's hand goes back to her scar, and there is some slippery truth in Astronaut's malevolent leer, in the terror on Jean's small face, and I am trying to knit it all together when Kessler behind me says "Enough" and pushes past me into the room, and Astronaut's eyes sharpen with recognition.

"Hey—" he says. "Jordan?"

"It's Agent Kessler, actually, you prick."

"Agent? Huh," and he moves to one knee and fires his pistol straight into Kessler's chest, and Kessler's whole body flies back into the wall, and I shout "damn it" and then "no" because Jean has opened fire, she jerks the trigger of her handgun and misses Astronaut by a mile—but a spark flies off the wall and catches the flammable atmosphere and explodes.

* * *

For a long minute the world is just fire. The sound of exploding bottles and the smell of burning, and the air is on fire and Kessler is and I am, blue and yellow fire is all around us, and I am batting at our bodies, slapping down the flames, while across the tiny room Astronaut's whole chemical-smoked body catches and bursts, and before he can react or move he becomes a pillar of fire, spiraling and falling. I get Kessler out of there with a few big heaves, cover his body with my body until we're both extinguished.

It's mostly our clothes, after all, Kessler's clothing is badly burned, as mine is—the real problem is the hole in his chest, a golf-ball-sized gunshot entrance wound geysering blood, and so with the heat still pouring out of the small room, the stench of burn and death, I am hunched over Kessler panting in the hallway, covering his chest with two flat hands, blood from his heart and chest flooding out around my fingers.

"Don't do that," he says, bleary, peering up. "No, please."

Blood bubbles up out of his mouth with the words, and in the glow of the fire behind me the blood looks black.

"Try not to talk," I say. "I'm putting pressure on the wound." I lean forward, flattening one hand over the other hand, flattening both hands over his gaping chest.

"Don't put pressure on the wound." He reaches up with surprising strength, pushes my hands off him. "Don't do that."

"Please remain quiet and still," I say, "until I can staunch the bleeding."

"I am going to bleed out and die."

"We don't know that."

"I *want* to bleed out and die. Palace! This is so much better than a—fucking—I don't know—*tsunami* or something." He laughs, coughing, blood spraying out. "This is the best-case scenario."

I don't like it. I shake my head. The idea of just *leaving* him here. "Are you sure?"

"Yes. God, yes. Did we get the monster?"

"Not yet."

"Well, go get him."

"Her," I say.

"What?"

The door to the room behind us is open, and Astronaut I can see in there, melted and smoldering, but it doesn't matter—it's Jean, it's Jean who rushes past in the corner of my vision, hoping I don't see her, but I do—I do.

4.

I don't know why it matters, but I know that it does. Getting the rest of the story, hearing a confession, checking off the final details.

Solving a murder is not about serving the victim, because the victim is, after all, dead. Solving a murder serves society by restoring the moral order that has been upset by the gunshot or knife strike or poisoning, and it serves to preserve that moral order by warning others that certain acts cannot be committed with impunity.

But society is dead. Civilization is burning cities, its terrified animals clustered around grain silos, stabbing each other at burned-down convenience stores for the last can of Pringles.

Nevertheless—even so—here I go, I go charging through the darkness toward the stairs, following Jean's frantic small form.

I don't yell for her to stop, because she won't stop. I don't yell

"Police!" because I'm not a policeman anymore, I haven't been for some time now. I hear her thin feet clanging up the stairs, hear the narrow metal stairwell rattling as she bolts for daylight. I charge across the floor and I follow her, hurling myself up the thin steps for the last time, putting the last of the pieces together, following Jean as she rattles up the stairway toward the clustered shadows at the top.

Look what you made me—

I sidestep small mounds of rubble still on the top step and into the garage and even among the horror of all that's happening, the desperation to catch up to Jean and get the rest of the story, still I feel a rush of gladness from being done with that bunker, that crypt. I burst up into the aboveground, drinking air and daylight like a surfacing diver.

I stumble across the three-car indoor garage, navigating the craters and piles, and then I'm in the hallway and I can see Jean, racing hopelessly a few paces ahead of me down the hallway, down the long corridor where I started my search, the corridor marked by my sister's blood and her blood, one trail in and one trail out.

I had to stop her, see—I had to—

I'm much faster than Jean. She's fast and desperate, but I'm tall and my legs are very long and I'm desperate too, and I do it—just as the glass front door of the police station is swinging shut behind her I push it back open and launch myself and catch her legs and get her down into the mud, and then I push myself back up so that by the time she turns over there I am, looming, full height with weapons drawn, the knife and the gun.

"Please," she says, her body trembling and her hands clasped together. "Please."

I glare down at her. We're surrounded by the overgrown bushes, blinking green in the daylight. The autumn wind riffles my hair, tickling up my shirtsleeves.

"Please," she says softly. "Do it quickly."

She is assuming my intention is to kill her. This is not my intention but I don't tell her that. I have no interest in her in any way. But I don't say that and I'm standing here with the butcher's knife and the SIG and I see that she sees those things, I see that she sees the flat look in my eyes. "Tell me," I say. My voice is flat also, flat and cold.

The flags ripple in the breeze, making a tinny *tink-tink-tink* as the ropes dance against the poles.

"I killed her."

"I know that."

"I'm sorry."

"I know that," I say again, and what I mean is "I don't care." Her sorrow is beside the point. I want answers, my chest is swollen with the wanting, my weapons are shaking in my hands. She thinks I am going to slay her where she lays, she thinks that I am vengeance-mad and bent on slaughter. But she's got it wrong, I don't want vengeance. Vengeance is the cheapest of motivations, it's a tin star on a shabby coat. I want answers is all that I want.

"He made you do it."

The word "yes" comes out softly and sharply, a little agonized rush of air.

"How did he make you do it? Jean?"

"I—" Eyes closed; breathing hard. "I can't."

"*Jean.*" She's suffered enough. I am aware of that. Everybody has, though. Everybody has. "How? When?"

"As soon as—" Her whole body spasms, and she turns her face away. I crouch down and seize her chin and turn her face back to me.

"As soon as you went underground?" Nod. Yes. "Between four thirty and five thirty last Wednesday. Let's call it five. Five o'clock on September 26. What happened then?"

"He said we were going to have a party. To celebrate our new lives. We can't be gloomy, he said. A new life. New time. We didn't even, you know. Didn't unpack. Or look around. It was just—as soon as we got downstairs we sat down."

"In the room marked LADIES."

"Yes."

Nodding, nodding. I won't let her become like she was in the jail cell, withdrawing, floating away like a space capsule drifting from the mother ship. I stay close, keep my eyes boring into hers.

"Did it seem strange to you? To be having a party at such a time?"

"No. Not at all. I felt relieved. I was tired of waiting. Parry wasn't coming. 'Resolution.' It wasn't happening. We all knew that by then. It was time for plan B. I was glad. Astronaut was glad, too. He poured drinks for everyone. Proposed a toast." A flicker of a smile rushes across her face, a vestigial fondness for the charismatic leader, but it dies fast. "But then he—he starts this speech. About our loyalty. About how we've lost discipline. How the hard part hasn't even started yet. He said our behavior outside, all the hanging out, while we had been waiting, it was bullshit. He told us we were weak. He spray-painted on the wall."

I listen. I am down there with her, watching his face contort with anger, watching the words appear on the wall: ENOUGH OF THIS SHIT.

"And then he started talking about Nico. He said, look who's not here. Look who abandoned us. Look who *betrayed* us."

Kessler was right about DeCarlo. He had him nailed. Suicide didn't fit the profile, but this: in group/out group dynamics. Cruel games. Tests of loyalty. And drugs, of course, Big Pharma and his clever hand with a concoction. He had resolved to kill all of his erstwhile coconspirators—he was doing it even then, merrily topping off everybody's tea—but first he was going to have some fun.

"Go on, please."

Jean looks at me helplessly, piteously. She is desperate to stop this line of conversation, desperate not to get to the end. To just lie in peace like Agent Kessler, waiting for the end.

I can see myself, a form of myself, floating up out of my body and running to get her a blanket, lift her gently, get her water, protect her. Young girl—recent trauma—curled in fear on the forest floor. But what I'm doing is nothing, what I'm doing is standing here clutching my weapons waiting for her to continue.

"The rest. Tell me the rest."

"He, um—he looked at me. At *me*. And he told me I was the worst. The weakest. And he told me what I—what I had to do. To *earn my place*." Her lip curls, her face tightens. The words are dull stones, she chokes them out one by one. "I said, 'I can't.' He said, 'Goodbye then, good luck. We are happy to drink your share of the water, little sister. To eat your share of the food.'"

She closes her eyes and I watch tears roll out from under the lids.

"I looked at the rest of them for help—or for, for pity, or—"

She looks down at the dirt. She got no help and she got no pity. They were as afraid as she was, all the rest of them, Tick and Valentine and Little Man and her old pals Sailor and Delighted, all as scared and confused, all just as firmly under the thumb of their leader. A week from impact and sharply aware of how isolated they had become, as the world narrowed to a pinpoint like the circle of darkness at the end of a Looney Tunes cartoon. As their leader and protector peeled off his layers, showing them the cruelty at his core.

So Astronaut tells Jean to go on now, he says get up, and she does, she gets up, she goes—and as she is telling me this story she is dissolving. She is seeing the memory complete itself out of the fog of forgetfulness, and it is *killing* her, I can see it. Every sentence is killing her. Every word. "I loved Nico. She was my friend. But as I was walking up those stairs my mind got—I don't know. Hollow. There was all this shouting, these weird voices shouting, and—like—giggling?"

"You were hallucinating," I say. "He drugged you."

She nods. She knows this already, I think. Weird voices and dark streaks from the cruel courage in her tea. Whatever secret ingredient he put in to add to his private fun. His game, his apocalyptic April Fool's Day joke. Given her overdose and the subsequent patchy spots in her memory, we're probably talking about a hallucinogen, some sort of dissociative anesthetic; PCP, maybe, or ketamine. But I can't say with certainty, it's not my area of expertise, and if it would do any good I would take blood, I would stick her with a needle and catch any lingering molecules still swimming in her veins. *Send it to the lab, boys!*

The rest of them got much worse, of course. This was Astronaut's real plan B. Food and water were limited, everything was limited, and he wasn't going to share any of it, not for a second.

So here comes Jean up the rickety stairs with Astronaut's sawtooth buck knife, shoved out of the hatch and told the price of her future. Surfing darkly, wild chemical horrors churning in her gut along with the terror. Looking for Nico.

"You know what?" She looks up at me with hope in her eyes, a small spark of joy. "You know what I remember? I remember thinking she's probably gone. Because she told me she was going to leave, on the stairs she told me. And then with the party, and the speech, I mean, we'd been down there for—I don't know, half an hour? He sat us down, he gave the speech, it had been time. If she was leaving she'd be gone already. I remember thinking that."

I've thought of it too. It's in the timeline I've got, up in my head.

"But there she was. She was still there," says Jean. "Why was she still there?"

"Candy," I say.

"What?"

"It was going to be a hard trip. She took what food she could find."

She took the time to empty that machine, to prop it with the fork and run a coat hanger or her skinny arms up there and empty it out, she took that time and it cost her her life.

"So you fought her."

"I guess."

"You guess?"

"I don't remember."

"You don't remember fighting her? And her fighting you?"

Her hand flies up to her face, her scratches and bruises, and then down again.

"No."

"You don't remember the woods?"

She trembles. "No."

I lean over her, the gun and the knife in my two hands. "What do you remember, Jean?"

She remembers afterward, she says. She remembers running back to the garage, and finding that it was sealed. And understanding, even in her dark and addled desperation, understanding what it meant. The whole thing had been a joke, he had known all along she wouldn't make it down there. Because Atlee Miller had already come and sealed up the hole, as Astronaut knew that he would.

And then there was just the sink. Just the sink and the knife and knowing what she had done and that she had done it for nothing—for *nothing*—and then cutting herself open like she had cut Nico open. Pressing the knife in as far as she could stand it, until the blood was pouring out of her and she was shrieking, and running, running from the blood, running out into the woods.

That's the story. That's the whole story, she says, and she's trembling on the ground, her face is streaked with grief, but I'm pacing back and forth above her, that's the whole story, she says, but there must be more, I have to have *more*. There are pieces missing. There has to be a reason, for example, that a slitting of the throat presented itself as the logical method—was that directed by Astronaut or was that an improvisation, the most effective means in the moment? And surely she was directed to bring back something. If she was supposedly earning her place in the bunker by killing Nico, there must have been a token to prove it.

I throw myself down in the mud and drop the weapons and grab her shoulders.

"I have more questions," I tell Jean. Snarling; shouting.

"No," she says. "Please."

"Yes."

Because I can't solve the crime unless I know everything and the world can't end with the crime unsolved, that's all there is to it, so I tighten my grip on her shoulders and demand that she remember.

"We need to go back to the woods, Jean. Back to the part in the woods."

"No," she says. "Please—"

"Yes, Jean. Ms. Wong. You find her outside the building. Is

she surprised to see you?"

"Yes. No. I don't remember."

"Please try to remember. Is she surprised?"

She nods. "Yes. Please, stop."

"Do you have the knife out at this point—"

"I don't remember."

"You chase her—"

"I guess."

"Don't guess. Did you chase her through the woods? Over that creek?"

"Please . . . please stop."

Jean's terrified eyes meet mine and it's working, I can see her seeing it again, being there, I'm doing it, I'm going to get the information I need, she's back there now at the scene with the knife handle wrapped in her palm, Nico's struggling weight beneath her. And where was I, I was on the way but I wasn't here yet, it took me too long, I should have been here to save her but I wasn't and it's burning, my blood is burning. I need more, I need all of it.

"Did she beg you for her life?"

"I don't remember."

"Did she, Jean?"

She can't speak. She nods, nods weeping, thrashes in my grip.

"Was she screaming?"

Nodding and nodding, helpless.

"She begged you to stop? But you didn't stop?"

"Please—"

"There are more things I need to know."

"No," she says, "no, you don't—right? You don't, right? You don't really, right?"

Her voice is altered, high and pleading, like a little kid, like a toddler, pleading to be told that something unpleasant isn't really so. *I don't really have to go to the doctor, right? I don't really have to take a bath.* Jean and I hold our pose for a minute, down in the mud, me clutching her shoulders tightly, and I feel it, suddenly, where we've gotten to, here, what's happening. What the asteroid did to her is done, and what Astronaut did to her is done, and now here I am, her last and worst terror, forcing her to stare into this blackness, wade through it like every detail matters, like it can possibly matter.

I let her go and she rolls her head back away from me, emitting low terrified moans like an animal on the slaughterhouse floor.

"Jean," I say. "Jean. Jean. Jean."

I say her name until she stops moaning. I say it softly, softer and softer, until it becomes a whisper, "Jean, Jean, Jean," a soothing small little whisper, just the word, "Jean."

I am sunk now into the ground beside her.

"When did your parents give you that bracelet?"

"The—what?"

Her right hand moves to the left wrist and she brushes her fingers over the cheap piece of jewelry.

"You told me when we first talked that it was your parents who gave you the charm bracelet. Was it on your birthday?"

"No." She shakes her head. "It was my first communion."

"Is that right?" I smile. I lean backward, balance myself with my fingers laced across my knees. "So you're how old for that?"

"Seven," she says. "I was seven. They were so proud of me."

"Oh, boy, I'll bet they were."

We sit there for a while in the mud of the lawn and she gives it all to me, painting the picture: the soaring nave of St. Mary's in Lansing, Michigan, the dancing lights of the votive candles, the warm harmonies of the choir. She remembers quite a lot of it, considering how young she was, how much has happened to her since. After a while I tell her a couple of my own stories, from when I was a kid: my parents taking us up to the old Dairy Queen on Saturday evenings for shakes; going to the 7-Eleven after school to buy Batman comics; biking with Nico all around White Park, when she first learned to ride and never wanted to get off the darn thing, around and around and around and around.

EPILOGUE

Wednesday, October 3

Right ascension 15 51 56.6
Declination -77 57 48
Elongation 72.4
Delta 0.008 AU

There's a memory I love. It's me and Naomi Eddes, it's six months ago, give or take. The last Tuesday in March.

"Well, I have to tell you," she says, looking across the table at me with a tiny tree of broccoli poised at the end of her chopsticks. "I am quite taken with you."

We're eating at Mr. Chow's. Our first and last date. She's wearing a red dress with black buttons down the front.

"Taken, huh?" I say, playing at bemusement, teasing her for the outmoded turn of phrase, which I actually find poetic and charming, so much so, in fact, that I am falling in love with her, across the smudged table, under the blinking neon sign that says *Chow! Chow!* "And why do you think you're taken with me?"

"Oh, you know. You're very tall, so you see everything from weird angles. Also—and I'm serious—your life has a purpose. You know what I mean?"

"I guess," I say. "I guess I do."

She's referring to a topic of conversation from earlier in the evening, about my parents, how my mother was murdered in a supermarket parking lot and my father hanged himself in his office six months later. And how my subsequent career, she suggested jokingly, has been like Batman's, how I've turned my grief into a lifelong sense of mission.

But it makes me uneasy, I tell her, that version of events, that way of seeing.

"I don't like to think that they died for a reason, because that makes it sound like it's okay. As if it's good that it happened, because it ordered my life. It wasn't good. It was bad."

"I know," she says. "I know it was bad."

She furrows her brow under her bald head and eats her broccoli, and I go on, explain the way I prefer to look at things: how it's tempting to place things in a pattern, name certain events as the causes of certain subsequent events—but then when you think again you realize that this is just the way that life happened to happen—like constellations, like you blink once and it's a warrior or a bear, blink again and it's a scattered handful of stars.

"I changed my mind," says Naomi, after I've been talking this way for a while. "I'm not taken with you anymore."

But she's smiling, and I'm smiling, too. She reaches forward and dabs ginger-scallion sauce from the corner of my mustache. She will be dead within forty-eight hours. It will be my friend Detective Culverson who calls me to the crime scene, at Merrimack Life and Fire.

"Can we agree, at least," she says at Mr. Chow's, still alive, still brushing sauce off my face with her thumb, "that you have *put* meaning in your life. Can we agree to that?"

"Sure," I say. She's so pretty. That red dress with the buttons. I've never seen anyone so pretty. "Okay. Yes. We can agree."

* * *

The remainder of Tuesday, October 2, I spend burying my sister in a shallow grave between the flagpoles on the front lawn of the police station. In lieu of a service I sing while I dig, first "Thunder on the Mountain" and then "You're Gonna Make Me Lonesome When You Go" and then a medley of Nico's favorites, instead of mine: ska songs, Elliott Smith songs, Fugazi songs, "Waiting Room" over and over until I feel like I've dug deeply enough into the police-station lawn to lay her body down and say goodbye.

For several hours after that I help Jean. I haul bodies up out of the bunker one by one; I move Astronaut's Bunsen burners into the general store so she can use them to cook up macaroni and cheese, if she wants; I push and roll loose stones and hunks of concrete back down onto that first step, sealing the stairwell back up as best I can. I don't know how long she'll last down there, or how she'll do, but that's the best I can do for her, it really is. There is a helicopter parked in some field somewhere in these woods, but I don't know how to fly one and neither does she, and where would she go?

She's got guns, in case she needs to use a gun.

And then I roll out, just after midnight on October 3, with that one particular memory, of me and Naomi at Mr. Chow's, threaded through my ribs like a red ribbon.

It's a quiet ride. Not a lot of people out on the road tonight; not a lot of action on the streets. Probably most places in the world are blue towns tonight, everybody deep into their last round of praying or drinking or laughing, doing whatever there is left to do before everything changes or dies. I roll through Rotary and pass by the house with the semicircular blast wall, the redbrick ranch house on Downing Road. I don't know if it's the same fella who shot at me with the machine gun, but there is some fella up on the roof, with a John Deere cap and a massive belly, surrounded by his family: a middle-aged woman in her Sunday best, plus two teenage daughters and a little boy. They're all up there on the roof, at rigid attention in the moonlight, saluting an American flag.

I find my way to State Road 4 going south. I remember the route. I've always been good at spatial geography: getting a sense of a place or a system of roads or a perpetrator's place of residence, registering the small details in my head and keeping them straight.

In a perfect world I wouldn't sleep tonight, of course, I'd stay up somehow, but my body doesn't know what day it is, and my eyes are bleary and I'm veering off the road. I find my same rest stop as before and I fold up my coat in the same way and after three hours of sleep I am awoken by the bright distinct howl of a train whistle, which seems impossible. But then I open my eyes and stumble to my feet and stand there watching it pass, way off in the distance, wondering if I'm dreaming. A long freight train rolling slowly across Ohio, smoke pouring from the engine.

I pee in the woods, get back on the bike, and keep on going.

* * *

Pink sky at sunrise, autumn morning chill.

I heard Officer Burdell once, in the kitchen at Police House, talking with Officer Katz about her plans for the last day. She said she was going to spend it thinking about "all the things that suck eggs about being alive. Having a body and that. Hemorrhoids and stomachaches and the flu."

I felt at the time like this was a bad strategy, and I feel that way now. I take one hand off the bars of the Schwinn and send the Night Bird an air salute, back in Furman, Mass. Send one along to Trish McConnell while I'm at it.

Then I put my hands back on the handlebars and make my turn at the fruit stand. Singing again, as loud as I can, each line caught by the wind and carried off over my shoulder, little snatches of melody, bits and pieces from *Desire*.

* * *

I hear the dog before I see him, three fine bright barks devolving into a growly canine coughing fit, cough/bark, cough/bark, then just cough, cough, cough as Houdini limps with determination from behind that shed out to see me.

"Here, boy," I say, and my heart swells just looking at him, loping and shuffling along toward me across the slight roll of the farmland.

The autumn corn is halfway through its harvest, half the stalks still burdened, half tilting, barren. There's a pumpkin patch I hadn't noticed before, in a dirt corner just to the right of the front porch, green winding vines and fat orange globes. Two of the women are up on the porch, two of the daughters or daughters-in-law, sitting on hard chairs in their long dresses and bonnets, sewing or knitting, working on blankets for the winter. They rise at my approach and smile nervously and take each other's hands, and I ask politely if I might speak to Atlee, and they go to fetch him.

Houdini ducks in and out of my footsteps, snorfeling at the dirt, and I bend and scratch the white fur behind his head, and he growls low and contented. Someone's given the guy a bath. Someone trimmed his fur, too, combed out all the bugs and burrs. He almost looks like he did when I met him, puckish little creature scampering around the filthy home of a drug dealer on Bog Bow Road. We look at each other and I smile, and he smiles too, I think. *You thought I was gone, too, didn't you, Hen? You did, huh?* Or not. Who knows? You never know what a dog is thinking, not really.

Atlee Miller doesn't ask after the outcome of my investigation, and I don't volunteer any information. We exchange nods and I point to the wagon.

"I brought back your jackhammer. Thank you."

He waves one hand. "Not sure I'll need it."

"My sister—she thinks we might all live. Somehow. So I thought it couldn't hurt to bring it back."

"Can't hurt," says Atlee, and he nods. "Can't hurt."

We're talking quietly out on the lawn. I can see the rest of the family behind him, the kids and the teenagers and the aunts and uncles and cousins, framed in the big windows of the house, reacting to my return.

"I thought I might stay for lunch," I say. "If you'll have me."

"Oh, sure," he says. Maybe even the hint of a smile somewhere in the gray of his beard. "Stay as long as you want."

* * *

In the busy hour before lunchtime I am mostly a silent presence in the house: the tall stranger alone in a corner like furniture. I smile politely at the women, make funny faces at the little boys and girls. I do not experience, as I had feared, any unwelcome rush of memory, no bloody moving pictures behind my eyelids. The house smells like bread. The children are giggling, carrying precarious trays of cutlery out from the kitchen. One of Atlee's sons has hurt his back farming, and so when there is difficulty in wrestling a heavy wooden table out from the kitchen, I get up and lend what strength I have.

We sit then for lunch. I have a seat right next to one of the children's tables, by one of the largest windows, wide and square, no curtain, a full view of the sky.

As the food is brought out, my courage suddenly drops out of me, and just for one awful minute my heart feels loose and floating and my hands start to tremble and I have to hold myself frozen by force of will, watching that big window, wide and square. I allow myself the last brief possibility that it will after all have been a dream, and that when I close my eyes tightly and open them again everything will be as it was—and I even try it, squeeze them shut like a child, press my knuckles into the lids, hold the pose until starbursts dance to life inside my eyelids. When I open them again Atlee's daughters and sons and their wives are bringing out the meal: stewed vegetables, braised rabbit, bread.

Atlee Miller bends his head and the room grows still as all of them silently pray over the food, the same as the last time, and the same as the last time I leave my own eyes open. I look around until I find her, and there she is, at her seat at one of the children's tables, young Ruthie with the strawberry braids, her eyes open like mine are open. Her face is pale and she sees me seeing her and I hold out my hand to the kid. I stretch my long arm and hold out my hand to lend her my courage and she holds out her hand to lend hers to me, and we clasp hands and look at each other as the sky begins to glow, and Atlee keeps his head down and the room continues in silent prayer.

I hold Ruthie's hand and she holds my hand, we sit like that, giving each other strength, like strangers on a crashing plane.

THANK YOU

This book, and this series, was built on a lot of input and help from a lot of smart and kind people, starting with forensic pathologist Dr. Cynthia Gardner, astronomer Dr. Timothy Spahr, and my brother, Andrew Winters.

Thanks to my wife, Diana; to my parents and her parents.

To early readers Nick Tamarkin and Kevin Maher; to everybody at Quirk Books, especially Jason Rekulak and Jane Morley; to Joelle Delbourgo and Shari Smiley and Molly Lyons.

To Don Mattingly of Mattingly Concrete; Katy and Tim Carter and their chickens; planetary scientist Professor Don Korycansky at UC Santa Cruz; everybody at the Concord, New Hampshire, Police Department, especially Officer Ryan Howe and Lieutenant Jay Brown; Detective Todd Flanagan at the New Hampshire Attorney General's office; Russ Hanser; Danice Sher (PA), Dr. Ratik Chandra, Dr. Nora Osman, and Dr. Zara Cooper; and Amish experts Professor David Weaver-Zercher and Professor Steve Nolt.